Praise for VENICE MIDNIGHT

'Stunning . . . a gem of a British contemporary novel that is a must-have for anyone whose idea of a good read is gossip, biography of stars, murder mystery, courtroom drama or the complex nature of human relationships under pressure . . . *Venice Midnight* is a rare piece of wonderment that is as forceful as it is endearing, as tricky as it is simple . . . I haven't stumbled across a more eligible candidate for my 'favourite' shelf in a decade' – David Hemmings

'Has the makings of a first-rate thriller' – Gillian Fairchild, *Daily Telegraph*

'A cracking good read . . . funny, stylish . . . Richard Faber and Maisie Rivers are amazing but totally real. It's brilliant' – Richard Barber, *BBC Radio Scotland*

'Like its polymath author, Gyles Brandreth's *Venice Midnight* is highly original, fascinating and multi-layered. On its most immediate level it is a gripping mystery concerning two star-crossed lovers (one, Richard Faber, a famous actor), set in three kinds of Venice (Italy, California, and our own Little Venice). But who, really, is Richard Faber?' – Charles Osborne, *Daily Telegraph Books of the Year*

VENICE MIDNIGHT

GYLES BRANDRETH

WARNER BOOKS

A *Warner* Book

First published in Great Britain in 1998
by Little, Brown and Company
This edition published in 1999 by Warner Books

Copyright © 1997 by Gyles Brandreth

The moral right of the author has been asserted.

A CIP catalogue record for this book
is available from the British Library.

ISBN 0 7515 2658 4

Typeset by Palimpsest Book Production Limited,
Polmont, Stirlingshire
Printed and bound in Great Britain by
Clays ltd, St Ives plc

Warner Books
A Division of
Little, Brown and Company (UK)
Brettenham House
Lancaster Place
London WC2E 7EN

'See how love and murder will out'

George Colman, *The Clandestine Marriage*

PART ONE

'A great man produces beauty, terror and mirth, and a little man produces cleverness (personality, psychology) instead of beauty, ugliness instead of terror, and jokes instead of mirth.'

Robert Louis Stevenson.
Laurence Irving's epigraph for his biography of his grandfather, *Henry Irving: the actor and his world*

ONE

Richard Faber was born early on the morning of Wednesday 5 October 1949, at the very moment, it turned out, when Donald Hume, small-time racketeer and double murderer, was tipping the segmented body of his first victim out of a light aircraft onto the Essex marshes.

Richard was born a thousand miles away from Essex, in Verona, in the sun-filled first-floor bedroom of the magnificent, medieval, arcaded, crumbling Villa Ortese on the Via Anastasia, a discreet alley and three side-streets away from the celebrated statue of Dante that dominates the Piazza dei Signori and an achievable stone's throw from the Casa di Giulietta, dedicated by the Verona Office of Tourism, even in 1949, as the traditional home of the Capulets. Richard's was an easy birth apparently, which was fortunate as the only midwife in attendance was his father who was nearly seventy and totally blind. Richard's mother was a noted Italian actress, then in her early thirties, Isabella Bertolazzi; his father, Theodore Faber, a distinguished Anglo-American poet whose reputation (still a considerable one) rested entirely on work published during and immediately after the 1914–18 war.

Looking back on his childhood, Richard's recollection of Isabella was of someone always laughing, of someone warm and soft and sunny. He claimed his first tactile memory was of the touch – and tickle – of her glorious red hair on his face when she bent over and kissed his tummy. He said for ever after the smell of hair – the right hair, of course, female, thick and long and full of curls – was better than anything, 'better than new-mown grass, better than freshly ground coffee, better than an English log fire'. Richard was a romantic, old fashioned, sentimental and nostalgic. He knew it, and knew too that it always coloured, and sometimes distorted, his view of the world. He conjured up an enviably rose-tinted portrait of his mother – in her simple silk dressing gown, preparing breakfast in the kitchen; putting the washing out to dry in the dazzling Veneto sunlight, humming Tino Rossi's hits; sitting on the edge of his bed, telling him the old story of *La Cenerentola* or the new one of Pinocchio, by the flickering yellow light of a candle they would blow out together on the count of three, *uno, due, tre* – and at the same time acknowledged that this rhapsodic picture was a bit odd, to say the least, because, by all other accounts, Isabella Bertolazzi was not

4

at all a happy person. She was a woman, like so many, who lived in a state of constant, unspoken, apprehension. She never relaxed in the moment because she was fearful, always, of what the next moment might bring. Nothing would last – her youth, her beauty, her career, her love for Theodore, more so his for her. It wasn't just that nothing is certain in this life; it was that everything is uncertain. Even as another royalty cheque arrived for Theodore, one that was unexpected, and handsome, a real bonus, it gave her no pleasure, and the spending of it caused her real anguish, because money today convinced her there would be, could be, no money tomorrow. 'She always feared the worst,' Richard said, 'so when her little car collided with a water lorry crossing the Ponte Navi and she was killed instantly, she wouldn't have been in the least surprised. It was exactly what she had been expecting.'

Richard called her 'the Italian Rita Hayworth', which was typical of Richard but quite absurd. She was nothing like as famous, she only made one internationally acknowledged movie (Vittorio de Sica's *Bicycle Thieves*) and her private life was as tame as Rita Hayworth's was spectacular. Isabella's hair was as sensational as Hayworth's, they were born in the same year, and there was a loosely comparable nervous energy in their performances, but that was about it. On stage, Isabella could blaze: she was forceful, fiery, feisty. At home, she simmered: anxious, watchful, wary. In performance, she could appear tremendously strong. Away from the theatre, she seemed vulnerable; in repose, she looked sad;

but even at forty-three, the age she was when she was killed, she was undeniably a great beauty.

It was probably Isabella's wistful pre-Raphaelite quality that appealed to Richard's father. As a boy in London he had met Burne-Jones and Holman Hunt and had held a torch for 'the Brotherhood' both when they were in fashion and when they were out of it. One of his favourite set-pieces was his account of the burial of William Morris: Theodore Faber, aged fifteen, had walked alongside the old farm cart bearing Morris's coffin as it trundled down the lane to Kelmscott churchyard in the autumn of '96. Jane Morris, Ford Maddox Brown, Max Beerbohm – he'd known them all. He was in Italy now entirely because Max had persuaded him.

For a sightless man Theodore Faber had an uncanny eye for beautiful women. Perhaps they chose him. He had not always been blind. He had seen the first of his three wives, the plainest of the six women he lived with during his long life. There was a general, lazy, unquestioning assumption that somehow he had lost his sight during the Great War. In fact, his sight didn't begin to dim until the 1920s. In a filmed television interview marking his ninetieth birthday, he revealed to Russell Harty that he 'last saw the colour of the world' on 8 November 1924, two hundred and fifty years to the day after the death of John Milton. The interviewer's upper lip moistened instantly in appreciation of the confidence bestowed and he turned to gaze out gratefully over a divinely timely Verona sunset. 'Cut.'

Theodore Faber enjoyed giving interviews. He was

happy to wrap himself in the mantle of the Grand Old Man of English letters. The older he got the grander they thought him. In his heart he knew that, at best, his place was at the forefront of the second division. He wasn't up there with Wilfred Owen or Siegfried Sassoon – but with Rupert Brooke? Possibly. 'I'm a set text on three continents, don't y'know,' he would purr, tempering the complacency with a self-conscious twinkle. Privately, and within limits, he was ready to send himself up. In public, he assumed the role of poetic sage and elder statesman. 'Self-deprecation is charming in the drawing room, but on the platform it's *gravitas* that sustains the sales, helps keep the Valpolicella flowing.' Secretly, he hoped that one day the Order of Merit might even come his way. He was vain, as well as delightful.

He talked like an Edwardian dandy and looked like a Welsh wizard. He was taller than Lloyd George – 'He never knew my father, but I knew him, knew him well for a while; I believe David Lloyd George was Merlin reincarnated' – and broader, bigger altogether, but, like Lloyd George, he let his soft white hair grow over his collar and he sported a similar silver-topped cane, broad-rimmed black hat and wrap-around cape.

Theodore Faber had no interest in politics. If he was fascinated by Lloyd George it was because of the Welshman's magic touch, his appearance, his way with words, his way with women. Theodore was a charmer who was drawn to other charmers. That was why Max Beerbohm (nine years his senior) loved him, and why he loved Max.

Theodore taught Richard the three rules of charm: Be courteous. Be carefree. And concentrate. 'Nine-tenths of the trick is good manners. People see them so rarely nowadays they're bowled over by them at once. *La cortesia, mio piccolo, sempre la cortesia.* And to succeed in this life, while you must try very hard, you mustn't *seem* to be trying at all. Your head may be thumping, your heart can be cracking, but easy, relaxed, *care free*, is what you've got to look. *Where* you've got to look, of course, is right in their eye. Concentrate, completely, utterly, resolutely, on whoever you are with and they'll be with you for ever and a day!'

He also taught his son what became one of Richard's favourite party pieces (and most useful bits of business): how to twirl a cane between his fingers, and then throw it nonchalantly over one shoulder so that it would slide effortlessly down over the other to be caught and kept spinning all the while. When he was seven Richard saw Fred Astaire and Jack Buchanan in *The Band Wagon* on a gigantic outdoor screen in the Piazzale Stefani and realised, with road-to-Damascus clarity, that with the skill of the one and the charm of the other he could be a bigger star than both. That night he told his mother that he was going to be 'a great actor and a famous film star'. Isabella hugged him and was terrified. Theodore roared his approval. 'Keep spinning the cane. The amateur practises until he gets it right. The professional rehearses until he can't get it wrong.'

The father also taught the son great chunks of epic poetry: 'Robert Browning for your mother's sake, John

Milton for mine.' Theodore Faber's only published work since the twenties had been a biography of Milton. It was magnificent, magisterial, and, amazingly, written in very creditable Miltonic blank verse. The book was well received, widely purchased, and universally unread. The publisher had seen the potential of the great blind poet of the twentieth century evoking the life of the great blind poet of the seventeenth. Faber admired Milton above all others: 'I don't love him like I love Shakespeare; you can't *love* him. He's a god, hard, austere, to be revered, not adored.' Faber, of course, was a cavalier, a swashbuckler, a ladies' man, so that, three wives and blindness apart, he and Milton had little in common. Even in their blindness they were different: here, and perhaps here alone, Faber was to be the more admired. Theodore never adverted to his blindness, in conversation or in his work. If he felt anger or self-pity, he never showed them. In his company you were barely conscious of his affliction. Even in his great old age, when for much of the year he lived alone, he never had the unkempt appearance or the decaying smell that you might have expected and would certainly have excused. '*La cortesia, mio piccolo, sempre la cortesia.*'

Richard enjoyed being the child of celebrated parents. In Italy everyone of a certain age had heard of his mother; in the English-speaking world everyone with a university education knew the name of Theodore Faber and many, thousands, hundreds of thousands perhaps, brought up in an era when learning poetry by heart was a natural part of education, could recite the opening lines of 'The

Mountaineer' or 'I Met a Girl in Mercy Street'. They were his 'Lycidas', his 'If', his host of golden daffodils.

Because they were famous, and because his mother was so beautiful and his father was so old, they were different from other children's parents. Richard liked that. Richard liked being different. He had always known he was different: he felt different (for a start he could speak two languages), he looked different (for minutes on end the mirror on the top landing told him how handsome he was), and when his friends played their childish games and told their silly jokes he took part quite happily but he knew that they were ordinary and that he was extraordinary. From as far back as he could remember Richard Faber had known that he was special. With Isabella he had been to Piazzale Stefani to see *Twenty Thousand Leagues Under the Sea* and had decided – he must have been eight or nine at the time – that when the day came for him to produce the remake it would be so much more effective if he played both the Kirk Douglas and the James Mason parts. From that night on too he saw himself gliding through life in a personal submarine, hidden just below the surface, secret, periscope at the ready, silent, invisible but all-seeing, unknown but all-knowing.

Richard was eleven when his mother died. Until that moment he had never known anything but calm waters, sunshine, happiness and love. He had cruised through his childhood securely cocooned in a Nautilus of his own making. As his father stood, gigantic and forbidding, at the side of his bed, like an Old Testament prophet blocking out the sun, and broke the dreadful news of the terrible accident on the Ponte Navi – 'Mamma is dead, *Mamma è morta*' – the little boy's world suddenly imploded: his impregnable vessel was holed and a great wall of black water, overwhelming and ice hard, raced along the galley towards him and, in an instant, engulfed him.

For days he lay on his bed, desolate, desperate, tossing, turning, sweating, crying, gasping for air, pushing away the water, fighting it, as it swept over him, wave after wave, calling out his mother's name as he lay drowning in grief and bewilderment. At last, he recalled, a young woman, a stranger, came to look after him: she was fair and pretty and gentle, and she stroked his head with her cool fingers, and she took off his clothes and washed him with a wonderful soapy sponge (it was hard and soft, and rough and smooth, all at the same time), and she dried him in a gigantic white towel, and dressed him in fresh pyjamas, and made the bed over him. Thirty years later he could feel the warm breeze of the linen as she threw it out over the bed, could see it still billowing like sand dunes as it floated gently down on top of him.

Jane Stanhope was a secretary with Theodore Faber's publishers in London and had been his occasional mistress for several years. Richard had no idea who she was or why she had come to Verona, but the moment he saw her and felt her touch he loved her and began to feel safe again. It was as if the storm had suddenly abated and he was lying on a raft, secure amid the wreckage, the gulls silent, the sea calm, the air clear, the sun warm once more. Years later, when he learnt the truth, when he discovered how Jane and his father had deceived his mother, off and on, for almost a decade, he felt a flash of burning anger and then let go of it at once.

Early one morning, it was just a month after Isabella's death, Richard's father came into his room and sat on the boy's bed and took his hand and said, 'No time for lamentation now, nor much more cause.' He smiled at his son and Richard, who often felt tongue-tied with his father, shy but not frightened, smiled back and gently squeezed the old man's hand. 'I'm going to send you home to England,' his father said. 'I'm going to send you to boarding school.' Somehow Richard had been expecting this. It had always been on the cards. An English boarding school. The words had filled Isabella with dread – the cruelty, the beatings, the separation – but Richard wasn't fearful. He was ready.

'Fresh woods and pastures new,' he said, wanting to please his father.

'Yes. Yes, that's it, *exactly*. It's my old school, don't y'know. You'll like it. We'll still have the holidays, but you'll make friends there.' Richard pressed his father's hand to show him it was going to be all right. 'Jane is going back to England soon. I have asked her to take you with her. When I was at school my best friend was a boy called Cyril, Cyril Holland. He was beautiful and kind. Like your mother. Like Jane. Like good friends should be. Cyril told me many marvellous secrets. His mother died when he was just thirteen and he must have felt then as you feel now. His father was a poet too. Not as good as Milton or Browning, to be sure, but' – he leant forward and let his voice drop to a playful whisper – 'keep this to yourself, *mio piccolo*, quite as good as your old papa. Cyril Holland was the son of Oscar Wilde. You've heard of Oscar Wilde?'

Richard arrived at Bedales School, near Petersfield in Hampshire, in the middle of the summer term, and found himself surrounded by the sons and daughters of distinguished poets. For years pride of place on Richard's fridge door went to a blow-up of a snapshot taken one Parents Day of his father and Robert Graves and Cecil Day-Lewis in earnest conversation. The head of English had taken the picture and liked to think they were debating Miltonic prosody. 'Three set texts discuss a fourth,' was the caption he gave the photograph when it appeared in the school magazine. Theodore told Richard he couldn't remember what they were talking about, but he supposed it was money. 'That's what poets usually talk about when they get together.'

Isabella had been wrong about Bedales. *Tom Brown's Schooldays* had sent out a false signal. At Bedales there was no deliberate cruelty: there were no beatings, just lashings of well-intentioned liberal education amid the invigorating Hampshire downs. Yes, there was separation. Of course. Inevitably. But, wherever you are, come eleven or twelve, isn't that when the long goodbye begins? Isabella had been wrong and Theodore was right. Fresh woods and pastures new. Good friends and marvellous secrets.

*   *   *

It was at Bedales that Richard met Adam Waterson.

Adam Waterson was unusual for a Bedalian in that he wasn't the son of poet, prince or rock star. His father was in the wool trade in Bradford, his mother was a housewife, but none the less Adam was by far the most sophisticated boy in their year. He smoked without coughing, he drank without side-effects, he had a wonderful way with women. He improvised a bed behind the wooden horse in the gymnasium store room and it was there, on top of the judo mats, on his thirteenth birthday, that Angela Roberts allowed him to touch her breasts and lick the roof of her mouth. Adam described this astonishing experience – and later, even greater triumphs – to Richard in beautiful detail and, while the stories delighted and excited him, they didn't embolden him to launch out himself on a career as a teenage Casanova.

'I was shy,' Richard confessed in a television interview, years later, 'or unlucky, or hamfisted, or something. Anyway, the first girl I fell for turned out to be called Sappho. Yes, it's true!' He laughed. Richard always laughed when he told self-deprecating stories, laughed and tossed his head back as though he was shying away from the light and heat of a burning sparkler. 'Sappho was lovely. She was the daughter of Lawrence Durrell. And looked it. There was something strangely Mediterranean and magical about her. She had almond-shaped eyes and silky olive-black hair and an air of contained Byzantine mystery. She was a year younger than me, but she seemed much older and, quite simply, unattainable. One evening, just once, I managed to catch her on her own, on the path leading from the girls' house to the library, and I presented her with a single red rose. Childish, I know. Embarrassing really. Hopeless. But she took it. She said nothing, but she smiled. Then she walked on, and turned back briefly and smiled again, and that was that. She was kind. If she tossed my rose in the bin she waited till she had turned the corner behind the bike sheds before she did so.'

At school Adam and Richard were a double act. They worked together, they played together. They produced the school plays together. Their desks were side by side; they contrived to be in the same dormitory; they didn't take quite the same exams (Adam took French for A Level while Richard took Italian), but they secured the same grades. They were more than good companions, they were comrades-in-arms, co-conspirators as well as best friends. There were differences, of course. Adam got into trouble, and Richard didn't. Richard was obviously handsome and highly ambitious. Adam wasn't.

In the summer before their sixteenth birthdays, each had an extraordinary experience that Richard liked to say defined the difference between them and illustrated the pattern of their lives. Adam had a sensational affair with the school nurse and Richard met Laurence Olivier.

The nurse, a French Algerian girl called Louise, was only twenty-one. At least, when he told the story Richard said she was called Louise. He couldn't really remember her name. All he could recall was that she had a delicious broken accent and a great and glorious bust. There wasn't a pupil or a teacher at Bedales who wasn't conscious of Louise's bosom. It was the most remarkable thing about her and during the first few days of her one term at the school it was a topic of excited and guilty conversation in dormitory and staff-room alike. Adam was ill that term, genuinely ill, and found himself alone in the sanatorium with Louise. She nursed him, then she kissed him, then she undressed him, then he undressed her, then they made love, and after five dangerous, thrilling, amazing weeks, the whole school seemed to know, the buildings throbbed with lust, Louise was fired and Adam was told that a repetition of anything similar would lead to his instant dismissal as well.

That same summer Laurence Olivier was appearing as Othello at the Chichester Festival Theatre, just an hour by bus from the school. For as long as Richard could remember, Olivier had been his idol. With his mother in the Piazzale Stefani he had seen *Richard III* and *The Prince and the Showgirl* and *Spartacus*, but it wasn't so much the individual performances that excited him as the *idea* of Olivier, the phenomenon, the icon. Richard booked a lone ticket for a Saturday matinee and wrote to Olivier, care of the theatre, explaining when he was coming and asking if Sir Laurence would consider signing his programme after the performance. It was like writing to Zeus. Richard's hand shook as he put the letter inside the envelope.

When the great day came – it was a brilliant English summer's day, golden and hot; Adam and Louise, up on Stoner Hill, quite naked, made love out of doors for the first time – Richard set off for Olympus full of trepidation. Richard knew his *Othello*, knew the entire play by heart. In his head, as he watched, perched on the edge of his seat at the back of the packed auditorium, surrounded by a thousand people but oblivious of them, he played Iago, Richard Faber played Iago to Laurence Olivier's Othello, every scene, every line, every word. And when it was all over, when Olivier, bare-footed, jet-black, colossal, had risen from his deathbed and raised his pale palms in gracious and final acknowledgement of the audience's wild roar, and then, gracefully, gently, had run, like a panther in slow motion, from the stage, Richard filed out with the other mortals and lingered in the foyer, drained, dazed and uncertain, wondering whether, after all, he dared make his way round to the stage door.

He knew where it was. He had located it before the performance. He left the theatre and walked towards the car park. It was only five o'clock. He stopped and turned back. He took up a position about ten yards from the stage door itself. There was a convenient tree for him to lean against. He could pretend to read his programme. He looked about him, casually, and checked his watch now and again, as though he was early for the evening performance and was waiting for a friend. At first there was a lot of movement by the stage door, comings and goings, banter, laughter, joshings, reprimands. Then, after half an hour, three-quarters maybe, a lull. He had watched them all come out, in gaggles or one by one, Brabantio and Lodovico, Roderigo, Emilia, Iago, stagehands, senators, Cypriots, Venetians, Cassio, Desdemona. Where was Olivier? Had he missed the Moor?

Quickly he ran forward, as though suddenly he was playing a game of hide-and-seek and was darting from one tree to the next before being caught. The door was wide open. He walked straight in. On the left was a sliding glass window and a little booth where he had expected to find the stage-door keeper. He had rehearsed what he was going to say. There was no one there. He pushed the inner door. It opened on to a narrow circular corridor. He stepped forward. To the left his path was blocked by a metal clothes-rail on castors packed with heavy costumes. He turned to the right, and then he saw him. Laurence Olivier was walking along the corridor towards him. He was carrying a small battered briefcase and a light fawn raincoat. He was wearing a business suit, and a trilby, and horn-rimmed glasses. He looked so small and old. And ordinary. He looked exactly, *exactly*, like Uncle Franco, his mother's uncle, who used to come to them each Easter, the manager with the Bank of Turin.

'Can I help you, my dear?'

'I wrote—'

'Oh yes?'

'I'm at Bedales—'

'Good. Good.' Olivier paused and ran his tongue along the inside of his lower lip. 'Marvellous school. Years since I visited. My first wife went there, don't y'know.'

He sounded like Richard's father. He had stopped immediately in front of the boy. Richard was standing face to face with Laurence Olivier. Zeus held out his hand and Richard shook it. It was quite soft.

'Will you sign my programme?'

'By all means. Name, rank, number?'

Richard didn't understand. 'Richard Faber. I want to be an actor.'

'Oh Christ!' Olivier laughed and, behind his glasses, Richard could see him rolling his eyes to heaven.

'I'd like to play Iago.'

Olivier smiled and gave a little growl. 'Mmm. You'd better see the stage then. Come.' And the mighty god put his hand on Richard's shoulder and steered the fifteen-year-old through a swing door that led straight on to the vast and empty stage.

'Here we are. Don't look down, look up. It's a difficult space this, tough nut to crack. You've got to take 'em all in with one sweep. You've got to make 'em notice you the moment you appear.' Gently he moved Richard towards a shallow step right at the front of the stage. 'I think this would be the best spot for you to come on. D'ye see?'

'And what about you?'

Zeus narrowed his eyes. 'Oh.' The eyes all but disappeared. 'Oh. I can come on anywhere!'

A burst of laughter, and then it was over. A softer chuckle, another smile, a second handshake, a never-to-be-forgotten pat on the left shoulder, a kindly dismissal. 'Good luck, young man. What was the name?'

'Richard Faber.'

'I like it. Good canopy name.'

'I am going to be a great actor one day.'

Olivier stood back a moment and looked at the boy. 'Yes,' he said, quite slowly. 'Yes, I believe you are.' He narrowed his eyes again and let his jaw fall open. 'But not too soon, my dear. If you don't mind.'

T W O

Within seven years Richard would see the words in print: COULD THIS BE THE NEW OLIVIER?

From the start Richard had an absolute sense of his own destiny. He *was* the new Olivier – and the new Marlon Brando – and the new Orson Welles. He knew it. He'd always known it. But that others might see it too, might commit themselves to it in print, in a national newspaper, that was good, that was very good.

The time would come when Richard would stop reading newspapers altogether, would recoil – recoil physically, flinch away – from the very sight of a news-stand, contriving the path through airport concourse or shopping mall least likely to bring him face to face with his fair-weather friends, the broadsheets, the tabloids, the celebrity magazines. But that was later. For twenty years, at least, Richard Faber took much delight in reading about Richard Faber. Just as you can hear your own name spoken in a whisper across a crowded room, Richard's eye could find himself instantly on a page of crowded print.

In their day Theodore Faber and Isabella Bertolazzi had been treated with consistent courtesy, kindness even, by an enviably indulgent press. Richard's mother had the twin advantages of being a beautiful woman and a serious actress, a quality pin-up meriting quality prose. Richard's father's age and blindness, and chosen profession, warranted respect, commanded veneration. He featured only occasionally in news items – at the time of Isabella's death; in a muddled protest with Bertrand Russell; collecting an honorary degree alongside Yehudi Menuhin and Diana Dors – but was regular, and wonderfully reliable, 'profile' fodder. He looked so striking in the full-page photograph. Karsh of Ottawa, Mark Gerson, Jane Bown, Jerry Bauer, Snowdon, great and varied were the classy snappers who lined up to immortalise the ancient bard. They brought diverse and substantial talents to their task, but, oddly, the end result always looked much the same: craggy, grainy, magnificent, lighting by Gregg Toland, styling by Old Father Time. Even the colour shots *felt* black and white. Eve Arnold, a fellow parent at Bedales, said: 'Theodore Faber was like Marilyn. You couldn't take a rotten picture. But, unlike Marilyn, every one came out the same. Whether you were trying for something casual or an action picture, it always turned out a formal portrait. The old boy had grandeur.' And, of course, for the profile writers, whether commissioned to produce a thousand words or ten (the Tynan piece for the *New Yorker* was the most verbose: 'I have been up the mountain to meet the blind man and I see more clearly now') the benevolence-inducing bonus was that their subject lived in Verona and entertained with style. The scribes came not as ruthless investigative reporters, but as literary pilgrims bent on being charmed at the shrine of the great war poet and grateful to be wined and dined (on expenses) up the hill ('my local trattoria') or down the lane ('I believe the *Observer* will want to feel it has treated us to the *crema caramel all' amaretto*, don't you? It is Ciccarelli's speciality and, if we are to speak of Ezra Pound, a just desert is called for.').

All the profiles told the same story, both because most profiles are merely a recycling of the chosen subject's cuttings file – so that layer upon familiar layer is built up over the years (the first lie is the one that counts) and this year's questions are simply based on last year's answers – and because Theodore Faber rarely varied his routine. The great man's set-pieces were not all that exceptional – indeed, of their type and time, they were all too predictable: the childhood encounter with Robert Browning, dying in Venice; E.M. Forster, not connecting in Florence; Pound, mad in Pisa; Maugham, gaga at Cap Ferrat; Max, incomparable at Rapallo – but the way he told them . . . ah, that was special. The confessional manner, the intimate touch, transformed barnacled anecdotes into fresh revelations, new secrets shared. Right to the end, Theodore Faber kept a firm grip on the three rules of charm.

Whenever a profile appeared Theodore asked after the photographs – and occasionally asked for copies of the photographs – but he rarely asked anyone to read him extracts and never troubled Signora Bosco (who lived in Vicenza and, for love not money, turned material into Braille as required) for a full transcription. When Richard started to be written about – at first in reviews, later in interviews – the son, unlike the father, devoured every word. He said seeing his name in print made him feel more real, gave him a sense of identity and definition. On the day the line appeared linking his name with Olivier's for the first time, with studied insouciance Richard sauntered into a dozen different newsagents to purchase a single copy of the same paper in each one. He checked the piece in all the copies. He read it first, standing in the hallway of his flat, frozen in a brilliant spotlight of his own imagining; then, slowly and deliberately, he made himself a pot of coffee and lay back on his bed to read it at leisure, again and again. He read it in one room, then in another, at different speeds, by different lights, at different times of day. He read it over and over again, in his head, out loud, *sotto voce*. He put it away. And then came back to it. Time and again. And again and again. The line was still there. It didn't go away. 'Could this be the new Olivier?' Yeesss!

Richard's photograph first appeared in the paper at the time of his mother's funeral. It was a striking picture of his father holding his hand as they walked alone together along the Sottoriva towards Sant' Anastasia. Old man and young boy united in grief. While Richard recognised it as a compelling image, touching and evocative, and tried to re-create it, years later, in his television film of Marghanita Laski's *Little Boy Lost*, it meant little to him, he didn't value it, because he knew he was in the picture not as himself but as the child of his parents. But when a school photograph of him, aged fourteen, playing Sherlock Holmes in his own adaptation of *A Study in Scarlet*, with Adam as Dr Watson, made the third page of the *Petersfield Post*, Richard felt his career – and, in many ways, his real life – had begun at last.

Adam was a solid Dr Watson. That's what you need with a Watson, after all. Richard, both at fourteen and when he came back to the part aged thirty-five (and played Holmes and Mycroft and Moriarty all in the one production!), knew he had all the qualities to be the definitive Sherlock Holmes. A bravura character required bravura playing. Even as a boy Richard handled the pipe and the violin and the syringe of cocaine not as clichéd props but as outward manifestations of the inner torment of the great detective and tortured genius. To his audience it might be a forty-minute end-of-term entertainment: to Richard it was more akin to a harrowing masterpiece emerging from the anguished bowels of Eugene O'Neill.

While Adam appeared in – and lit – every one of Richard's school productions, both of them knew that Richard was destined to be the star, and Adam wasn't. In due course Adam went off to Oxford (to St Catherine's, to read Law, to secure an unsurprising Second), while Richard, more unexpectedly, made his way to the Bristol Old Vic Theatre School. He wouldn't apply for any of the more famous London schools because he had determined that when the time came for his first appearance on a London stage it would be in a leading role capable of making him a star.

At Bristol he joined a good crowd. It was a good year. His contemporaries included Jeremy Irons, Tim Pigott-Smith, Simon Cadell. But while they shone, Richard blazed. From day one, he was the front-runner. He got the parts, he stole the notices, he won the prizes. All the same, the others seemed quite to like him, though later they claimed they didn't really know him. 'He wasn't knowable,' said Simon. 'He didn't let you in. We weren't jealous. You aren't jealous of people like Richard. They've got it. You know it. They know it. In a way, that's that. We thought he was a bit mad, of course, but then Olivier was mad, Sir Ralph was mad. Look at Edmund Kean! But Richard wasn't just obsessed – we were all obsessed, more or less. Richard was *possessed*.'

In his third term at Bristol a boy called Stefan told him he had fallen in love with him. Richard was profoundly embarrassed, not by the declaration, which touched and rather pleased him, but by the realisation that when Stefan (who was playing Curio to Richard's Orsino in the end of year *Twelfth Night*) turned to him in their shared dressing room and stammered, 'Richard, I think

I've fallen in love with you,' Richard had no idea what the poor boy was called.

'You're too ego-centric. It's not healthy to be so self-absorbed.' That was Emma's verdict. 'I'm not saying you're egotistic. That's different. You're just too wrapped up in yourself.'

Emma Irving was the jolly, jaunty, genially bossy girl with whom Richard shared a tiny flat above the launderette at the Clifton end of Whiteladies Road. She was a year older than Richard, loud but likeable, opinionated but not dogmatic, chaotic but pleasantly domesticated: she had brought her own basil plant from home. There was a comforting Big Sister feel to her manner, a touch of hockey sticks and horses, and a boyishness in her *jolie laide* appearance that made her quite appealing at twenty-one and left her quite plain at forty. Richard called her 'a public school Rita Tushingham'. He'd been drawn to her at once by the rumour that she was a direct descendant of the first theatrical knight, Sir Henry Irving, which was wonderful, and then by the fact that she had a room to let in the right place at the right time, which was convenient.

Richard and Emma became good friends, what Richard, with his deliberately old-fashioned way with words, called 'best chums'. Emma was quite ready for something more, and there were the halting opening moves of what might have been a first affair for both of them. They would sit late into the night, a coy caricature of sixties students in bedsit-land teetering on the brink of the age of permissiveness, hunched up in front of their wheezy, spluttering gas fire, drinking hot chocolate from earthenware mugs, letting the crumbs from their digestive biscuits fall and settle into the gutters of their books, hers by Carl Jung, his by Stanislavski.

She didn't pretend to understand the Jung (it was *Memories, Dreams, Reflections*) but for some reason it was on their reading list and it felt right. It felt good. What's more, it gave her the excuse to tell Richard about her dreams and invite him to reciprocate. On Sundays, their only day away from the school, a difficult day for Richard, Emma's favourite day by far, they got up late, and after brunch (Emma loved the word, loved the idea) they went for long walks around Clifton, talking, laughing, planning. When they held hands for the first time – they were standing looking into the window of an antiques shop on St Michael's Hill – Emma felt a charge of electricity that took her breath away. She looked at Richard's reflection in the window and her eyes sparkled. Richard looked back and smiled a gentle, kindly smile. He squeezed her hand and felt it was good to have a friend. Nothing more.

One clear, cold night in July, a night with a chill and a full moon, 'a night for mystery and romance', said Emma, 'a Daphne du Maurier night', said Richard, a night to remember anyway, it was the last night of *Twelfth Night*, it was after they got in from the cast party (at which Stefan had vowed to commit suicide, and failed miserably, and Richard had sung 'You're the Top', and succeeded triumphantly – Bristol had not seen the routine with the cane before), it was late, very late, nearer four than three, and their earthenware mugs were filled with a final draught of the deep south. Richard was lying on the rug in front of the fire, quietly drunk, mug balanced precariously on his chest, hands clasped loosely behind his head. He was gazing at Emma. It was a look she hadn't seen before. It was a look she hardly saw now the flickering firelight was so dim. She was on the sofa, facing the fire, her face burning, her legs stretched out in front of her, her bare toes pressed hard up against Richard's thigh. The hiss and crackle of the gas were comforting. She slid lower on the sofa and slowly pushed her feet up and over his leg so they nestled in his lap.

'Isn't it about time we went to bed together?' she asked.

As she spoke Richard realised that he had just been reflecting that she was a competent Viola, technically accomplished, but completely ordinary. 'She can do it, but she hasn't got it. There's no magic there.' He rolled on to his side, and spilt the wine, and said, 'I'm sorry, I think I'm going to be sick.'

In the morning Adam turned up and, by lunchtime, Adam and Emma were lovers.

Richard didn't ask for the details, let alone an explanation, but Adam was ready with both. 'I want it. She wants it. You don't.'

Richard and Adam were still best friends. Adam visited Bristol. Richard travelled to Oxford. They spent vacations together in Verona where Richard told Adam of his dream to create a world-famous Shakespeare Festival in English in the Teatro Romano on the bank above the Adige, and Adam told Richard of his dream to make love to all the women in the world. They each thought the other ridiculous. They knew each other by habit; being alone in each other's company was easy because it was uncomplicated: there was no striving, no strain, no play-acting. And the fact that their preposterous preoccupations were so different meant that neither felt threatened by the other. They were like brothers, without sibling rivalry. And Theodore played the foolish, fond old grandfather to both of them. He was now so ancient that his wives, his mistresses, his cronies had all died. There really was no one left. Jane still came, but far less frequently and, though determined not to, she spoilt the visits by wondering out loud why she was still coming. 'Is it duty or nostalgia?' It was no longer love.

While Theodore Faber still got a faint charge out of wooing and winning the pilgrim profile writers – all gratifyingly gobsmacked at how shrewd and sharp and erect and agile the Great War relic appeared to be – he had completely lost interest in himself. There was nothing more he could say or do that would surprise or intrigue him, so that the 'visits from the boys' were his reason for living. He was immensely proud of Richard, and swore he wouldn't die, couldn't die, until he had seen 'the lad' play Hamlet at Stratford-upon-Avon.

'Beerbohm-Tree was my first Hamlet,' he said, tapping the tips of his spindly fingers together in delight at having a licence for legitimate reminiscence. 'William Gilbert said it was funny without being in the least bit vulgar!'

'And the best?' asked Richard, knowing full well what he was prompting.

'The best is yet to be!' gurgled the old boy. 'That's what you want me to say, my son, and I do – with pleasure, with conviction, because I know it to be true. The last Hamlet I saw, actually saw with my own eyes, was Sarah Bernhardt. I went with Max. We sat stony-faced and rigid for four hours. We daren't look at each other because we knew that if, for a moment, we caught sight of one another we couldn't have contained ourselves. One laugh in that dangerous atmosphere and the whole structure of polite solemnity would have toppled down burying beneath it the national reputation for good manners! That was the *Hamlet* when Max told me he had at last realised that talking to oneself is a bad sign.'

'One day I shall do a one-man show as Max,' Richard said.

'Why don't you do a one-man show as me? I'm a set text, y'know. Max isn't. I'll waive my royalties.'

'I am going to do *Samson Agonistes* with you, Papa.'

'You will be Samson?'

'Yes, Papa. And you will be Old Manoa.'

'And I shall screw Delilah,' Adam said. And they all drank to that.

Theodore adored Adam. He loved his lewdness: he

encouraged him to talk dirty. It reminded him of his own randiness.

'Who have you had today?' was his customary greeting as they gathered for their six o'clock Prosecco. 'I want all the details. Spare me nothing. For a start, how old was she? You know my rule. Never more than half your age plus seven years. I've stuck to it all my life. Trouble is, now there seems to be a shortage of willing fifty-two-year-olds!'

'I don't think Mother was half your age plus seven years.'

'We weren't speaking of mothers and wives, boy. We were speaking of lovers and mistresses. Who was it who told me "Never have your wife in the morning in case something better turns up during the day"?'

Richard had been surprised to discover this Priapic aspect to his father's character. It didn't disturb him, or hurt him, but it didn't interest him that much either. It was what his father and Adam had in common. That was all. As a child Richard had worshipped his father in a simple, childish way, as primitives might have worshipped a pagan god, as the folk over the rainbow worshipped the Great Oz. When the truth dawned, when Richard came to realise that the intellectual Titan was also a dirty old man, there was a flash of disappointment, a flicker of disgust, and then a pushing of the issue to one side. 'So what?' he thought, and determined to think of it no more.

Before the end of his final term at Bristol Richard was

offered his first professional engagement. The production was a revival, in Manchester, of R.C. Sherriff's classic account of life and death in the trenches of Flanders, *Journey's End*. Theodore Faber, ancient but upright, flew to England for his son's first night. 'I knew Robert Sherriff,' he said, 'knew him well. We lost touch when he went to Hollywood and wrote *Goodbye Mr Chips*, but I knew him in the trenches. We were friends. He was with the East Surrey Regiment, commissioned at eighteen. We were wounded together at Ypres.' Whether or not there was any truth in what Theodore said about Sherriff hardly mattered: that the sole surviving poet of the Great War should come to Manchester and endorse the play was just what the box office needed. The six-week run sold out as it opened and the pre-publicity ensured that the critics from the nationals stood down the stringers and left their deputies in town while they covered the production themselves. Richard played the part of Henry Stanhope, the war-weary young captain who turns to drink to disguise cowardice. It was the role Olivier had created in the original production in 1928, when he was twenty-one. Richard was just twenty.

Richard won the *Evening Standard* award as 'most promising newcomer', and when the play transferred to the West End, found his name above the title in a typeface larger than the author's. He stayed with it for nine months and, each night, as he stepped into the warmth of the stage lighting, he felt he was coming home. 'In the wings I was terrified. The moment I stepped onto the stage I felt utterly secure. This was where I belonged.'

He left *Journey's End* on a Saturday in June and the very next day travelled back to Manchester to start rehearsals for another twenties revival that would turn into another personal triumph, and another West End transfer. In *The Vortex* Richard played the Noël Coward part (John Gielgud had played it too, in 1925; and Ivor Novello in the silent movie version; Isabella had seen – and adored – Dirk Bogarde in the revival in 1952; Richard loved the heritage of the role as much as the role itself). This time the critics were divided about the play, but unanimous when it came to the leading man. 'It may be melodramatic mush, and too dreadfully dated, my dears, but never mind all that, Richard Faber makes it a must-see. He is magnificent.' They liked the look: tall, dark, handsome; they liked the voice: the precision, the touch of huskiness, the occasional crack; they liked the manner: arrogant, theatrical, unexpected.

At the age of twenty-two Richard found himself making his debut with the Royal Shakespeare Company in Stratford-upon-Avon: Sebastian in *Twelfth Night*, Berowne in *Love's Labour's Lost*, and the title role in *Henry V*. 'Richard Faber is rapidly establishing himself as the pre-eminent classical actor of his generation. He has a great deal going for him. He is handsome, with chocolate-box good looks, sophisticated rather than sweet, more Bendicks than Black Magic. He has an outstanding pedigree: his mother was one of the leading ladies of the Italian cinema in the immediate post-war years and his father is one of the century's great poets – which may help explain young Faber's wonderful facility as a verse speaker. What is most extraordinary about him, and not so easily explained, is his sheer stage presence. He has an authority that belies his years. Richard Faber is an heroic actor who appears to spring from an ancient tradition. What is odd is that what he does doesn't seem stagey and old-fashioned. On the contrary, it feels natural and thrillingly new.'

On the first night of his son's first *Hamlet*, 23 April 1973, Theodore Faber sat in the stalls of the Shakespeare Memorial Theatre and let the warm salt tears run down his face. After the performance father and son stood in Richard's tiny dressing room and hugged one another as they had not hugged one another for ten years or more. Richard was taller than his father now, stronger, much stronger, but he clung to him as a little boy.

'This is my boy.'

'Funny old Papa.'

'If only Max could have seen you. Think how he'd have written you up! If only Isabella could have seen you.'

'Perhaps she could. Perhaps she can. I believe in angels, Papa. Don't you?'

'Sentimental child. Why not? Nothing is too wonderful to be true.'

As he flew back to Verona, for the last time as it turned out, Theodore Faber sensed the nervous tension in the passenger on his left. 'You're quite right to feel anxious,' he thought. 'This flight may well not make it. Indeed, this could be the perfect way to go. Perhaps the good Lord will dash the plane from the skies. "From morn to

35

noon he fell, from noon to dewy eve, a summer's day; and with the setting sun, dropt from the zenith like a falling star." I have heard my son play Hamlet a hundred yards from where Shakespeare lies buried. I am content.' Out loud he said, 'I don't mind if I die now. Do you?'

They hit a little bit of turbulence and Theodore Faber's unhappy fellow traveller threw up.

For seven years Richard Faber worked in the theatre without pause. He went from one production to the next. He never stopped. He never took a holiday. He never looked back. In Stratford he had a one-room flat in New Street. In London he and Adam shared an extraordinary apartment in the old St Pancras hotel.

He learnt about it while he was doing the voice-over for a television documentary series on England's 'Hidden Glories', neglected architectural gems (Leighton House, Alexandra Palace, the Spitalfields Synagogue) and oddities (the Abbey Mills Pumping Station at Stratford East, the Maharajah's Well at Henley-on-Thames) that would have made John Betjeman's heart skip a beat and provided an uncomplicated half-hour of Sunday afternoon viewing for middlebrows too mean to invest in membership of the National Trust. Richard spent only two days on the project, sitting in a suffocating studio in Shepherd's Bush, but he was so taken by the sound of the St Pancras hotel – four hundred empty rooms in a deserted palace by King's Cross, a glorious, grandiose Gilbert Scott masterpiece, once the pride of the London Midland and Scottish Railway Company, from the 1870s to 1935 a bustling station hotel, then offices, now nothing, Sleeping Beauty's castle on the Euston Road – that he asked to see it and then, amazingly, persuaded the property services people at British Rail to let him live in it.

He was given a five-year lease for a peppercorn rent because he agreed to cover the substantial costs of restoring plumbing and electricity to the three suites that he and Adam commandeered on the first floor and because the estate manager was a fan who managed to convince his bosses that, until the redevelopment plans were finally agreed, having Richard Faber as a tenant would 'send out the right signal'.

Richard loved living in the St Pancras hotel, not so much for the rooms that made up the flat, as for the thrill of having the run of the rest of the place. For Richard the chief glory of the building was the grand staircase, a marvel of high Victorian engineering, flight after flight of stone steps rising up in one heady sweep the whole height of the building, with elaborate wrought-iron balustrades, stone dragons standing sentinel on each floor, gothic arches, and bizarre niches painted with wonderfully romantic murals. Richard would stand and talk to the figures in the paintings. He would run up the stairs like Errol Flynn in pursuit of the Sheriff of Nottingham, dance down like Fred Astaire in *Swing Time*, leap an entire flight like Olivier in his film of *Hamlet*.

On television Richard allowed his voice to be heard, but he wouldn't let his face be seen. 'I will not be a television actor. One day I shall be a film star, but until then if you want to see me you will find me in the theatre.'

He was offered television work almost every week and, two or three times a year, a small part in a film. He turned them all down. 'I don't want to play a minor Nazi in a Hollywood blockbuster. If I want to play a baddie I'll have a go at Richard III at the National, thank you very much.'

'What about the money?'

'I don't need the money!'

'What about the women?'

'You can have the women.'

And Adam did. Richard was not yet famous, but among those who love the theatre he had an extraordinary following: most nights there were girls lingering at the stage door and, on the evenings when he went to the theatre to meet up with Richard after the performance, Adam would usually manage to bring one of them back to St Pancras with him. They worshipped Richard Faber, but they went to bed with Adam Waterson. As they made love, they talked of Richard. Sometimes, when a girl was reluctant, Adam would say, 'Richard has asked me to sleep with you. We are doing this for him.' Apparently, instead of bursting out laughing, or slapping him across the face, they mostly obliged. Perhaps the poor creatures believed him.

Richard did not need money. Richard did not need sex. And then he met Maisie, and everything changed.

THREE

Richard Faber first set eyes on Maisie Rivers on 5 October 1979, his thirtieth birthday. He was struck at once by her amazing looks. Everybody was. Maisie Rivers was sensationally beautiful; and full of contradictions. Tall yet slight; naturally blond with strong, dark eyebrows; that fabulous, full, ever-smiling mouth quite at odds with those wide and shining ever-mournful eyes; handsome high cheekbones either side of an absurd baby-doll nose; the catwalk presence with the kittenish allure; a boyish look inside a girlish figure. Compelling, and confusing. Seductive, and elusive. Wonderful, and very strange.

Richard recalled their first conversation exactly.

'What's your name?'

'Maisie Rivers.'

'That's unusual.'

'I'm unusual.'

'No, I meant "Maisie" is unusual, not very modern.'

'I'm not very modern.'

'You look as modern as they come to me.'

'It's Miranda really, but everyone calls me Maisie.'

'I like Miranda.'

'You would.'

'How long have you been acting then?'

'I haven't. This is my first audition.'

'How old are you?'

'Oh, God. I'm not going to have to sleep with you, am I?'

That night, over his birthday dinner at the Ritz, Richard recounted the exchange and Adam laughed.

'You really haven't slept with anyone, have you?'

'It's not that remarkable.'

'It is. You're thirty.' They had known one another more than half their lives. Adam gazed steadfastly at Richard through the flickering candlelight and the haze of Fleurie (they were on to the second bottle now) and smiled. 'You're not gay, are you?' He asked it playfully, with affection. 'People have secret lives.'

Richard smiled. 'I have no secret life,' he said.

It was true. All that Richard Faber was and did was there for all the world to see. He was an actor. That was his life, the totality of his life. He had embraced his vocation as a young postulant for the priesthood might, but there had been no vow of celibacy, no tormented struggle with the lure of the things of the flesh. He had simply never fancied anyone sufficiently to do anything much about it. He hadn't made time for love, and lust had never claimed him. It was a relief really, to have been spared the distractions of desire. The likes of Adam, for whom voracious screwing was a way of life, might think him freakish: he accepted he was unusual, he doubted he was unique.

'Well then,' said his friend, with a suitably wolfish leer, 'are we going to engage this Maisie Rivers?'

'I think so.'

'Isn't she too tall?'

'Probably.'

'But we're going to book her all the same?'

'Yes – if you don't mind. And, if you don't mind, you're going to keep your hands off her. Okay?'

Adam raised his glass. 'Anything you say, birthday boy. You're the boss.'

In fact, they were equal partners. They had fifty shares apiece in St Pancras Productions, a £100 off-the-shelf company, managed by Adam and designed to market Richard's talents as actor and director. They produced plays (which occasionally won awards and regularly lost money); they made films for television (and, reluctantly, Richard now agreed to appear in them: the plays had to be subsidised somehow); they planned to make movies. Within five years they had created a business of some substance. The enterprise had been Adam's idea. Four years out of Oxford, he had worked out that life as a solicitor was fine, fine and dandy (especially if you were one for detail, and convivial lunches, and golf), but limited. With Richard, there was uncertainty, and no golf, but the food and wine were plentiful and the possibilities appeared infinite.

They were both about twenty-five – it was during the run of Richard's first *Hamlet* – when Adam came up with the idea for *Murderer*. It was a simple enough concept: a series of one-hour dramas using documentary techniques to tell the lurid tales of some of the world's most notorious murderers.

'This is the story we start with.' Adam was brandishing a sheaf of newspaper cuttings. 'The incredible case of Emil Edmund Kemper III.'

'A Ruritanian prince?' Richard loved dressing up.

'A multiple murderer from Santa Cruz – and he's exactly your age.'

Richard looked at the photograph. 'He's hardly my *size*. He must be twenty stone.'

'Twenty-one. It'll show off your versatility.'

'Try Orson Welles.'

'I'm serious. This is what you need.'

Richard was flicking through the cuttings. 'This is gross, Adam.'

'It's real, Richard. It's a true story.'

'It's sick. "She had a rather large forehead and I was imagining what her brain looked like and I just wanted to put a bullet in it. One side of me says, 'Wow, what an attractive chick, I'd like to talk to her, to date her.' The other side of me says, 'I wonder how her head would look on a stick.'" I can't believe you're showing me this. You want me to play some sort of serial decapitator?'

'I want you to get inside the mind of a psychopath, Richard Faber – and amaze and terrify the world!'

'It's revolting, Adam. This fellow chops off his own mother's head.'

'Yes.' Adam smirked and retrieved the cuttings. 'On Easter Saturday. And to stop her nagging he cut out her larynx and tried to stuff it down the waste disposal. But it wouldn't go. "Even when she was dead," said Kemper, "she was still bitching at me." What a line!'

'Dear friend and partner, when I want good lines and I choose to play the part of a fat man with a weakness for beheading women, I'll have a go at King Henry the Eighth.'

'Keith Michell's already doing it, and it's selling across the planet.' Adam raised a patronising left eyebrow: 'Don't you want a worldwide success?'

'I do, Adam, I do. But not with this.'

In the event, Richard did become famous the world over for playing murderers, but Emil Kemper wasn't one of them. Adam developed the script (with a first draft by John Osborne, no less), but the money men baulked at the scene where Kemper invites his mother's best friend to tea, crushes her head with a brick, cuts it off, and then makes love to the torso. 'The violence was fine,' said Osborne with glee. 'It was the sex they couldn't cope with.'

Over four years Richard portrayed a total of twenty-six true-life murderers, ancient and modern, old and young, hideous and handsome, infamous and virtu-ally unknown. His versatility was given full rein and his international celebrity (and his and Adam's bank balances) grew as the series was taken up by country after country right around the globe. He started with Donald Hume, petty and pathetic, and finished with Dick Turpin, swashbuckling and heroic. Richard used to say if it hadn't been for Donald Hume he'd never have met Maisie Rivers. Donald Hume was certainly the key that unlocked the door to worldwide fame and fortune. 'They were a motley bunch our murderers, all monsters, of course, in different ways, all loathsome, but not all obviously crazy like Hume or Haigh or Charles Manson. Some were apparently quite sane – sophisticated – stylish even. I'm ashamed to say I had a lot of fun with the Venezuelan count who murdered his wife for a bet. And Dick Turpin's death, his public execution . . . it was a wonderful scene to play. We filmed it in York, on the race course, virtually on the spot where it happened in 1739 or whenever. Turpin was about thirty-four, oh-so-gorgeous, and oh-so-conscious-of-it. He bought himself a brand-new suit to wear to the gallows. He hired mourners at his own expense. He wooed the crowd as he was carted through them, chatted amiably to the hangman, and then, cool as a cucumber, climbed the ladder and, with a final graceful wave, jumped nonchalantly to his death. He went in triumph – and a legend was born! Yeesss!'

In all, *Murderer* was dubbed into thirteen languages and sold to thirty-two countries. Even now some channel somewhere is recycling it still and, to this day, getting on for a quarter of a century after the first frame was shot, the video sales produce a tidy and regular return. The series won huge audiences, but no awards. It gave Adam a position, recognition, status. He was only in his twenties, remember. ('What do you do?' 'I produce *Murderer*.' 'Wow!') It made Richard a copper-bottomed, gold-plated internationally bankable television star. But that wasn't what he wanted. Patrick McGoohan was not his role model. Richard Faber was the new Olivier. That was his destiny.

Adam wanted more of *Murderer* 'because the networks want more because the public want more'. Richard wanted something else. 'In 1946 when Olivier triumphed with Oedipus what did he follow it with?'

Adam knew the answer (Adam had picked up quite a bit of Olivier folklore through his years with Richard), but he wanted to tease, so he said, 'Caligula? Great idea.'

'No.'

'He should have done Caligula.'

'He did Puff.'

'As in the magic dragon?' Adam was happy to play the caricature philistine.

'As in Sheridan's great comedy *The Critic*, you idiot.' Richard looked at his friend indulgently. 'Before the interval Olivier had it away with his mother and tore out his eyes and the audience wept buckets. And twenty minutes later he was back, camping it up in a regency romp, and the audience roared. Oedipus and Mr Puff. On the same stage. On the same night. Think of it, Adam!'

'I am thinking of it. If you want to go back to the theatre—'

'I do.'

'Maybe you *should* do Caligula then. Your public like you as a psychopath.'

'I am going to do *Alice in Wonderland.*'

'Christ Almighty.'

'As a musical.'

'And you'll be the Mad Hatter, I suppose?'

'Yes. And Lewis Carroll.'

'Jesus wept.'

'And for Alice we shall find ourselves a brand-new star. We shall take the world by storm!'

They were in the large drawing room at St Pancras. They called it 'the hall' and Adam had it furnished and lit in the style of Bluebeard's Castle: Hammer Horror meets Metro-Goldwyn-Mayer. Suddenly Richard took a silver-topped cane from the stand by the stairs – the one he'd always said was Edmund Kean's sword-stick – and threw it in the air, and caught it, and spun it, and tossed it over his shoulder, and caught it again, and brought it crashing down towards Adam's head. At the moment of impact the cane dissolved into a fantastic bunch of multicoloured feather flowers, and the two men roared and clashed their palms together, and late into the night the champagne flowed.

On reflection, of course, Adam saw the merits of the *Alice* idea. On reflection, Adam always agreed with Richard. And did his bidding. That was the deal. It was unspoken, but binding.

The open auditions for the title role in what became

known as 'Richard Faber's *Alice*' were held on the stage of the London Palladium on the first Thursday and Friday of October 1979. Margaret Thatcher was newly ensconced in Downing Street preparing to confront the trade unions and emasculate them, if need be personally, with her own teeth; in Bradford the so-called Yorkshire Ripper claimed his twelfth, and youngest, victim; in County Sligo the IRA, having murdered 316 soldiers in the current spate of 'troubles', was now celebrating 'the execution of Lord Louis Mountbatten'; on the other side of the world, in Cambodia, Pol Pot and Leng Sari were condemned to death *in absentia* for the mass murder of *millions* of their fellow countrymen; but cocooned in the darkened stalls of London's premier variety theatre Richard Faber sat serene, utterly absorbed in the wonderful world of white rabbits and lobster quadrilles.

The world of politics – in truth, the world outside the theatre – made little impact on Richard. He rarely watched the television news; he never listened to the radio; most days he looked at *The Times*, the *Daily Mail* and the *Evening Standard*, but he only glanced at the front page, never turned to the back, and only gave any concentrated attention to the arts pages and the obituaries. That month he took on board the suicide of Jean Seberg, because she was an actress, because Otto Preminger had cast her as Saint Joan, because Richard had met her once and been struck by the texture of her voice and her faraway look; the thought of her dead, cold, alone, in the back seat of her car abandoned in some Paris side-street appalled and touched him; about that he cared; the suggestion that she had been driven to suicide by the FBI because of her alleged involvement with the Black Panthers registered with him not at all. That was politics. That wasn't for him.

According to the *Mail* eighty thousand young hopefuls had applied to play Joan in the Preminger movie. The would-be musical Alices were rather fewer in number. Even so, over the two days, some five hundred girls, of varying ages, shapes, types and talents, made their anxious ways to Argyll Street in anticipation of instant stardom. Richard had never held an open audition before. Customarily he cast among friends. When he met and worked with an actor he liked and trusted, he did his best to work with them again. He took on new talent as well, brought on unknowns, but as a rule they came to his notice by way of established agents, or because he'd seen their work himself and sought them out, or because Adam had spotted them at the bus stop and effected an introduction. Never before had Richard Faber – *the* Richard Faber, 'British theatre's new *wunderkind*' (*Time* magazine), 'TV's murderous heart-throb' (the *Sun*) – simply invited all-comers to beat a path to his door and strut their stuff. He did so because *Alice* was different. He had not been involved in a musical before. He wanted to discover a new star. And Adam believed the publicity would be good.

Adam was right. All they did was place a modest advertisement in the back pages of *The Stage*, alongside the ads for topless showgirls looking for openings in

Algiers and pictures of Humphrey Bogart and Elizabeth II lookalikes, and at once the calls came flooding in, not just from agents, managers, mothers, but from the press and radio stations and local TV news magazines offering to run stories, features, competitions to find the 'Alice in Wonderland for our times'. A satisfactory amount of gentle *Alice* fever was generated and the advance takings at the box office began to lift.

The scene appealed to Richard because it came straight from several of his favourite movies. He and Adam sat in the auditorium of the Palladium, in virtual darkness, at a makeshift table in the centre of Row M, sustained by Mars bars and flasks of coffee, their notes lit by a single Anglepoise, taking it in turn to say (not entirely unselfconsciously), 'Thank you! We'll let you know . . .' and, 'Next!' The Crazy Gang, Danny Kaye, Liberace, Laurence Olivier – oh, yes – they'd all capered on these boards. Was the new Judy Garland going to come on next? If she was, you'd know it at once. Either they've got it or they haven't. Maisie had it all right.

'I'll never forget that audition.' Richard would tell the tale in much the same way in interview after interview down the years. (It became a set piece and, once established, not an inflection or a pause was changed. Looking back at the cuttings now you can be sure the slight variations in turn of phrase reflect the transcription skills of the journalists concerned rather than inconsistencies in Richard's performance.) 'She came on looking like a street urchin, torn jeans, T-shirt, bare feet. At first, she seemed a little confused, baffled, almost uncertain of where she was, as if she'd just woken from a deep sleep. But the moment she hit her mark, bang centre stage, she turned out front and smiled that amazing smile of hers. She was extraordinary. Beautiful. And different. Quite different. She didn't introduce herself, give her name or anything. She offered a slight bow and just went straight into her piece. We had no idea what to expect. What do you think we got? "To be or not to be", for God's sake! "To be or not to be, that is the question . . ." Can you imagine? We were casting Alice in Wonderland. We'd had two days of Shirley Temples and Bonnie Langfords – and now this! It was outrageous. It was absurd. But, believe me, it did the trick. We asked her to sing. She couldn't sing that well – she'd had no training to speak of – but the way she did it . . . I tell you: it was tingle-up-the-spine time. And when she danced . . . Oh, yes, if you want to know, all at once my heart stood still. No question: it was love at first sight.'

Adam told much the same story: 'Richard was transfixed immediately. Maisie was so unlike all the other girls. For a start she didn't turn up in a traditional Alice outfit, which was a pleasant surprise. She wore jeans and a T-shirt and sneakers. I think Richard imagined the bare feet. But she wasn't just different, she was *totally* different. She was like an enchanted creature from a Celtic fairy tale – but in modern dress. Right from the start, you sensed there was something strange and quite wild about her, something dangerous as well as beautiful. It was the danger as much as the beauty that attracted

Richard. He denied it – vehemently – but Richard was always drawn to danger.'

Alice, The Musical was a triumph. The critics were kind – Richard was still at the stage where it seemed he could do no wrong – and the audiences packed every performance for the three-month run because at first the notices and then the word-of-mouth made it clear they'd be getting what they wanted: gloss, glamour, class, warmth, sentiment, style, strong tunes, clever lyrics, sensational sets, pace, polish, panache, an award-winning cameo from Emma Irving as the Queen of Hearts ('Best Supporting Performance in a Musical'), a sensational debut from a new babe on the block ('A Star Is Born': the *Daily Express* has never shied away from clichés), and a show-stopper for the finale that from first preview to last night produced a standing ovation: a number when Maisie danced with both Lewis Carroll and the Mad Hatter simultaneously. If you saw it from the wings – mirrors, doubles, dry ice and all – you had to admit it was very clever stuff. If you saw it from out front, it made you believe in make-believe. 'Richard Faber and Maisie Rivers – magic!' *Daily Mail*, 4 December 1979. Of course, London hadn't seen Richard's routine with the cane before.

At the end of the performance on the first night, Richard stepped forward and, with some ceremony, presented Maisie to the audience who were happy to pretend they were in a movie too and rose to their feet and offered up what old troupers like to call 'the Palladium roar'. It rolled around the stage, it filled the flies, it swamped the wings, and, as it reached its crescendo, through it Emma heard Richard shouting, 'Where the hell's Adam got to? Where are the frigging flowers?' And then, in the nick of time, on waddled Tweedledum and Tweedledee laden with suitably overblown bouquets, two for Maisie and one each for the other ladies billed above the title.

Richard's dressing room was quite close to the stage, through the fire door, up a short flight of stairs. In he burst, still triumphant: 'Is the champagne poured? Is my partner ready and waiting? We need to celebrate! Where is he?' The champagne *was* poured. God, it looked good. Richard paused, took a deep breath and raised his glass. 'Yeesss!' God, it felt good. 'But where the fuck is Adam?'

'I'm here.' He was standing behind the door. 'I've got bad news.'

Richard knew at once. 'Papa.'

'Yes. I'm sorry.'

'When?'

'I don't know. Last night, this morning.' They looked at each other and smiled. Adam had been crying. Richard put his hand up to Adam's cheek and stroked him with the backs of his fingers.

'I think you'll miss him even more than I will.'

'Yes,' said Adam. 'I loved him a lot.'

'And he loved you.' Richard filled a second glass and passed it to his friend. 'No time for lamentation now.'

'He was very old.'

'He was *ancient*! He was a hundred and one.'

Adam laughed. 'Almost.'

'Let us raise our glasses – to my papa – and your friend.' And, quite suddenly, exhaustion overwhelmed him and he put his arms around Adam and started to sob uncontrollably.

The funeral was held ten days later at St Stephen's, Gloucester Road. Theodore Faber might have preferred it to have taken place at Santa Maria Antica, the little Romanesque church on the Via Arche Scaligeri, five hundred metres from his own front door. The notion of being laid to rest amid the celebrated Scaligeri tombs, Verona's masterpiece of fourteenth-century funerary art, had appealed to him since intimations of mortality first struck around the time Richard was born. However, the old boy would quite have understood that for Richard, now, 'the show must go on,' and if the choice was between bringing a dead poet to London or robbing a West End smash of its main attraction there was no contest. Also, as Richard tried to explain to Jane Stanhope, who had suddenly resurfaced, pinched around the mouth, puffy around the eyes, *in loco* grieving widow, 'St Stephen's, Gloucester Road, is a poets' church. Masefield, Eliot, it's their church. And it's Anglo-Catholic. It's ideal.' Jane, who had once seemed to Richard so fresh and full of sunlight, and now seemed so dowdy, so drear, so prone to pathetic attacks of the poor-me's, was not to be appeased. 'It's very far from ideal,' she muttered. 'It's just you being selfish. Sorry.' And she hung up.

At the funeral mass Richard sat alongside her, together with Adam and the Poet Laureate, just the four of them in the front pew, and Richard was conscious that while she sniffed noisily – irritatingly, and the tip of her nose was moist and red and ugly – and Adam appeared patently grief-stricken and John Betjeman beamed seraphically through plashy tears that streamed and tumbled down his cheeks, he, the only son, the only child, felt nothing, nothing at all. Numb is how he felt, remote from the present proceedings, distant from those around him. Given that he had always loved his father, this complete lack of sensation in the presence of his coffin was perplexing. And when the line from Ecclesiasticus came – 'Let us now praise famous men and the fathers that begat us' – he was alarmed to realise that at once his mind turned not to the great blind poet of the Great War but to himself, to Richard Faber, to his own fame, his own place in history.

Afterwards, in an appropriately faded hotel on the Gloucester Road, ham sandwiches and Riesling were served to around fifty favoured mourners. Richard pulled himself together and quietly worked the room. Jane stood by a window, drinking steadily, smoking slowly, feeling sorry for herself and certain that she would never see Richard again, and didn't want to. 'And some there be that have no memorial.' The Poet Laureate was blowing his nose. 'Pure Barbara Pym,' he gurgled at Adam who, wisely, chose not to respond.

Richard was the first to leave. Everyone understood. It was Wednesday and there was a matinee. Richard never missed a performance. Richard never missed a beat. Sentimentalists in the company sensed a difference in him: that afternoon, they said, his Carroll was more wistful, his Mad Hatter more manic. The audience, having read of his father's death, sustained their ovation as never before: Richard sensed they were standing a little straighter and had added a touch of gravitas to their loud hurrahs.

When the curtain fell the rest of the cast burst into spontaneous applause. They loved him, and he loved them, both for themselves and for their sweetness in loving him. By most accounts, and by the standards of a zonking great star, Richard was remarkably easy to work with, surprisingly tolerant and exceptionally generous to fellow performers. He was demanding, of course, but no more demanding of others than he was of himself. He wanted to be the best and to be surrounded by the best. He was an actor's director: he had a clear picture of what he wanted, he cast well and then let them get on with it. He was a fine leader of men and women: his company loved him, admired him, trusted him. The younger ones were in awe of him, the older ones respected him without resentment; given what he achieved on stage, they had little choice. He led from the front and played it as though Kipling's 'If' was not just a party piece but a personal mission statement. He had no favourites. Apart from Adam Waterson, and to an extent Emma Irving, he had no special friends. Then Maisie happened and everything changed.

*　　　*　　　*

Between shows, almost two months into the run, Emma found herself alone with Richard and unable to stop herself from saying what she'd been wanting to say for weeks: 'You know you're making a fool of yourself, Richard. She's a child.'

'I haven't touched her.'

'But you'd like to.'

'You don't understand.'

'I understand exactly.'

'I hardly ever speak to her.'

'But you look at her. And she looks at you. I can see what's happening. We all can. We're not blind. All I'm saying, Richard dear, is be careful. Please.'

It was true. Richard hardly ever spoke to Maisie, and they were never alone, except on stage, at every performance, and, just the once, in the wings. There was a small quick-change area in the opposite prompt corner, a tiny makeshift roofless room, created by two screens, equipped with a single low-voltage lamp and a full-length mirror. It was there because Richard had two quick changes in the first half and Maisie one just before the finale. On the last Monday of the run, during the interval, Richard went down on to the stage and into the quick-change area to collect something. Maisie was there, alone and completely naked. She looked up at him and smiled. 'It's all right. It doesn't matter. It's us and we're different.'

The show completed its sell-out season and closed as planned on the first Saturday in April. Richard and

Adam hosted what was destined to become a legendary end-of-show cast party at the St Pancras hotel. The *Alice* company had a ball: they laughed and loved, and rocked and rolled, and ate and smoked and drank till dawn. Emma watched Richard and Adam spied on Maisie. Now and again the star-cross'd lovers passed – on the great stairway, in the hall, queueing for the loo – and Richard raised his glass to Maisie and Maisie smiled, but through the night they spoke to one another no more than twice. At six in the morning, however, as arranged, they met outside, in the Euston Road, and drove to Heathrow, and caught the eight thirty flight to Verona. Richard, you'll recall, was thirty. Maisie was not quite sixteen.

FOUR

'Of course it caused a fucking scandal. That's because nobody understood. Or tried. Or wanted to. We *were* star-cross'd lovers. We were fated for one another. That's the way it was. We were meant to be.'

Right from the start of the affair, it's clear, Richard Faber pictured himself as a figure of true romance, the latest in a long line of legendary lovers stretching back to Tristan and Isolde, Abelard and Heloise . . .

'Cinderella and Prince Charming?' Whenever they talked about it together – and in the early years they talked about it all the time – Emma liked to tease him. She was jealous, of course. He didn't mind. He was happy.

'Mock if you must, you bitch.' He said it tenderly and sighed through a smile, and then laughed, and drew his head away and narrowed his eyes. 'I think, Emma, I prefer Elizabeth Barrett and Robert Browning as an analogy, if you don't mind. Real people.'

He knew it made him appear faintly ridiculous, but he didn't care. He now believed – passionately – not just in love but in love-at-first-sight. 'Yup, darling, the flash of lightning, the *coup de foudre*. At once, there and then, then and there, wham, bam, the whole damn thing. Not simply the sudden infatuation that may or may not develop into something deeper, the momentary attraction that does or doesn't sustain: no, they happen too, of course, all the time. But *love* at first sight – complete, profound, absolute – and immediate. It happens. I know, because it happened to me. When I stood in the stalls and saw Maisie for the first time I realised *at once* that this was it, no turning back, no dipping a toe in the water. The only possibility was the headlong plunge.' It was Emma's turn to smile. 'Oh, yes, darling, by all means, dismiss it as women's magazine mush . . . I defy your cynicism. I'm simply telling you how it was.'

And how did Maisie feel? Was it love at first sight for her too? 'I don't speak for Maisie. You'll have to ask her yourself.' And over the years, they all did: inquisitive friends, prying colleagues, insolent journalists, even once, memorably, Oprah Winfrey. But answers came there none. Richard talked about Maisie. Endlessly. Maisie didn't talk about Richard. Ever.

But what about Maisie's age? Wasn't that a worry? 'I didn't think about it – not for a moment. *It did not cross my mind.*' He closed his eyes and slowly,

wearily, shook his head at a petty, prurient world –
thin-lipped, tight-arsed, small-minded. 'Yes, indeed, as
it turned out I thought she was a little older than she
was, but only because when we engaged her she lied
to Adam about her date of birth. She wouldn't have
got the job otherwise. But in terms of our relationship,
our love for one another, her age, my age, that didn't
come into it. It simply didn't. Not for a moment. We
were *different*, and we knew it. And from the instant
we had acknowledged it to one another there was no
holding back, and no turning back. And, best of all, no
fear either. Cry freedom! Suddenly I thought, why can
I only do dangerous things in the theatre? Why must the
magic only happen out there, under the lights, in front
of three thousand people? If you can be brave on stage,
lad, you can be brave anywhere! So we took our chance,
seized our moment. Grabbed it. It was just for us, after
all. This was our affair. And we did it our way. Let people
say what they will, think what they like – spit where they
must. Nobody really cares about you except yourself and
the one you love.'

'Except possibly your parents?' This was Emma as
big sister.

'I didn't have any parents any more.'

'And Maisie?'

Richard paused, and turned, and looked into the middle distance. 'Yes,' he said slowly, 'Maisie had Jack.'

Jack Rivers, Maisie's remarkable father, is a key figure
in all that follows.

*　　　*　　　*

At twenty-one, a hero of the Sicily landings (mentioned in dispatches); at twenty-four, a published (and acclaimed) war diarist; at thirty, a member of parliament (the Aldershot Division, pukka) and, soon after, the youngest member of Winston Churchill's last administration; Jack Rivers was now, in 1980, at fifty-eight, out of politics and into money, big money, and in a serious way. He was an international financier with wide interests, immensely successful, immensely powerful, immensely aware of his own significance. On the whole, the world respected Jack Rivers; those who knew him, feared him; those who didn't, admired him. He was, after all, a war hero and a significant achiever. He was also a noted and generous patron of the arts. Richard Faber found him utterly ridiculous. Within moments of their first meeting, Richard recalled Lord Alfred Douglas's dismissive remark to his own father: 'What a funny little man you are.'

When Richard had been a child there was a popular comedian on television in England called Charlie Drake, a squat, coarse, pug-faced little man, with a high-pitched voice and an irritating giggle. This is how Richard saw Jack Rivers. The world saw the great financier rather differently. Certainly, you could say he was ugly, but only because his face had been reconstructed in 1943, in the aftermath of the assault on the bridge at Catania: at first encounter the shiny, immobile features, the hairlessness, the way only the eyes showed expression, made the appearance disconcerting, grotesque even, but for most it was a reminder of past valour not an excuse for contempt.

He was small rather than tall, but slim, loose-limbed and dapper. Was he a touch too fastidious when it came to his clothes? Probably. His kit was always impeccable. The elegance was studied: the cut of the cloth just so, the knot of the silk tie never out of place, the buttonhole always seasonal but never overblown. And his voice was far from high-pitched or squeaky: it was smooth, velvety, ever-measured, never raised; he spoke aphoristically, his gnomic utterances on *Any Questions?* felt memorable at the time. 'Lessons aren't given – they're taken . . . All rising to a great place is by a winding stair . . . Truth is the safest lie . . .' Jack Rivers gave the impression of breadth and depth, of knowing things you didn't know, of having access to the room beyond. He was ruthless in business, but no one said he wasn't honest. He was certainly kind to his horses and devoted to his daughter.

The horses were kept in the country, at the moated house outside Oxford. Maisie didn't go there any more. She didn't like it: she'd grown out of horses; she had no friends in the country; she felt lonely and bored. She was happy in London. The house in South Kensington was Victorian, vast, truly ambassadorial – six floors, thirty rooms, with 'extensive reception areas ideal for large-scale entertaining' – and the feel, consequently, much more Grand Hotel than Home Sweet Home. But all her life Maisie liked grand hotels, the more opulent the better. She liked beautiful things too and at Dabney House there was no shortage of those: the Louis XVI escritoire with the secret panel where she hid her diary; the exquisite Yuan porcelain on display in the Yellow Drawing Room – blue and white dishes, fourteenth century, desperately delicate, apparently priceless – on which she took daily delight in impressing her fingerprints, both for the hell of it and to see how long it took for the staff to wipe the dishes clean; on the landing at the top of the grand staircase, the painting entitled 'The Beautiful Lady' by Sir John Lavery. Maisie had discovered who she was: Maria Carmi, an actress as well as a model, also known as Madame Volmuller and, later, as Princess George Matchabelli; she appeared as the Madonna in *The Miracle* at the Olympia Theatre in 1911 and as Princess Miranda in *Venice Midnight* at the Palace in 1912 – the year of the portrait. Whenever Maisie came down the grand staircase she tried to float down as she imagined The Beautiful Lady would have floated: she held her head high and her arms outstretched. And, on her way to school, as she walked down Cromwell Place and passed the house where Lavery lived – she knew exactly where it was: her father had been instrumental in securing the commemorative blue plaque – she wondered whether Lavery and Maria Carmi had been lovers. She knew Lavery was a ladies' man.

She suspected her father was a ladies' man. She didn't know. She hoped so. There was no evidence to suggest he was: his bedroom, his bathroom, his dressing room, his sitting room (all of which regularly she explored) had to them entirely a bachelor feel. But she didn't know what he got up to in Oxford each weekend. And he didn't know what she did alone in London.

She wasn't quite alone. Her mother had died before her first birthday, there were no brothers or sisters, no cousins and aunts, no relatives, close or distant, but there had always been servants. Loving, giving, ageless Filipino women, so fond of her, once so free with her, so giggly and affectionate, now, still adoring, but quite frightened. When she was small they had called her 'Little Miss Maisie-Daisy' and played with her like a doll. When she turned from ten to twelve she transmogrified from Cabbage Patch Kid to in-your-face Barbie and the good women of Manila recognised at once that they would be playing with her less and praying for her more. Over the years too there had been a succession of nannies. Jack had meant well and tried the lot – formal Norland, informal Australian, mad Greek. None had lasted. But they served their purpose, as Jack said. 'Running down the nannies was something Maisie and I could do together. Even when she was quite small, we conspired against them. It was our talking point, our common cause. And when we got rid of the last of them, it was a pity really. We found we didn't have anything to talk about any more.'

They didn't talk together about Miss Cooper, the housekeeper, because, to Jack, she was indispensable, an essential part of the furniture, and to Maisie, she was ugly, an irritant and an intrusion. In fairness, while Miss Cooper was no great beauty, she was not so much plain as nondescript, not careless of her appearance, but not careful of it either; set in her ways, a little prissy, sometimes spiky, often awkward, easily bruised, of her type, of her time; not an apple-cheeked flour-fingered housekeeper from the comfortable, comforting Mrs Hudson mould, but not a Mrs Danvers either. And no fool. She ran the house superbly, she kept the books assiduously, she completed *The Times* crossword without fail. She didn't have a pet to resemble, but she was very like the tiny, pale water-colours she collected and occasionally attempted: old fashioned, restrained, accomplished, not very memorable. In her small sitting room in the basement of Dabney House, with half an eye involuntarily checking the usually silent area steps, she read and re-read Elizabeth Taylor, admiring her style, feeling at home in her world, readily recognising herself (with private amusement) in a variety of the dowdier, spinsterly characters, older than their years, quietly pained, secretly pining, but no longer hoping, either put-upon or overlooked. Almost her first job had been as Jack's constituency secretary at the House of Commons in the early 1950s. She had traditional virtues. She was true to her man, loyal to a fault, utterly discreet. (About a year before he stood down from parliament, Jack was charged with reckless driving. Witnesses swore they saw him at the wheel of the Humber as it went the wrong way round the roundabout. Miss Cooper swore that she, in fact, was the one at the wheel: the MP and war hero was at her side, in the passenger seat, fast asleep. Thanks to her testimony, Jack was cleared and, as no one had been injured, the police decided to let the matter drop.) Miss Cooper had lived her adult life at Jack Rivers' beck and call. His manner with her was consistent: he took her for granted. He was always courteous, but never considerate. He had no idea about her hopes, her fears, her dreams, her birthday, the colour of her eyes. This is not necessarily a devastating criticism of him. He was only a man after all. He had no idea he had no idea. Jack relied on Miss Cooper and was grateful that he could. Beyond knowing that he didn't want to lose her, he gave her almost no thought. And knowing that he could rely on her without thinking about her was why he valued her.

Miss Cooper was fond of Maisie. She loved her, she said, 'not as a mother loves a child, because that would be impertinent and, of course, I've never been a mother, but as a good godparent loves a godchild, as a maiden aunt loves a precocious, wayward niece'. It is doubtful whether Maisie knew, or cared much, about the quality and depth of Miss Cooper's devotion. When she was small, Maisie was happy to be cocooned by the cossetting Filipinos, and kept herself away from Miss Cooper, aware of her but wary. As she grew older, and came down from the nursery and up from the kitchens, and began to regard the whole of Dabney House as her domain, she became less fearful of the resident housekeeper, more irritated by her presence, cross when she saw her coming down *her* staircase, looking so insolently at home. When her father was away, which he seemed to be most of the time, Miss Cooper was the figure left in authority, but as far as Maisie was concerned it was an authority whose writ did not run very far or wide.

By the time she was ten, Maisie had worked out that, as her father's daughter, she was the one with the ultimate upper hand, and she asserted her supremacy over Miss Cooper by ostentatiously ignoring her in her presence and by playing practical jokes on her behind her back. When Miss Cooper spoke to her, Maisie didn't respond. When they passed in the corridor, Maisie looked the other way. One memorable day, when Miss Cooper was out, having her afternoon off, visiting the Wallace Collection once again, Maisie, with her friend Odile as accomplice, raided the housekeeper's bedroom and stole every pair of her knickers. The two ten-year-olds then hid the knickers in the freezer with a piece of paper pinned to them on which Maisie had typed, using Miss Cooper's own Remington, 'Life is basically tragic and futile and the only thing that matters is making little jokes. E. Lear.'

When the hapless housekeeper came home and discovered her loss, and a little later, and quite by chance, and in the presence of a pair of profoundly embarrassed Filipinos, discovered the missing underwear, frozen with message attached, she guessed at once what had happened. She was hurt, but she was helpless. She knew she should raise the matter with Jack, but how could she? Jack Rivers was the last person on earth with whom she could discuss the issue of her disappearing knickers. She tried to raise it with Maisie who, at first, denied any involvement, then acknowledged it all with some pride, and finally flattened poor Miss Cooper by saying superciliously, 'Can't you take a joke?'

'On the first of April, maybe, Maisie, but this . . . this
. . . this is unkind.'

'It was supposed to be funny.'

Miss Cooper's humiliation left Maisie not simply
in the ascendant, but in command. She knew now
she could ignore the housekeeper with impunity. And
she did.

Throughout her school life Maisie was a pupil at the
French Lycée in South Kensington. When she was a
little girl, nannies, Filipinos and the housekeeper took
it in turns to walk her to the school gates. By the time
she was twelve the nannies had all gone, the Filipinos
were cowed, and Maisie, now a good two centimetres
taller than Miss Cooper (and particularly pleased to be
able to look down on her in every sense), made her own
way to school – usually on foot, sometimes by bicycle,
occasionally not at all, as her whim and fancy took her.
Maisie was a law unto herself. The school complained, of
course, but they complained to Miss Cooper. There was
no one else to whom they could complain. When they
telephoned Dabney House it was Miss Cooper who took
the call. When they wrote to Jack it was Miss Cooper who
drafted the replies. 'If Maisie wouldn't go to school, what
could I do? I tried talking to the child, but she wasn't
going to listen to me. I tried raising it with Jack, but
much as he loved his daughter, he wasn't interested in
her education.' Surprisingly for a scholarship boy, Jack
hadn't much time for school.

Maisie was playing truant the day she went to the *Alice*

audition. When she got the part, reactions were predictable. Miss Cooper was appalled, Jack was delighted. Miss Cooper saw it as the beginning of the end: 'I knew we would never get her to go back to school. I sensed right away we'd lose her altogether. What good could possibly come of it? It had to end in tears. It had to. I tried to reason with Jack, but he wouldn't listen. I didn't say anything to Maisie. There was no point. I never understood why, but I accepted that the pretty little girl I loved so much had become a wilful young woman who despised me. Whatever I felt for her, she felt nothing for me. As far as she was concerned I was at best a total irrelevance, at worst an interfering old baggage. She was so beautiful, so alive, so headstrong. She thought she knew everything, but she knew nothing. She had the veneer of sophistication, of course, but she was just a child.'

She was just a child to Jack Rivers too, but she was *his* child and the idea that his offspring, his pride and joy, his own daughter, bearing his own name, should have been chosen in an open audition to play the title part in a West End production devised and directed by the internationally celebrated television star and acclaimed classical actor Richard Faber, this was flattering to the House of Rivers. 'Of course, she must do it, it'll be an education in itself,' he said to Miss Cooper, confirming her worst fears.

One Sunday, during the run of previews, three days before the official First Night, on Maisie's behalf Jack threw a party for the *Alice* company, the entire cast and crew. It was Dabney House at its most elaborately informal: 'just brunch' – but brunch on the Jack Rivers scale: salvers of tropical fruits and tureens of proper porridge, side after side of smoked salmon, baskets of bagels and cornucopias of cream cheese (oh yes, literally – cornucopias carved out of ice stuffed with cream cheese), and scrambled eggs, and poached eggs (poached correctly), and individual omelettes, and the crispiest bacon and the lightest kedgeree. It was colour supplement heaven. There was a Bloody Mary bar and a champagne fountain and, as the clocks struck one, precisely, the host and his daughter, Jack and Maisie in complementary white linen suits, Daddy Shwabucks and Alice in Wonderland, stood together at the top of the stairs and raised their glasses to the assembly. 'You do me great honour coming to my house today,' said Jack. 'You are important people. You are the entertainers, so often taken for granted, but so vital to a civilised society. You are the splash of colour on the hard road we have to travel. I salute you all – with a special thank you to three people without whose contribution we'd have no cause for today's celebration. To the shade of Lewis Carroll' – and he lifted his glass in the direction of the magnificent chandelier above him – 'And to the substantial presence of this fabulous production's distinguished producers, Mr Richard Faber and Mr Adam Waterson.' At the foot of the stairs Adam beamed inanely and Richard offered a wintry smile with a hint of Clark Gable in *Gone With the Wind*. 'On Wednesday,' Jack concluded, 'break a leg! Today, enjoy yourselves! I give you *Alice*!'

'What a lovely speech,' said Emma.

'Yes,' said Miss Cooper. 'Jack's a very special man.'

In the conservatory a pianola played Victorian parlour songs. Upstairs, in the drawing room, a young man played Gershwin and Cole Porter. Fresh, strong coffee came accompanied by jugs of thick pale-yellow cream, silver bowls of multi-coloured sugar crystals and big boxes of Bendicks' bitter mints. A cartoonist looking like Mark Twain was wandering about giving impressively recognisable lightning sketches as souvenirs to the guests.

'This is very generous,' said Adam.

'This is very vulgar,' said Richard, switching from sardonic Rhett Butler to sneering Mr Darcy. 'I imagine there's a lady in the loo playing the Harry Lime theme on the zither.'

On the landing at the top of the grand staircase an easy, affable Jack Rivers was giving a small audience the story of 'The Beautiful Lady', his beautiful daughter at his side.

'What have you got against him, Richard? Why don't you like him?'

'I don't dislike him. And I've got nothing against him – except he's a phoney. I don't trust him, that's all. Do you?'

'I've no reason not to. I've hardly met him.'

'He looks like Charlie Drake but he's poncing about like Tom Wolfe.'

'He can't help his appearance.'

'I know, I know. My response is quite irrational. I

apologise. But there's something creepy about him all the same. Remember A.H. Fish?'

'As featured in the first series of *Murderer*, conman and serial killer?'

'Yes.'

'Richard, this isn't irrational. It's ridiculous.'

'Yup, I know. I just don't want to have to see him too often.'

After the first night, for the length of the run of *Alice* Richard Faber didn't see Jack Rivers at all. The proud father came to the show more than once, but Maisie's dressing room and Richard's were on different floors so the paths of the great financier and the great star didn't cross and, midway through the season, when Jack invited Richard and Adam to join him and his daughter for a late supper at Le Caprice, at the last minute Richard sent his regretful excuses and a grateful Emma in his stead. And eventually, when the fateful last night came, that Saturday in April, Jack was away for a long weekend, in Stockholm, on business.

On the Sunday morning, when Miss Cooper realised that Maisie hadn't come home, she was neither particularly surprised nor unduly alarmed. The captious child regularly stayed over with Odile or one of her other friends without giving prior notice. Miss Cooper was disapproving but impotent. When Monday came and still Maisie hadn't reappeared at Dabney House, Miss Cooper began to feel anxious. She called Odile, she called Marie-France, she called Emma Irving.

On Tuesday morning Jack got back.

'How are things, Miss C?'

'Fine.' She tried to say it lightly. 'Except that Maisie seems to have disappeared.'

Jack was unperturbed, standing at his desk, doing what had irritated Miss Cooper ever since she'd known him: concentrating wholly on the papers in his hand, not in the least on the person he was addressing. 'Since when?'

'Since Saturday,' she said. 'I think we should call the police.'

'Mm.' He turned over a page.

'Jack, I said "I think we should call the police".'

He looked up. 'Don't be absurd, woman. She'll be at some party. Have you called her friends?'

'I've tried.'

'What do you mean "you've tried"?'

'Exactly that. I've got through to one or two, but—'

'Oh, for God's sake.' He dropped the papers on the desk. Miss Cooper could be so infuriating. 'You need to go through her address book, name by name, one by one.'

'I can't.'

'Oh, for crying out loud, woman, don't be so precious—'

'No, I mean I can't because it's gone. The address book is missing. She's taken everything.'

Like the rat from the trap, the bat out of hell, suddenly frantic, Jack ran from the study, across the hall, up the grand staircase, up again, and again. He swung round on the top landing, breathing hard, and, with quite unnecessary force, like a cop on a raid, burst violently into his daughter's room. It was filled with brilliant sunshine and the lingering aroma of joss-sticks, but it was unnaturally tidy, just as a loving Filipino would have left it, and at once he could see that Maisie, and all of her treasures, had gone.

'Get me Faber. Get me Waterson. *Now.*'

Miss Cooper, trembling, had the number already in her hand. Within moments, Adam was on the line.

Jack's shiny face glistened with sweat, but his voice was dry and steady. 'Where's Maisie?'

'I don't know.'

'When did you see her last?'

'Saturday night, Sunday morning. At the party.'

'Where is she now?'

'I don't know. Truly.'

'Where's Faber?'

Adam paused. 'I don't know.'

'If you don't, Mr Waterson, I do.'

He said nothing more. He replaced the receiver and pushed the telephone away. He took a small key from his waistcoat pocket and unlocked the top left-hand drawer of the desk. Out of it he took a blue-black metal case, the size of a large cigar box. He was much calmer now. 'Miss Cooper, get on to the office, would you? Cancel today. Cancel everything.' He turned and stared out of the study window. The gentlest breeze rustled the cherry blossom. 'That bastard. He's abducted my daughter.'

By nightfall Jack Rivers was in Verona, ensconced in the austere splendour of the Verdi suite of the Hotel Due

Torri at number 4 Piazza Sant' Anastasia. As he heard the church clock strike the quarter, he clambered off the high, hard, Napoleonic bed and lifted his battered leather briefcase from the chair by the window on to the dressing table. He checked his watch, then with ceremony and adroit fingers, like a jeweller displaying prize stock, he opened the briefcase, pulled on a pair of surgical gloves and removed the blue-black metal box. He unlocked it, and, with care, took out and loaded a smallish long-barrelled hand-gun. He then folded the weapon neatly inside a copy of the *Financial Times* and replaced it in the briefcase which he snapped shut.

He went to the bathroom, peeled off the gloves, peed, washed, straightened his tie, put on his jacket, adjusted his buttonhole, and checked his watch one more time. At four minutes before ten, he collected his briefcase and made his way along the dark corridor and down the clattery tiled stairs to the hotel's huge and celebrated reception hall. In the season, after the opera, this is where *le tout monde* gathered for the post-performance buffet: Prosecco and a cold collation. It was quite deserted now. Jack crossed the echoey hall to the little bar set beneath the massive tapestry on the left-hand wall. He put down the briefcase, took up his position on one of the tall stools, and waited.

He ordered an *espresso, doppio,* and, after a couple of minutes, as the coffee was being served, he looked up and saw Richard coming towards him across the hall. And Richard saw him, and hesitated.

'Mr Rivers – Jack. What are you doing here?'

'I might ask the same of you.' Jack stirred his coffee with a tiny spoon.

'I was looking for Adam. I had a message to meet him. Odd.' He looked around the deserted hall. 'I suppose it was you. I should have thought.'

'Yes.' Jack smiled. 'I imagine you can guess why I've come.'

'Yes.'

'I'm looking for Maisie. You know where she is?'

'Yes, Jack, I do.'

'I thought so.'

'She's here. With me.'

'Why?' He shifted round on his stool and gazed at Richard.

'Because I love her.'

'She's a child.'

'She's not a child.'

'You're old enough to be her father. It's obscene.'

'Not so.'

'Have you slept with her?'

'No, Jack, but I have married her. Here in Verona, where Romeo married Juliet. This afternoon. Your daughter is now my wife. And there's an end on it.'

'Fuck you, Richard Faber. Fuck you.'

FIVE

Richard stood his ground for no more than a moment then turned and, without hurrying, walked away, across the hall, past the porter's polished oak desk – '*Buono notte, Signor Faber*,' the old concierge knew him a little, had known his father well, remembered his mother with sentimental reverence – and out through the revolving glass door into the still, warm night. Jack watched him go, and did nothing.

In London it was a little after nine fifteen and as cold and wet as a fish-monger's slab. The brilliant morning sunshine in South Kensington had given way to lunchtime drizzle right across town and now, on the dreary, wind-swept Euston Road, while the black cabs bleakly plied their trade through the steady downpour, up in a turreted corner of the St Pancras Hotel, there high on the fifth floor, in Richard's fabulous bed-room (Regency stripe wallpapers and a *trompe l'oeil* Wordsworthian sky ceiling, an amazing conjunction that worked completely), on Richard's fabulous bed (once, a hundred-and-some years ago, the property of the actress Rachel Felix to whom the Prince de Joinville sent the note 'Where? When? How much?' and received the reply 'My place, tonight, free') in total silence Adam Waterson and Emma Irving were making love. They were disconcertingly expert.

Adam, of course, was an habitual lover. He had sex once or twice a day, every day, without exception, without fail, and, interestingly (and this for many was the annoying bit), without giving offence. He seemed never to approach a reluctant potential partner, he never appeared to have to do more than give a nod and a wink to make his intentions plain, he never had any problem finding a discreet and readily available venue for his brief encounters. 'Clearly I've got a nose for it' was his little joke. He seemed to have the rest of the necessary physique as well. He wasn't obviously handsome in the way that Richard was – Richard had classic good looks: brilliant blue eyes and movie-star bone structure – but while Adam's face was oddly lopsided, his mouth and chin were out of true, and the puffy bags under his eyes made him look permanently exhausted, from shoulder to thigh he was, by all accounts, magnificent. His body was firm and muscular, wonderfully free of blemishes, incredibly smooth. He was strong and fit and skilful. 'The one thing you can say about Adam is that he fucks you fantastically.' That was Emma's line – said, mainly, in her head, to herself, and occasionally, in her cups, to friends.

She lay beneath him as he came thinking of Richard – she always thought of Richard when she made love – but thinking too that this time it felt specially good, specially easy, because they both knew Richard wasn't there. Emma liked making love with Adam because it was uncomplicated, it was comforting, and, often, it felt sensationally good. Adam liked Emma because so many of his women were virtual strangers and she was familiar. She was thirty-something too, older than most of his conquests these days, broader, with a rounder stomach and fuller breasts, and he liked all that. He rolled off her. 'Where's my post-coital Craven A?' she said. They lit their cigarettes and gazed up at the blue sky and fluffy white clouds.

'Do you think he's made love to her yet?' They always talked about Richard at times like this. She pushed her head back into the pillow and relished the moment, enjoyed shaping her mouth to slowly, softly blow her cigarette smoke up towards the clouds. 'Do you think they're at it right now?'

'No,' he said, smiling. 'No, I don't.'

'Why not?'

'I don't know. He's strange about sex.'

'She's very beautiful.'

'Yes.'

'Do you think she's a virgin?'

He paused. 'Well now, that's—'

'You haven't?!' She lifted her head from the pillow and turned sharply towards him, appalled, excited, amused.

'God, no.' He laughed. 'She's a child.'

'You don't fancy her then?'

'No. Not at all.' She watched the pale grey cigarette smoke filter slowly out of his nostrils, curling up like wispy mammoth's tusks. 'She's too tall – and scraggy – and *young* for me.' With his thumb and forefinger, quite tenderly, he pinched the inside of her thigh.

'Thank you.' She nestled closer, putting her head on his shoulder. 'This is good.'

'Yes,' he said. 'Best ever.' Not only was he expert in his love-making: with Emma, for some reason, he also made an effort with the small-talk. She was grateful and did her best to reward him by being as complaisant as possible. She never nagged, she never grumbled, she never asked for more. Her aim was for him to feel at all times she was available, indulgent and fun.

'What's the worst thing about oral sex? Have you heard it?'

'The view! Boom boom! The old ones are the best . . .' He stubbed out his cigarette (in Gerald du Maurier's ashtray on C.B. Cochran's bedside table) and stretched over her to switch off the light. In the sudden dark he lay close beside her and kissed her gently on the cheek and laid his hand, comfortably, fingers spread wide, across her stomach.

'If he's not going to make love to her,' she whispered, 'why has he run off with her?'

'He does strange things,' he whispered back. 'He's a strange man.'

'He loves her though, doesn't he?'

'Yes. He loves her.'

She listened for a moment to the world outside, the distant cabs trundling past, the ones closer by turning into the station forecourt, the insistent swishing of the rain. 'It's strange that we make love but don't love one another, and Richard . . .'

With his fingers Adam lightly traced the line of Emma's appendix scar. 'What is this thing called lurve?' he murmured.

'Do you think he's mad?' she asked.

'No, not mad. Not certifiable anyway. Possessed perhaps. Driven. He's done it, but he doesn't know why, hasn't thought it through.'

'It's like his acting. He doesn't know how he does it. It's sort of magic.' Her eyes had adjusted to the darkness and she could see the outline of a cherub in a corner of the ceiling. 'What happens now?'

'We go to sleep and when we wake up I break the habit of a lifetime and make love to the same woman twice in a row.'

'Good.'

In fact it was the throb of the rush-hour traffic on the Euston Road that roused Emma in the morning. Adam had gone. She wasn't surprised. He came. He went. That was the deal. She knew. She understood. She didn't mind. Well, no, she minded, but she accepted. It was just as she accepted what was happening to her career, her looks, her life – it was all okay, fine, good really, but not that special, not quite what she'd hoped for, not what she'd expected, more down than up, let's face it, more grey than gold. It's the same for everyone, you could say, more or less. You could say it, but it isn't so. Is it? Richard, her one-time flatmate, her friend, the finest actor of his generation, no question, had gone off with one of the most beautiful girls you'd ever seen. Of course he had. That's what happens. That's what really happens. That's life. And she knew there was more of it to come. Every day she could see it all a bit more clearly. She would end up in bed with Adam less often, with a cat that needed to go to the vet more frequently, with a perfectly pleasant flat, a good long lease, yes, and near the river, but with ever-encroaching crows' feet around the eyes, and an ever-more-useless agent, and china that looked dated and didn't altogether match, drinking too much camomile tea from mugs with little chips on them. As she fumbled with her lenses she stared into the mirror and felt sorry for herself and desperately jealous of the sheer beauty of Maisie, the unadulterated happiness of Richard and Maisie, the golden sodding sunshine of Verona.

And in gilded Verona that morning how brilliantly the sun did shine! After breakfast, early, Richard took Maisie by the hand, like a child, and led her out of the Villa Ortese, across the road, down one side street, then another, under arches, through piazzas, through the fish market and the flower market, past the famous statue of Dante, past colonnaded palazzos, past churches great and small, through all the streets and squares of his childhood.

Once or twice he stopped for a moment to tell a story, to conjure up the past. The little bakery, now a shoe shop, where his mother sent him to collect the Christmas *panettone* and he'd dropped it in a puddle on the way home. The tucked-away tiny Romanesque church, Santa Maria Antica, where Isabella Bertolazzi *always* stopped to light a candle until the never-to-be-forgotten year when the fool of a priest cast someone else's blue-eyed boy as Joseph in the nativity play. The amazing Palazzo della Ragione with its sensational Renaissance staircase leading straight from the street to the law courts above. 'That's the Palace of Reason. My father called it the Palace of Varieties. And you know my routine with the cane, the one we used in *Alice*? I think I was seven when I first did it dancing down those very steps! "The amateur practises till he gets it right. The professional rehearses till he can't get it wrong."'

Maisie let go of his hand and put her arm through his. 'Where are we going?'

'Somewhere,' he said, hoping to sound mysterious. She raised her amazing dark eyebrows. 'Over the river.'

'Juliet's tomb?' she guessed.

'No. We'll go there later. And often. It's wonderful, but it's the other side of town. If you're happy to, right now we're going to climb up into the hills. I want to show you something.'

'I'm happy to do *anything*, Richard. And I want you to show me *everything*.'

All in all it took them less than thirty minutes to reach the river from Richard's house. They crossed the Ponte Romano and the small embankment beyond. The sun was getting higher and hotter as they started up the dusty main road that led from the city towards the hills. After about two hundred metres they turned into a narrow side road that gradually narrowed further and then changed from cobbled street to sandy lane and led them to a pair of huge, ornate, rusting wrought-iron gates set into a high red brick wall and loosely held shut by a broken padlock and chain. Richard unravelled the chain and pushed open one side of the gate. 'Welcome to Paradise,' he said.

It was immediately cooler here. They climbed up and up through an immense deserted garden, where the faded grandeur of the lower ornamental terraces, with unraked gravel paths and neglected box hedges, gratefully gave way to overgrown woodland that grew wilder the higher they went. There was no discernible path, but Richard made a way for them through the tall rough grass, through the bracken, through the encroaching forest of cypress and olive trees. 'This is Sleeping Beauty country,' said Maisie, and Richard laughed and at once drew a make-believe sword from its sheath and cut through the air with a flourish that would have done Prince Florizel proud.

Eventually, they reached their destination: a small shaded clearing on a natural terrace high up on the hillside, close to the summit, with a sudden and spectacular view of the blue-green ribbon of the river Adige way below and the little domes and towers and terra-cotta rooftops of the medieval city beyond.

'In fair Verona where we lay our scene . . .' cried Maisie, bang on cue.

'Exactly!' Richard was in ecstasy. 'And look, down there, right down, this side, by the river, the Roman amphitheatre. See! It's two thousand years old – and perfect. That's what I wanted to show you. That's where we're going to do it. *Romeo and Juliet.*'

'*Romeo and Juliet*,' she repeated.

'Yes.'

She laughed. 'With the fabulous Fabers!'

He was more cautious. 'Yes – if that's all right?'

'If that's what you want.'

'It's what I'd like,' he said carefully. 'It would be a dream come true.'

'Oh,' she said, teasing, smiling, tilting her head a little to one side, 'then we must do it. Richard, from now on, all our dreams come true. That's the point.'

'That's settled then.' He seemed so pleased.

'Good.' She nodded. 'And when do we do it?'

'September, October. Rehearse July, August.'

'And who'll come?'

'The *world* will come!'

'Of course. Silly me.'

'And it's silly-you they'll be coming to see. And me, I hope. And, if we can get him, Simon as Mercutio. And I think Emma as the Nurse, don't you? You will be a perfect Juliet, Maisie. One of the greats. Apart from anything else, you're the right age.'

She narrowed her eyes and pulled a face. 'Age, Richard Faber, is not important. In plays perhaps, but not in life, not in our lives. It may be important to *them*, but not to *us*. Who cares if I'm fifteen or sixteen or you're thirty or forty? People always think I'm older than I am, but it doesn't matter. Okay?' She slowed down and put her hand up to his face to stroke it. 'You know you seem a lot older than thirty most of the time.' She grinned and put a finger to his lips. 'More like a hundred and thirty.'

'He was born with the gift of perpetual old age.'

'Who? You?'

'No – my father's friend, Max Beerbohm. You've never heard of him, have you?'

'I know everything – and nothing. And you know nothing – and everything. That's why we're a perfect match.'

'I'll take you to Rapallo. We'll visit Max's old house. You'll love it.'

'Will that be our honeymoon?'

'Our life will be our honeymoon!'

'Well done! You're getting the idea.' And she clapped her hands and spun round with delight. When she came to a standstill she peered down at the amphitheatre below and said, as though wondering out loud, 'I take it we're doing our *Romeo and Juliet* in English.'

'Yes, you fool. Do you speak Italian?'

'Not yet, but I could do it in French and everyone else could do it in Italian. It'd make it different. And we like to be different, don't we?'

'We do, but they already do Shakespeare in Italian

here. If we do it in English we'll be different anyway.'

'I'm easy.'

'I'm happy.' He meant it.

'Good.' She meant it too. 'And don't forget, you're free now as well, completely free.' They were standing by the low stone wall that formed a kind of parapet around the terrace. She took him by the lapels and pulled him towards her. 'Come here, you funny old-young man, and look into my eyes. Look right in, look right inside me. That's it. Hold that. You're inside me now. And I'm inside you. It's just us against the world – our secret. And we two, we can do anything, anything we like, anything we want, *anything*.'

'You're strange.'

'Thank you. You're pretty weird yourself. That's why we're together. We are strange and amazing and—'

'I love you.'

'I love you. I love you. I love you. Say it again. Whisper it into my ear.'

He did exactly what she asked him, then and always. 'Ours,' she said, 'is a fairy-tale romance.'

'Which means?'

'Which means that not only do extraordinary things happen to us in extraordinary ways, but we also get to live happily ever after.'

'That's nice.'

'It's essential. What is equally essential,' she said, letting go of him and squinting up at the sun, 'is my mid-morning *tiramisu* and *caffè macchiato*.'

'You do speak Italian.'

'When I'm hungry and happy I can do anything. And I'm always hungry – and I eat like a horse – and I never get fat. And now I've got you I'm always going to be happy. You must believe that.'

'I do.'

They clambered down the hill and found the little café near the bridge that Richard had remembered going to with his father all those years ago. 'He loved that climb up to the Secret Terrace. That's what we called it.' When the coffee had been served and Maisie had wolfed down her *tiramisu* and Richard had set light to the little squares of tissue that were wrapped round the *amaretti* biscuits and they'd watched them float up, up and away over the river, Richard said, 'Can we talk about your father?' He had told her what had happened the night before.

'We can talk about anything.'

'What are we going to do, Maisie?'

'I love my father,' she spoke very deliberately. 'I won't hear a word against him – ever – promise?'

'Promise.'

'But I can't go home – there's nothing I'll miss at Dabney House, except "The Beautiful Lady". Daddy's never there, so he can't really complain. And I can't stand Miss Cooper – he knows that – and, anyway, I'm Mrs Faber now. "Mrs Faber". Sounds funny, doesn't it? And when you get your knighthood I'll be "Lady Faber". That sounds a bit better. Poor Daddy. You'll just have to tell him. Of course, he's cross. He's been crossed. And he doesn't like that. He's not used to it. He's hurt, that's all, but he'll get over it. And when he does, we'll all be friends again. It'll be easy. You'll see.'

'I thought you said you knew everything.'

'And nothing.'

When they got back to the Villa Ortese he was there, standing outside in the street, a little man in a white suit with a folded *Financial Times* under his arm. Did he look sinister or did he look absurd? To Richard, of course, he looked utterly absurd – 'white suit, grey fedora, little yellow rosebud in his buttonhole, co-respondent shoes, Herbert Lom plays Hercule Poirot, I wonder he wasn't wearing spats!' – but press photographs of Jack Rivers taken at the time tell a different story. Stocky, disfigured, too carefully groomed, but with sharp, intelligent eyes, a ramrod back, broad shoulders, the sense of a powerful physical presence, a figure of substance not a figure of fun.

The moment they saw him as they came out of the side street into the Via Anastasia Maisie shrank back, pulling Richard with her. Jack hadn't seen them. He was staring up at the house. He checked his watch, looked up and down the street, and took a few steps in their direction. Still he didn't see them. He stopped, turned back and looked up again at the shuttered windows.

Maisie pulled Richard further back into the doorway of the corner *pasticceria* where they were hiding. 'I can't talk to him, not now. Give him my love. But tell him I won't see him, I can't see him, until he accepts you, accepts us. Tell him. Please.'

'I'll tell him.' He put his hands to her shoulders and his face close to hers. 'Don't worry, little girl.'

'Don't call me that. Please.'

'Sorry.'

'It will be all right, won't it?'

'It will be all right.'

They arranged to meet up within two hours by the statue of Dante – 'Sooner if you can', 'Much sooner if I can' – then Maisie pushed Richard out of the doorway into the street towards her father. When Richard reached the kerb and glanced back, she'd gone. He dodged through the traffic, just missed a collision with a frog-faced priest on a bicycle, thought suddenly of Fernandel and of sitting in the cinema in the Piazzale Stefani with his mother, and then heard himself calling out, 'Good morning!'

Jack turned towards him quite casually and said, in a pleasant way, as though continuing a well-established if inconsequential conversation, 'This is a very handsome building. The iron work's remarkable.'

Richard looked at him, bewildered.

Jack continued affably, 'Well, now you're here, aren't you going to invite me in?'

Richard hesitated. He had no plan. He was confused. 'I – no – I don't think so.'

'I'm sorry.'

'Yes, I'm sorry, I—'

'Is she here?' Jack glanced up again at the shuttered windows.

'No. Jack . . . Mr Rivers . . . She's asked me to tell

you she doesn't want to see you – not for the moment. She sends you her love.'

'It is not as simple as that, Mr Faber. If I can't see you here, will you come back with me to the hotel?'

They walked together along the crowded street, making desultory small-talk about the history and architecture of the Veneto as they went. Jack asked intelligent tourist's questions and Richard, uncomprehending, on automatic pilot, came up with cogent, well-informed tour-guide replies. As they neared the hotel, Richard suddenly found himself saying, 'Have you been inside Sant' Anastasia? It's very beautiful.'

'And very peaceful,' added Jack as they stepped under the glorious Gothic portal out of the hot square into the vast cool cavern of the deserted church. They wandered through it in silence, past the famous fading frescos, under the startling carvings of the grimmer moments of the life of Saint Peter the Martyr, and stopped together at the entrance to the sacristy, gazing up at the church's celebrated fifteenth-century show-stopper, Antonio Pisanello's 'Saint George and the Princess'.

'Maisie will like this,' said Jack. 'She'll see herself as the fair Princess of Trebizond. Looks a little like her, don't you think? She's a great romantic, our Maisie. Girls of her age often are. She'll certainly see you as Saint George, Mr Faber, ready to mount your steed and charge off to slay the dragon. You may even picture yourself as Saint George. But there's a slight problem here, isn't there? I'm not a dragon waiting to be slain. I'm not a mythical beast of any kind. I'm just a father. And this is life, not art.'

Richard flinched as the small man with the shiny, unreal face moved closer to him and touched his arm and smiled a little patronising smile. 'Come, let's sit here for a moment. It's appropriately near the confessional.' They sat, side by side, awkwardly, on hard church chairs deliberately designed, Richard felt, to encourage you to spend the maximum time on your knees. He looked at Jack, so close to him now, and could only see a caricature, Peter Sellers as Dr Strangelove, Donald Pleasence in *You Only Live Twice*. The man couldn't help his face, of course, but there was something equally unreal, unconvincing, contrived, about his manner, the way he moved, the way he talked. 'Let me start with an apology.' This was just bad acting, wasn't it? The not-so-gifted amateur doing *Listen with Mother:* 'Are you sitting comfortably? Then we'll begin.'

'I lost my temper last night and I should not have done so. I was angry and I was hurt. I am sorry for the way I spoke.' Richard nodded blankly. Why was he listening to this old phoney? Why was he letting this happen to him? 'Now let me explain the reasons why I believe my daughter should return to London with me. Today, on the evening flight.' He laid the newspaper carefully on his lap and felt in his jacket pocket for an envelope. 'I have a ticket for her here. I want her to come home because she is only fifteen and I am her father and her legal guardian and I love her and I understand her—'

'But I have married her—'

'So you say. But in Austria the law would have allowed you to marry her if she'd been twelve. Because it is legal

92

does not make it right. She is too young, Mr Faber –
and you are too old. It won't last. It can't last. I want
to protect her—'

'No, Mr Rivers, you don't want to give up what you
believe to be yours. It's an old story. Read *The Merchant
of Venice.*'

'I have – many a time and oft.' He smirked and looked
Richard directly in the eye. 'Let me come straight to the
point. We are both men of the world, Mr Faber. I have
a proposal to make to you.' He fished in his pocket
again and produced a second envelope. 'I intend to
give you half a million pounds. Here – now – this
morning.'

Richard tried to move. 'I can't believe this is happening.'

Jack held up his hand. It was small and pale and
beautifully manicured. 'Hear me out, please—'

'This is pathetic,' hissed Richard. 'Are you actually
trying to buy me off?'

'No. Please listen. I am trying to buy time. That's all.
You see, I believe time is on my side. At close of business
today I shall pay into your London account – I have the
details . . .' He waved the envelope.

'What details? How?'

'I spoke with Adam Waterson this morning.' Richard
closed his eyes. 'Hear me out, Mr Faber. The half million
you get today is simply the first instalment. For every
month that you do not see Maisie you will receive a
further one hundred thousand. At the end of five years,
if you keep away from my daughter throughout that

time, you will then have six and a half million. As Mr Waterson said, "Not bad, eh?"'

'It's obscene.'

'It's a great deal of money, certainly.'

'What happens at the end of the five years?'

'I'm glad you're intrigued.'

'I'm not in the least intrigued, Mr Rivers – except at the way your mind is working.'

'At the end of five years Maisie will be almost twenty-one and she will be free to do as she pleases. She can run off with you then if she is still so inclined – and you are still interested. Put it to her.'

'No.'

'Put it to her. I know my daughter. You may find my idea appeals to her fairy-tale view of life. She can see herself as Sleeping Beauty. Some day her Prince will come – and if it turns out to be you, thanks to me he'll have a decent dowry.'

'I reject your proposal – on my own account – and on behalf of my wife.'

'It is a generous offer – particularly when you consider that I am the injured party.'

'It is absurd. You are absurd. I know she loves you – as a daughter should love her father, I suppose – but I despise you, Mr Rivers—'

Quite suddenly Jack moved, turned sharply towards Richard, and as he did so the newspaper on his knees shifted and the hidden pistol, black and shiny, slipped out, fell from his lap and clattered on to the stone tile floor. Jack moved to retrieve it, but Richard moved much faster. He bent down and grabbed the gun and held it high, out of Jack's reach. 'For Christ's sake, what kind of a lunatic are you?'

Jack shrugged and waved his hands dismissively. 'It's just a wartime souvenir. But I keep it with me for protection. I have to be careful. I'm sure you understand.' He opened out the *Financial Times* and held it towards Richard who dropped the gun on to the newspaper, and shook his head.

'I don't begin to understand you, Mr Rivers. All I know is that, for some reason, you fill me with contempt. You can take your gun, you can keep your money, but I shall have your daughter. Now and for ever.'

'Oh no, Mr Faber. I will get her back. However long it takes, I will be revenged on the whole pack of you.'

SIX

Within a week the world knew of Maisie Rivers and Richard Faber, of their sudden elopement, of the flight to Verona, of the anger and anguish of a father cruelly abandoned and betrayed. The world knew and the world was taking sides. Jack, who broke the story at a press conference in the garden of Dabney House on Thursday morning, was confident he would win the media battle, and for the first seventy-two hours of the campaign all the spoils were his. He particularly relished the headline in the *New York Daily Post*: 'MURDERER' ABDUCTS 'ALICE'.

The press were bidden to the Rivers' South Kensington mansion for ten forty-five am where, in the ambassadorial splendour of the main hallway, uncommunicative Filipinos offered them a choice of coffee or iced tea and, at eleven fifteen sharp, Miss Cooper appeared to gather them up and lead them, clipboard held aloft like a tour guide's umbrella, through the green drawing room, through the yellow morning room, through the mock-Edwardian conservatory and out on to the wide, white, wrought-iron end-of-Raj verandah that overlooked the sunny garden where, all forlorn, their photo opportunity awaited them. Jack Rivers stood alone by the empty child's swing that hung from one of the branches of the spreading ilex tree. With one hand he held the rope of the swing, with the other he clutched a bedraggled teddy bear. When the fusillade of clicking had subsided and he'd responded to the cries of 'Can you sit on the swing, Mr Rivers?' 'Hold the bear to your face, would you?' 'This way, sir, just one more, thanks', he moved forward towards the verandah and made his statement: 'Ladies and gentlemen, I am grateful to you for coming here this morning. I am making this statement following consultations with my solicitors and with the police. The plain fact of the matter is that Mr Richard Faber, the well-known actor, has absconded with my daughter Maisie. She is a child and he is old enough to be her father. Only a few weeks ago Mr Faber was a welcome guest here at my house. He has abused my hospitality and my friendship. I fear he is now abusing my little girl. He has kidnapped her. I say that advisedly because what else can I say? He has refused to let me see her or speak to her. I am hurt, angry and heartbroken. More than that, I am fearful for the safety of my child.' He turned directly to the television cameras now and held the teddy bear close to his chest. 'To Mr Faber I say, "Let my daughter go. Please." And to Maisie I say simply, "Come home, darling. Growler and me, we're missing you. We love you, baby."'

Among the several million viewers of the early evening news, a handful of hard-bitten seen-it-alls from the theatrical community greeted Jack's statement, carried *in extenso* as the lead item, with cynical squawks and derisive cries of 'Pass the sick-bag, Mabel!' Most, however, were rather more sympathetic in their response. Many were plainly moved.

On Friday morning every newspaper in Britain carried the story. Because Jack was a star in their firmament even the *Financial Times* ran his picture on the front page. Inevitably the tabloids, notably the *Daily Express* and the *Daily Mail,* had most to say – and show. As well as the shots of Jack on the swing and close-ups of Growler, they had two pictures of Maisie – the only two available at that stage: one a still from *Alice,* the other (supplied by Miss Cooper on Jack's instruction) a formal school portrait taken at the Lycée when Maisie was eleven and looked it – and a glorious rogues' gallery of Richard Faber, TV star, playing half-a-dozen celebrated killers including, fortuitously, one child molester (Albert King, executed 1927) and Terence Livingstone, the notorious 'Babes in the Wood' murderer (detained at His Majesty's Pleasure in 1950 and, in the spring of 1980, still languishing in the hospital wing of Strangeways Prison, Manchester). Only the picture editor of the *Guardian* managed to avoid the cliché and unearthed a striking study of Richard in his first Stratford *Hamlet*.

By Saturday the story was running in virtually every country in the world where *Murderer* had been screened and, in the UK, the leader writers and the columnists were beginning to have their predictably sanctimonious say. Everybody was on Jack's side; Richard was universally condemned; but interviews with Odile and other friends of Maisie's from the Lycée were now giving the rapacious reader just a hint that the 'kidnapped heiress' wasn't quite the wide-eyed innocent her unhappy father fondly imagined. The young dancer who played the White Rabbit in *Alice* was quoted in the *Sun* as saying: 'Maisie's a really lovely girl, but she's not a kid. She's mature. She knows her own mind.' This, plus supporting visual evidence in the form of some fun snaps taken recently by Odile on the steps of the Albert Memorial, gave a fresh spin to the features being prepared for the Sundays. Jack's assertions that his daughter had been abducted – repeated in a further statement on Saturday morning – were still given coverage, but the big space went to pages bemoaning the demise of childhood and the loss of innocence ('Where have all the children gone?') and asking 'Why DO men go for these teenage nymphs?' The broadsheets came at it at a tangent. Alongside the latest pictures of Maisie, the *Observer* ran the familiar *Lolita* still of Sue Lyon sucking her heart-shaped lollipop and invited Vladimir Nabokov's thirty-five-year-old son Dmitri to defend his father's controversial masterpiece: 'It's a work of art in which Humbert's love is a sort of poetic fixation.' The *Sunday Times* tracked down Beverley Aadland, Errol Flynn's 'darling Woodsie', so called because she reminded the great swashbuckler of a wood nymph. She was fifteen and he was forty-eight when they met on the lot at Warner Bros. The movie, of course, was *Too Much, Too Soon.* For two years Flynn travelled the world with his darling Woodsie at his side, until he died of a heart attack in October 1959. Twenty-one years later, Beverley had no regrets, 'except that we didn't have a longer time together'.

The news pages of the Sundays had more of a problem. It wasn't the competition from other stories ('Thirteen government ministers executed by firing squad' – but in Liberia): it was how to give a new impetus to this one. A diligent search of the cuttings files turned up nothing of note. A series of fishing expeditions among Richard's acquaintance proved no more productive. Frustratingly, at least so far, the errant actor appeared to have no previous form either as Lothario or Big Bad Wolf. In Verona the shutters of the Villa Ortese remained firmly closed. The hacks and the paparazzi stood sentinel at the gate, but no one came or went. In London Emma Irving was saying nothing. The telephones at St Pancras Productions went unanswered. Adam Waterson had apparently gone into hiding.

In fact, on Thursday, within an hour of the story breaking, Adam had shut up the office and driven to Portsmouth en route for Le Havre. By nightfall he was in Alençon, staying at Le Grand St Michel in rue du Temple and sleeping with the obliging young waitress who proved the perfect complement to the 78 franc *menu gourmand*. All Friday he drove through France, hard and fast, reaching Le Metropole in Beaulieu-sur-Mer too late for dinner and, to his own astonishment, too weary to exploit a chance encounter in the bar with a comely ex-patriate novelist whose vaguely familiar name he could never remember but whose pet poodle he would never forget.

'What's he called?'

'Willis.'

'Willis?'

'As in "Willis is barking". As opposed to "Barkis is willing".'

Theodore Faber would have loved the joke. It was Theodore who had introduced Adam and Richard to the elegant old-world charms of Le Metropole a dozen years before. The old boy had treated them to a wantonly extravagant guided tour of the Italian lakes and the Côte d'Azur as a joint birthday present in the summer of the year they both turned eighteen. Adam thought a lot about Theodore Faber that Saturday as he pushed himself and the Mercedes across the border and on through northern Italy.

He reached Verona around ten and as he drove down the Via Anastasia was amused, and impressed, to see the half-dozen photographers hovering at the front of the Villa Ortese. He thought better of parking in the piazza – some of the hacks would be staying at the Due Torri and the right-hand drive and number plate might arouse unnecessary interest – and drove on to the municipal car park in Via Zappatore. He walked back through the silent half-lit streets, reflecting how early Verona goes to bed outside the festival season, and when he reached the top of the Via Anastasia automatically turned down the little alley that led to the Villa Ortese's anonymous side door. He had his own key.

He closed the door, locked it behind him, and stood quite still on the threshold of the storeroom, waiting for his eyes to adjust to the gloom, enjoying the familiar smell, ripe apples and paraffin, remembering his affair with Gina, one of the best, consummated in this very place, Easter Sunday, 1967 – forty-eight hours later than anticipated. He'd tried to have her on Good Friday, naïve sod. Worth the wait though. Through the darkness he could now see the faint wisp of ochre light delineating the door on the far side of the room. Gingerly he felt his way across, expecting to bruise his shins at every turn. He didn't and, better still, the door wasn't locked. He pulled it open and, quickly, lightly, two at a time, ran up the long, narrow flight of stone steps that led from the ground floor straight into the main hall on the *piano nobile*. And there they were, centre stage, as pretty as a picture – no, much prettier, but *looking* like a picture, the young lovers, seated side by side at Theodore's writing table, reading the poems of Elizabeth and Robert Browning to one another by candlelight.

They were thrilled to see him.

'Adam!'

'Richard! Maisie!'

They stood, all three together in one embrace, and

hugged and hugged, and Richard whispered, 'Welcome, Adam, welcome', and kissed his friend, and Adam, for the first time, kissed Maisie on the mouth.

'Watch it!' Richard laughed. 'She's a married woman now!' He went through to the kitchen and returned at once, a bottle of Prosecco in his hand.

'So I understand.' Adam was smiling. 'You must tell me all about it. Every detail. A blow by blow account. I want to hear *your* side of the story. And I'm not the only one.' Lightly he brushed the hair from Maisie's forehead and with the back of his hand gently stroked her face. 'She is so beautiful,' he said to Richard. 'Congratulations.'

Richard had the bottle open. 'And I'm pretty damn gorgeous myself, aren't I?'

'Exquisite.' Adam claimed his glass. 'You're the perfect match.'

Maisie went over to her husband and put her arm around his waist. 'We are the perfect match.'

'A marriage made in heaven,' said Adam, tilting his wine towards them.

'Exactly,' said Maisie.

'Here's to heaven,' cried Richard. And they raised their glasses to heaven – and to each other – and to love – and to the Brownings – and to Emma – and to Gina – and to Willis – and to Theodore Faber – and to absent friends – and to love again – and again – and to the past – and to the future—

'Most of all, to the future!' Richard moved off to collect a second bottle. '"Ah, but a man's reach should exceed his grasp, or what's a heaven for?" Robert Browning is a genius.'

Adam smiled at Maisie. 'Before he turns maudlin I think we should have a word about your immediate plans.'

Richard refilled their glasses. 'My immediate plan is another toast:

> "The year's at the spring,
> And day's at the morn;
> Morning's at seven;
> The hillside's dew-pearled;
> The lark's on the wing;
> The snail's on the thorn:
> God's in his heaven—
> All's right with the world!"'

'Ah, yes, well, would that it were.' Adam pushed his face towards a candle to relight his cigarette. 'Word may not yet have filtered through to your little love-nest, but I'm here to tell you that your new father-in-law is far from being a happy bunny. He seems to think you've kidnapped his daughter. Stolen his child. He fears for her safety.'

Richard was peering into his glass.

> '"All her hair
> In one long yellow string I wound
> Three times her little throat around,
> And strangled her. No pain felt she;

104

I am quite sure she felt no pain."'

Adam moved behind Maisie and whispered in her ear, 'He's a little odd, isn't he?'

She laughed. 'He's a little drunk, isn't he?'

'Methinks I am in wine,' admitted Richard, emptying the bottle with a sudden flourish.

Adam was amused. 'Does he often get like this?'

'I don't know,' said Maisie. 'We've only been married a week.'

'Don't worry.' He stubbed out his cigarette. 'I do know. Your husband is my oldest friend. We both love him – in our different ways. He won't ever let you down. You are quite safe with Richard Faber.'

'I know.'

'That said,' with his palms Adam beat a soft tattoo on the table, 'you can't go on hiding in here for ever, holed up like naughty schoolchildren.'

Richard stirred. 'Oh, I don't know. The cellar's full and the freezer's well stocked.'

'You've got to face the world.'

'Have we?'

'Yes.'

'When?'

'Tomorrow,' Adam said with finality. 'Leave it to me.'

They left it to Adam. And Adam did them proud.

He was up and dressed before seven and had conceived, developed, organised, stage managed, delivered and wrapped up the entire operation within twelve hours. He left the house just twice and spent the rest of the day on the telephone.

'Who are you calling?' asked Maisie as she supplied him with his umpteenth *espresso*.

'I'm calling the world!'

From five pm that Sunday evening, he was ready, on parade in the courtyard of No. 27 Via Cappello to welcome the world, to assist them with their every enquiry, to supply their wants, to furnish their needs, to hand out their press pack, to allocate them their position for the photo shoot. At six pm, when the courtyard was packed and could take no more, Adam stood on the top step, under the arched entrance to the old house, and clapped his hands, and said, first in Italian, then in English, 'Ladies and gentlemen, thank you for your patience. May I present –,' and he turned and with his right arm extended (in a gesture he'd rehearsed with Richard) indicated the small marble balcony above him – 'Mr and Mrs Richard Faber.' And for the first time together as man and wife, Richard and Maisie, the fabulous Fabers, stepped out on to Juliet's balcony, and took their call.

You've seen the pictures. You know how wonderful they looked. So beautiful, so happy, so easy, so natural, so young, *both of them* so young (that was the trick, that's what clinched it), so open, so radiant, *unquestionably* so in love. SO IN LOVE. That was the headline in the *Mail* on Monday morning. It was replicated, more or less, in headlines and captions and over-the-top opening paragraphs and under-the-credits closing moments in TV news programmes around the world. They conquered the world that week did Richard and Maisie. Took it by storm. With a little help from their friend, as he liked to remind them.

Adam was right to be content with the way it had gone. As he said afterwards, 'It looked so easy in retrospect. And in a sense, given the setting, the pictures *were* easy. Richard looked like a god, after all, and within the year Maisie was universally described – and accepted – as the world's most beautiful woman. I knew once we got the location, and the look, the pictures would work, had to work, and I'd hoped that the triumph of the pictures would swamp the words. In fact the words worked too. The journalists stood in the courtyard calling out their questions. If there was one they didn't like Richard and Maisie could have pretended not to hear. In the event I think they answered everything. And they didn't put a foot wrong.'

First reporter: Congratulations.

Richard: Thank you.

Second reporter: Are you happy?

Richard: Completely.

Maisie (putting an arm around Richard): What do you think?

Third reporter: What about your father, Miss Rivers?

Maisie (from the heart): Send him my love. I'm thinking of him.

Third reporter: Were you thinking of him when you eloped with Mr Faber?

Maisie (smiling, arms held out to the world): Love conquers all.

Fourth reporter: Have you heard that Jack Rivers is threatening legal action against you, Mr Faber?

Richard: I'm sure that's a mistake.

Fourth reporter: Have the police been in contact with you?

Richard (smiling): Of course not. I've done nothing wrong.

Maisie: And everything right.

Second reporter: Mr Faber, can I ask you – would you like *your* daughter to get married at fifteen?

Richard: I don't have a daughter, but I hope one day I will and, if and when I do, I would like my daughter to marry for love. And when the time was right for her. (As an afterthought) And, by the way, my wife is sixteen.

Second reporter: That's not what we understand.

Maisie (laughing): Have you checked?

Richard: Her birthday was last week. (Laughing) My father always forgot my birthday too.

*   *   *

It transpired that Jack had held his press conference, whether knowingly or not, on the morning of Maisie's sixteenth birthday, Thursday 24 April 1980. Somehow this revelation changed everything. From wronged father, righteous in his indignation, overnight Jack Rivers was transformed into something quite other, at best foolish fond old pantaloon (old Capulet of Verona), at worst vindictive, thoughtless, selfish old devil (Mr Moulton Barrett of Wimpole Street). Either way, the story was dead. And it was game, set and match to the fabulous Fabers.

From the vantage point of the newsdesk the song was over, but for the feature writers, for a week or two at least, the melody lingered on. Guided by Adam, Richard agreed to a number of interviews – the best by far was with Lynda Lee-Potter: the Prosecco flowed, the karma was good, the copy a dream – and Maisie (who Adam felt at this stage should be seen more than heard) accepted two modelling assignments, one of which led to her appearing on the cover of the September issue of American *Vogue*, photographed by Franco Pisani no less, the other to an offer to become 'the face of Passion', a new French fragrance where the perfume didn't smell quite right to Maisie and the money didn't smell quite right to Adam. 'We can do better than that,' he said. 'There's no rush.'

That first night Adam slept in his old room up in the attic, but since Richard and Maisie were now established in Theodore's old quarters, sleeping in Theodore and Isabella's notorious old bed ('It hath done the state some service,' said Theodore in the Tynan interview in the *New Yorker*. 'In Verona, y'know, we say bed is the poor man's opera'), later in the week Adam allowed himself to be persuaded to move down one floor to Richard's childhood bedroom, for some reason the coolest and lightest room on that floor, and just across the hall from the master suite. Adam moved into Richard's room, into Richard's clothes (he'd brought almost nothing from London), into Richard's pyjamas, and, now and again, into Richard's and Maisie's bed. It was all quite innocent: at breakfast-time, when he arrived with the *caffè latte* and the brioches and apricot jam, he just clambered in. It felt right. It was cosy. It made Richard think of Noël Coward and the Lunts in the last Act of *Design for Living*.

Adam set up what he described as the 'European Office' of St Pancras Productions in Theodore's library, ordered notepaper, installed a new phone line, and set about masterminding the next phase in their careers. 'The sky's the limit, *mes amis*. It's been good, it's getting better, the best is yet to come.'

'The best is yet to be.'

'What? What are you saying?'

'"Grow old along with me, The best is yet to be!" It's Browning. "Rabbi ben Ezra".'

'Of course. I should have known.'

Maisie became a director of the company and, morning, noon and night, fuelled by coffee and nicotine, Prosecco and Bardolini, they plotted and planned, schemed and dreamt their golden future – shows, plays, whole seasons – movies, lots of movies, art films that Isabella would have been proud of, blockbusters to make them rich and famous. They took to referring to 'the fabulous Fabers' as though they were people other than themselves, not quite creatures from another planet, more an all-conquering troupe of spangle-suited fire-eating trick cyclists who could juggle their way through a three-ringed circus – including riding the high wire over the lions' den – and then give you *Waiting for Godot* as the encore. With the fabulous Fabers anything was possible. Within the month they had announced their forthcoming *Romeo and Juliet* at the Roman Amphitheatre, opening 2 September, and while Adam took charge of the pre-production nuts and bolts in London and Verona, Richard took Maisie off on a lovers' tour of the Veneto plain.

Montagnana, Valdobbiadene, Cittadella, Marostica, Conegliano, they drove a bit, stopped a while, wandered here and there, down the cobbled streets of walled medieval towns, up the cypress-covered slopes of the foothills of the Dolomites, through vineyards, across piazzas, into churches, around Palladian villas (designed by Palladio himself), they took the tourist trail. In Grappa they drank *grappa*. In the narrow streets of Asolo they walked in the steps of Robert Browning. 'He loved this place. He wrote his last poem here, "Asolanda". It was published, you know, on the very day he died.'

She didn't know. She liked not to know so he could tell her.

'Did he die here then?'

'No, he died in Venice.'

'When are we going to Venice?'

'Not yet. Do you mind?'

'I don't mind anything,' she said. And then, calling out to the reverberating hills, she cried, 'I – love – you!' And there, halfway along the Via Santa Caterina, to the evident disgust of a couple of local widows, muttering crones who gazed on fixated and appalled, she put her arms around his neck and swung her legs around his waist and kissed him with a passion Emma Irving would have greatly envied and Adam Waterson much admired.

They were conspicuous because they were happy. Also, of course, because to some they were now recognisable. Over the past five years or so Richard had got used to the sideways glances, nudges and murmurings from passers-by to whom his face seemed familiar. Mostly he enjoyed it. It was trying late at night on the London Underground, on the Northern Line, when louts would call out '*Murderer!*' as they shambled off the train (it always happened as they got off, as the doors were closing), but gratifying when intelligent-looking students approached him in the street to tell him how much they admired his work in Shakespeare. Now he was parading the most beautiful girl in the world, with long legs, short skirts, and a look that Pisani had photographed and Passion craved for, so of course heads turned.

In Vincenza, as they explored the Teatro Olimpico and Richard told Maisie the story of Europe's oldest surviving indoor theatre, they were spotted by a small group of elderly English tourists who came into the auditorium and saw them standing centre stage and, suddenly recognising them, spontaneously burst into a smattering of applause. In Padua, sitting over coffee in the Caffè Pedrocchi, taking it in turns to tell one another tales from their childhood, they were approached by an old man, tall, elegant, upright, Roman nose, patrician bearing; even as he looked up at him Richard cast him as John Gielgud in *Providence*. The old gentleman inclined his head towards Maisie and put his hand out to Richard.

'I recognise you. May I take the liberty of introducing myself?' He was clearly Italian, but his English was impeccable, precise, considered, colloquial but from another era. 'Please forgive the intrusion, Signor Faber, but many years ago I was a friend of your dear mother.'

He sat with them for a few minutes and dazzled them with his charm. He was seventy, but still teaching at the university. He had been an artist, an actor, but was now 'a dull academic, a dry old stick'.

'You are very beautiful,' he said to Maisie with another gallant little bow, 'and your husband – he is terrifically handsome, don't you think? We must thank his parents. Isabella Bertolazzi was a great actress, you know, as beautiful as she was brilliant, and she was very brilliant.' He looked benevolently at Richard. 'I was more than a little in love with her, which is probably why I never really hit it off with your father. Jealousy. Beware the green-eyed monster.' He got up to go.

Richard got up too. 'Do you live in Padua?'

'No, no. This is just where I work, where I teach, where I sit in the library. Scribble scribble scribble. I live in Venice, almost the last Italian who does.'

'Is that where you come from?' Maisie asked.

'Oh, no, originally I come from the south, from Sicily, from Catania.'

'My father was in Sicily during the war,' said Maisie.

'Yes,' he said, widening his eyes a little, 'I know.'

SEVEN

When they got back to Verona they found there were two letters waiting for them: one was from Jack Rivers, the other from Laurence Olivier.

It was now mid-May. They had only been away two weeks. Thirteen nights in fact. Maisie was ready for more. Maisie, naturally enough, was ready for Venice, for her first ride in a gondola, for her first sight of San Marco, for Harry's Bar, for the Lido, for the Cipriani . . . But Richard was wanting to get back to work. As Maisie quickly learnt, Richard was always wanting to get back to work. In Asolo he had told her the story of Caterina Cornaro, sometime 'Queen of Cyprus, Jerusalem and Armenia, Lady of Asolo'.

They were standing in brilliant sunshine, high on the hill, by the ruined remains of Caterina's castle. 'She lived here, ruled here, five hundred years ago. This was her domain.'

'I like it,' said Maisie.

'Wait till you've heard the whole story,' said Richard. 'She was a Venetian by birth, "a daughter of the Republic", beautiful, we assume, from a good family, plenty of money, and, in 1472, conveniently married off to the King of Cyprus.'

'When do we start making the movie?' (This was a game they played all the time.)

'Hold on. Within a year of the marriage, the unfortunate king is bumped off – poisoned, poor bastard, so that the State of Venice can claim Cyprus as its own.'

'This is harsh.'

'Especially on Caterina as, at a stroke, the fair queen is robbed both of her king and her kingdom.'

'This is sad.'

'She is brought here to live in exile.'

'This is good.'

'Well . . .'

Maisie surveyed the scene. 'This is good. Look around, Richard. This is heaven.'

'It's certainly better than St Helena, but is it good?'

'Take it from me, husband. Asolo is good.'

'Wife, I have successfully brought you to the point of my story! One of Queen Caterina's courtiers was a man named Pietro Bembo, a cardinal, a poet—'

'This is who you'll be playing. I get it.'

'No you don't. Listen, Maisie. This is the point. This is the man who, watching Caterina in her gilded exile,

116

coined the verb "*asolare*" to describe the bitter-sweet life of idleness in paradise.'

'"*Asolare*".'

'It's not for us.'

'Oh no?'

Oh no. Richard could never be idle. He couldn't lie in the sun. He couldn't snooze in the hammock. He couldn't sit still – unless the part called for it. He couldn't view a landscape without framing it for the screen. He couldn't see a painting without making it a backdrop. He couldn't read a book without assessing its dramatic potential. Unless he was the director, he found filming near to unendurable because of all the hanging around between takes. Yes, he could – and would – unwind (especially with wine) but only with pleasure, only properly, if it was a reward at the end of a day of endeavour. He could even take a break, go away, stay away, but he needed to know it was time-limited and, to his conscience, he needed to justify it as a necessary 'recharging of the batteries' in anticipation of the coming fray. First and foremost, Richard lived to work. That was his nature. That's what his restless mind and body and spirit demanded. Richard also worked to live. That was his upbringing, the legacy of Isabella's life of anxiety. He quoted Noël Coward: 'Work is more fun than fun.' He quoted the Book of Proverbs: 'A little sleep, a little slumber, a little folding of the hands to rest and poverty will come upon you like a vagabond and want like an armed man.'

Maisie, of course, had never wanted for anything. Her

father was already fabulously wealthy by the time she was born and, together, over the years, she and Richard earned huge amounts, hundreds of thousands in the early years; in time, millions. Emma said, years later, 'I envied her her beauty and her talent, but most of all I envied her her wealth – not the money itself, but the fact that, from the moment of her birth, she had never, not once, not for a moment, had to consider the cost of anything. Can you imagine? A life without money worries? No scrimping, no saving, no making the hair last another week, no eking out the grant, no crawling for the overdraft. No dread of brown envelopes. No stomach churning. No sleepless nights. It's inconceivable. You know, if I hadn't ever had to worry about money I could have been beautiful and talented too.'

Jack's letter was largely about money. He told Maisie he loved her, missed her, wanted her, needed her, forgave her, understood her – and asked her in her turn to understand, forgive and love him too. Then he explained that, under the circumstances, she would appreciate that, unless and until she came home, he couldn't support her financially, would have to reorganise the trusts to ensure that nothing came her way, would have little choice but to leave 'The Beautiful Lady' to the Wallace Collection—

She banged her coffee cup down on the table. She was pacing the spacious old-world kitchen at the Villa Ortese, scuffing the tiles with her heels, reading the letter out loud, gently sending it up, 'performing' it for her husband's benefit. 'God, what an idiot. He just doesn't get it, does he?'

Richard was near the window, with his back to her, standing in front of the huge walnut dresser, reorganising the famous Faber crockery, all from Murano, acquired by Isabella, preserved by Theodore, cherished by Richard who liked to see it correctly stacked and displayed according to design and size. Adam had been in sole command of the kitchen for a fortnight and, oddly, Adam, so precise with a balance sheet, had no sense of domestic order.

Richard turned, with an appropriately theatrical sigh (it was his stock-in-trade, after all), and started to say, 'He's a first-class—'

'Don't say a word. I forbid it.' She ran over to him and pushed her broad bright-eyed face right into his. 'He's *my* father. I can say what I like. You cannot say anything. You stole his daughter. You're in the wrong. And you have promised me faithfully never to say anything, *anything*, against him. Remember?'

She put her hands behind his head and dug her fingers hard into his thick hair and pulled herself up towards him and kissed him fiercely, as though she was embracing the Cup Winners' Cup itself.

Just as abruptly she broke away from him, reclaimed her coffee and resumed her moved reading. On the second page of the letter her father furnished her with the full details of the generous offer he had made to Richard by the confessional in Sant' Anastasia, and went on to say that the offer was still on the table and would remain there until the end of June, but not beyond. She stopped in her tracks again and put down the coffee cup once more. 'Do you realise: Miss Cooper must have typed this. Can you believe it? Can you believe it?'

Richard smiled and decided that the giant fruit dish was too precariously balanced and needed to go on a broader, lower shelf. 'I'm not saying anything.'

She shook her head and waved her hands, acting dismayed-young-girl-in-state-of-shock-and-disbelief. 'It's just amazing.'

Richard was rearranging the tiny coffee cups, hanging them on little hooks so the handles were all turned in the same direction. 'You've probably never heard of an actor called Peter Lorre, but I'm thinking we'll have to have him in the movie.'

'What happened to Charlie Drake?'

'Altogether too classy.'

He expected her to laugh and when she didn't he turned and saw a stranger standing there, pale and trembling, tears streaming down her face. Richard always said Maisie looked so strong and sure, so certain, so fearless. Now, quite suddenly, the strength had been drained from her, the warmth had turned to cold. She looked childish and frightened. He came to her, but she pushed him away. He took the letter from her.

The final page was a long postscript, handwritten in a large, ungainly, childlike hand.

'Maisie dearest. I think I ought to try to explain to you WHY I'm doing this. It's not just selfishness. It's not just me being pig-headed and possessive. That's what RF thinks, I'm sure. "Jack Rivers has to have his own way – he always has to have his own way." That's what he's saying, isn't it? I know it is. The truth is, Maisie, I'm doing what I'm doing BECAUSE I HAVE TO – I have no choice – and what I need you to know is that it's to do with your darling mother as much as with you. We don't talk about her much, I know. We don't talk much, period. I know that too. We can change that. We WILL change that when you come home, I promise. We don't talk about your mother, but we both think about her a lot, don't we? I think about her most days, Maisie, and I feel that I should tell you something about her you may not know but you may have guessed at. I loved her very much. You have seen pictures of her so you will know how lovely she was. What you cannot know is how special she was to me. She was everything to me and I was everything to her. We depended on one another – but I feared for her always, right from the day we met, because she was not what they call "a well woman". As my mother would have said, she suffered from her "nerves". Her mind played terrible tricks on her. One day she'd say she felt fine and the next she'd tell me her brain was racing, racing, round and round, like a Catherine wheel spinning out of control. On days like that she said she felt she was possessed by demons! It wasn't just the "brain fever" as the doctor called it – physically she was always weak as well. We were told we shouldn't have children, but she wanted a child more than anything. That's what you need to know. She wanted YOU more than anything! Conceiving you wasn't easy! Giving birth to you put a great strain on her. On the night you were born she was convinced she was going to die. That night she made me promise to look after you always. She made me repeat it like a cub scout promise. You know that in the end she took her own life, don't you? She said she simply couldn't cope. She felt inadequate. She said she couldn't be a good mother and told me that I would have to make up for it by being the best father instead. Maisie, before she died I promised your mother to look after you ALWAYS. I want to keep my promise. That's all. Love you. DAD.'

Richard folded over the letter and put it down on the kitchen table. He spoke quietly. 'The man's a monster.'

'Don't.'

'You don't believe any of this, do you?'

'I don't know, I—' She was bewildered, but the tears had stopped and she let him come to her and fold his arms around her.

'It isn't true,' he whispered. 'I know it isn't true.' He held her to him and with loving fingers softly stroked her golden hair, soothing her, calming her, as you might a child after a tantrum.

'Richard . . .'

'Shh . . .' He hushed her and held her close, swaying with her. 'Don't ask me why he's doing it. I don't understand any more than you do. It's emotional blackmail. That's all it is. It's pathetic.'

'What do I do?'

'Forget it.'

'Hold me,' she whispered.

'To have and to hold from this day forth . . .'

She closed her eyes. 'For richer, for poorer, for better, for worse . . .'

'You're safe here. Always. It's just us, remember.'

'It's just us.'

'It's just us!' roared Adam, full of cheer, loaded with shopping, standing at the wide-open kitchen door. 'It's just *us!*' He was in exuberant mood. The work was going well, the box-office advance was already growing nicely, and Jinny, the gap-year girl at the Bureau de Change by the Arena, had made it transparently clear that morning that she fully understood the nature of his currency requirements. 'Welcome home, young lovers! How was the honeymoon? Where did you get to in the end? Firenze?'

'No.'

'Ravenna?'

'No.'

'Venezia?'

'No.'

'For God's sake, what's the point? You're wasted on him, Maisie. He's got no idea. Clearly I'm going to have to be the one to show you a good time. Stick around.' He dumped the bagful of groceries noisily on the table and embraced them both. If he noticed the blotchy tear stains on Maisie's face he didn't say. He looked at her indulgently. 'I imagine, poor girl, Richard has forced you back from your honeymoon prematurely, lured home, bless his cotton socks, by his sixth sense telling him there was a letter waiting for him here from his great hero, the one and only . . .'

Richard was gazing at his lifelong friend appraisingly. Adam raised an eyebrow. 'Well? And what does his lordship have to say?'

Richard made to tweak his nose. 'Don't tell me you haven't looked?'

Adam confessed. 'Well, as it happens, I have – but I sealed it up again to give you the pleasure of opening it for yourself.'

With suitable ceremony Richard reopened the envelope.

'My dear Faber,
      By all means, I'll tell you what little I can recall. I may have the music you want. And some other bits and pieces. I'm not sure. It was a disaster, you realise. I made a really ridiculous fool of myself. Please call my secretary. It will be a pleasure to meet you.
      Yours aye,
      Olivier.'

'A little cryptic, but a royal summons all the same. I think you'd better go.' Adam took Maisie's right hand and brought it to his lips. 'I'll stay and look after your young bride. She'll be quite safe with me.' He attempted a self-mocking, caddish leer and Richard, amused (he loved him still), set about casting the moment at once: the look was Peter Sellers, the tone George Sanders, the effect Terry-Thomas.

Maisie said, 'Who's George Sanders?' Of course she

124

did. All Richard's references, always, sprang from another era, another time, another place. He was puzzled by it sometimes too. Here he was in 1980, not yet thirty-one, and yet his points of departure came not from the world around him, not from his childhood, from his own roots, but from a world half a century away. It wasn't just that he saw himself in some great romantic line – the sword handed on from Garrick to Kean to Irving to Olivier to Faber – it was as if he kept himself safe from the terrors of this world by living in another one. He could play a contemporary character with complete conviction, but he couldn't be one. And when it came to women, while Adam knew the current form ('Form of choice: 34B/24/35 – ho-ho'), studied it, savoured it, could flick through a magazine checking off his fantasies (Carla Bruni ahead of Estelle Lefebure ahead of Talisa Sotohe now tieing with Jane March), Richard's feminine ideal was neither supermodel nor superwaif, it was silver screen and proscenium arch, it was Maisie and Merle Oberon, Greer Garson and Vivien Leigh.

He knew all their stories. He knew that Vivien Leigh and Laurence Olivier had starred together on Broadway in *Romeo and Juliet* in 1940, the year they married. He knew that Olivier had composed the music for the production. He wondered what had happened to it. He had written to him. He had wanted an excuse. He had found one. And now, in his hand, here it was: an invitation from Zeus in person.

He called, he fixed the date, Thursday that week, half an hour, no more, mustn't tire him, a cup of tea in the

125

flat at Victoria. He need only be away twenty-four hours. Adam would look after Maisie.

When Thursday came he took the day-break flight to London. It was odd to be back. Unsettling. Unreal. Lonely. In Verona it was warm and light and the sky was cloudless and properly sky blue (Zeffirelli country); London was cold and grey and overcast (Sidney Lumet). There was no fog, no Basil Rathbone peasouper, but Richard said he managed to conjure one up and struggled through it, not knowing quite where he was going, feeling apprehensive and uncertain but not knowing quite why. He went to St Pancras. Adam had left chaos everywhere. He went to Somerset House and, without difficulty, within an hour, for £1.25, secured a copy of Maisie's mother's death certificate. He went to Horseferry Road, to the Westminster Coroner's Court, where a helpful young man (Murray Melvin in *A Taste of Honey*?), with a high, whiny, alarmingly penetrating voice, and an unnerving knowing wink, recognised him and was more than happy to assist him in the filling out of an application form requesting a transcript of the report on the inquest into the sudden death of Georgiana Hope Rivers held on Thursday 20 May 1965. 'Fifteen years ago to this very day,' mused the young man, a disconcerting finger suddenly inserted inside his shirt collar. 'Is that a coincidence?'

By way of reply, Richard managed to look confused and said, 'Do I have to come in to collect it?'

'No.' The finger was working its way round the neck. 'We can send it to you if you pay the postage.' Richard handed over the money and, with relief, made his way to Victoria for his cup of tea on Mount Olympus.

Olivier hadn't played Zeus at that stage. *Clash of the Titans* was a treat in store.

'I've just done General MacArthur. "I shall return." Christ, I hope not! That said, impressive make-up, don't you agree?' He showed Richard a still of himself as the great American general and the commanding look, high brow, hawk eye, eagle nose, lantern jaw, was certainly all that the producers could have wished for. 'God, what we do for money!' In the flesh, he looked frail: still Uncle Franco from the Bank of Turin, but so much older, smaller, shrunken, the voice thin and reedy, the eyes mournful, anxious, cherry stones in watery albumen. He had no recollection of his encounter with Richard at Chichester. He'd seen his work. Naturally. And admired it. Greatly. If Richard had then hoped for godlike murmurings of appreciation of his Richard Bolingbroke or his Hamlet or his Henry V he was to be disappointed. It was *Murderer* that Olivier remembered best. With affection and respect.

'And I've been following your marital capers.' He brought the tea cup a little unsteadily to his mouth and looked over it, the eyes, now kittenish, narrowing. 'Vivien and I knew something of the kind.' The eyes opened wide and rolled to heaven. 'Bless me, Father, for I have sinned. Heathcliff and Scarlet O'Hara. A dangerous affair. A secret wedding. A great furore!' He put down the cup and waved his right hand from the wrist, an odd circular wave, as though he was trying to conjure something from the air.

'It was darling George Cukor's idea. Take advantage of all the fuss. Make a little money. Make a little splash. That's what we thought. Stake our claim as Shakespearians as well as film actors. Ralph was against it. "*Romeo and Juliet* – a bit too luxurious for wartime, eh, cockie?" The gods were against it. And the critics, my dear . . . Not a bad cast – Wesley Addy, a beautiful actor, for Benvolio, Edmund O'Brien for Mercutio, remember him? Dame May Whitty for the Nurse – but you couldn't see them and you couldn't hear them because of the fucking set!' He clapped his hands and let his jaw drop. His voice was stronger now. 'I must tell you I had conceived the most wonderful revolve designed to sweep us effortlessly through all twenty-one scenes. It was quite magnificent, but built on such a scale that to fit it on to the stage it had to go right, right at the back so the poor audiences felt they were watching the piece from another building – and that was a Turkish bath! The heat and the humidity were terrible. The stage was an oven. I was soaked. The wig (those dark Italian locks!), the putty on the nose (that fine Italian profile!), the costume (has to have a bit of weight to hang right), the corset – sshh, whisper it not! – I had a bit of a tum on me! I was drenched. And I was shattered.' He sat back and blinked at Richard from behind his thick glasses. The jaw went slack, he looked from side to side, and then summoned up new forces to complete the tale. 'I was producing it, directing it, writing the music – such flourishes! – designing the set. Oh, yes, and essaying the title role!

'We opened in San Francisco – a memorable night for one and all, except for dear old Ben Webster, our Montagu, who came on, made a dignified cross to confront me and hissed, none too quietly, "Give me me word, give me me word!"' Both hands were waving now. The pace was quickening. 'It got worse. When the moment came for my little hop-skip-and-jump, my vault over the wall out of Capulet's garden, I ran at the wall, such *élan*, leapt up, got my fingers on to the top and suddenly realised I hadn't the strength to go further. I just had to hang there, helplessly, kicking, gasping, sweating, entirely unable to move in an upward direction. Oh God, forgive me. After a century the curtain came down.

'When we got to Broadway we were not welcomed with open arms. Clearly we'd got the publicity all wrong. We were advertising in movie houses – "See real lovers make love in public!" Can you believe it? My dear. And I don't suppose the production was entirely right either. We got the most terrible notices. Here, here.' He had them ready to show Richard. He seemed quite proud of them. The worst, he seemed to like the best. '"Jumpo and Juliet" . . . "The worst Romeo ever" . . . "Laurence Olivier talks as if he were brushing his teeth" . . . The morning after we opened there were queues around the block – demanding their money back! And we gave it to them! Christ, whatever you do, don't give them their money back!'

*　　*　　*

There was no need. When Richard Faber's production of *Romeo and Juliet* opened at Verona's Roman Amphitheatre that September, with Maisie Rivers as Juliet, Simon Cadell as Mercutio, Emma Irving as the Nurse, with settings by God and music by Laurence Olivier, the season was a complete sell-out, the reviews, without exception, were written with pens dipped in honey and champagne, and a standing ovation greeted each and every one of the twenty-seven performances. You might say that was the month when the legend of Richard and Maisie, of Faber and Rivers, was born. Okay, so the scandal of their runaway romance fuelled the sensation, but the success was real – substantial – and extraordinary. As Adam said: 'The fabulous Fabers have now arrived. And I think we'll find they're here to stay.'

They were. Yet you're right, of course: the history of entertainment is littered with the been-and-gone names of celebrated couples who once wowed the world – and how! Henry Irving and Ellen Terry, Fred and Ginger, Tracy and Hepburn, Burton and Taylor, Cruise and Kidman, Ken and Em, Bruce and Demi. And more. Some stayed the course. Some dazzled and fizzled. So, yes, it's happened before, it's happened since, it'll happen again. But on this one Adam wasn't wide of the mark: the fabulous Fabers were in a league of their own. Truly. The closest parallel would have to be Olivier and Vivien Leigh – Richard knew that – except that Richard (by common consent) was better-looking (and stayed better-looking) than Olivier, and Maisie would have seen herself more as Marilyn Monroe than Vivien

Leigh. Adam used to say, 'There was a lot of Marilyn in Maisie.'

So forget the comparisons. Just accept it. The fabulous Fabers were unique. They were a fantasy couple leading fairy-tale lives. They were beautiful and brilliant. So young and so happy. As all the world could tell, they were gloriously, hopelessly, helplessly, head-over-heels in love. And the more evident their love for each other the more the world seemed to love them. They could do no wrong. They made the stars shine more brightly. They quickened your pulse. They warmed your heart. And everything they touched turned to gold.

And when, in the summer of 1981, their daughter, Sarah, was born, quite surprisingly, it didn't spoil it at all. The magic held.

Eight

Adam said, years later: 'Until Richard married Maisie, I had not really fancied her. She was very obviously fanciable – the hair, the eyes, the mouth, the figure, she really was sensational – but there was initially something that made me keep my distance – beyond the fact that Richard had told me to, beyond the fact that she wasn't much more than a child. She didn't seem to connect. It was as if she was some strange, wide-eyed, wayward spirit from another world, an enchanted creature from a Celtic fairy tale. There was something wild about her, anarchic almost, something disturbing, dangerous as well as beautiful. I think in part it was the danger that attracted Richard. Richard was always drawn to danger.

'I wasn't. During the run of *Alice* I kept away from her. I could see the effect she was having on Richard, we all could. I wasn't jealous. I was a little afraid. She overwhelmed Richard, swamped him, took him by storm. She took the audiences by storm too – they clearly loved her, from the word go – she had an amazing stage presence, bewitching, there was energy and vulnerability, she had a special quality, no doubt about it, and she could do it, she could do the business – and the others in the company, especially the wise old birds like Emma, they all seemed to get on with her fine. But while she and I were perfectly friendly, we remained distant, and the once or twice when we happened to be alone together it felt uneasy, awkward. In Verona it was different. Totally. Sharing the house with them, I saw her all the time, of course. And she seemed . . . it's difficult to know how to put it . . . not more ordinary, but more *real*. As we all know, Richard just lived to work, but it became crystal clear to me during that glorious, golden Italian summer that Maisie lived to live. She wasn't normal, she was still odd, changeable, moody, still *strange* but, to me at least, no longer a stranger.

'The more I saw of her the more remarkable she became. I was struck by the way she was beautiful all the time: on stage and off, morning and night, dolled up for dinner at Il Desco or in her jeans and T-shirt struggling with her lines, after a week in the sun or a night on the tiles, she *always* looked so *good*. She was just gorgeous. And she knew it. And I think she liked it. Why shouldn't she? She knew she was fanciable and I flatter myself that she had no objection to being fancied. Seeing her at close range, looking at her – she liked

you to look at her, it didn't disconcert her at all —
I was fascinated by the way her body was changing,
day by day, week by week, partly of course because she
was growing older, growing up, partly because she was
working on it, and working especially on her voice, her
breathing, her diaphragm. Under Richard's direction she
did hours of exercises every day, literally hours. Olivier
had told him that when they did their *Romeo* Vivien's
voice had been slammed by the critics — it was thin,
weak, unsubtle, *inaudible* — and Richard was determined
that his Juliet wasn't just going to look the part, she was
going to sound it too.

'Whether Maisie became careless or easy, or whether
it was just the way she was, I don't know, but quite
quickly I could tell that she didn't mind when or
where I saw her, or how. Very soon after I moved
in, it was the week Richard went to London to meet
Olivier, it was late in the morning, nearly lunchtime,
and I walked into their room without thinking and
there she was, standing in front of the mirror, quite
naked. It was amazing — not simply because she looked
so incredible, so delicious — forgive me — but because
she stayed so still. Come across any other girl like that
and . . . well, over the years I've noticed it, particularly
with the very young ones, and the slightly older decent
middle-class married ones embarking on their first illicit
liaison, catch them with their kit off and they shy away,
their shoulders come forward, they hide their breasts,
they want to disappear under the duvet. They want
the dark. Maisie stood there, the sun pouring on to

her, and simply turned towards me and smiled. She was fantastic.'

Wisely, Adam did not mention this incident to Richard. Less wisely, some months later, it was not that long before Sarah was born, it was late in the evening and they were quite drunk, as often they were, and Maisie had just left them to go to bed, and as she had closed the door, Adam had gazed after her and, unthinking, by instinct, on automatic pilot, said something coarse and blokeish and typical about fancying pregnant women, and added, laughing, 'I suppose it's the beautiful big tits – look at Maisie!'

Richard closed his eyes and his head whirled and he whispered, 'Don't, please don't', and let it pass. Outwardly, between them nothing changed, but inwardly they both knew it was a defining moment, the first crack, tiny, almost invisible, but acknowledged silently between them. However long the journey might take, and it took many years, they both knew from that night there was no turning back. The crossroad had been passed: the paths were separate now, apparently parallel, imperceptibly diverging, so for many miles they could still walk and talk together as if all was all it had ever been. But it wasn't. They knew that. This was the beginning of the end.

In the coming years Maisie became a universal object of desire, but somehow – amazingly, given the prurience of the times – she managed to keep the details of her sex life to herself. Plough your way through that fat airport classic *The Intimate Sex Lives of the Rich and Famous* and you'll find more than all you'll ever need to know about Marilyn and Madonna and Princess Stephanie and Princess Di – who they had, and when and where and *how*. Mae West is there, and Paula Yates, Demi Moore and Barbra Streisand, the Spice Girls and Vivien Leigh, the almost-forgotten and the near-immortal. Marilyn rates ten pages. Maisie Rivers doesn't feature. Marilyn, after her first encounter with Marlon Brando, is reported to have murmured huskily, 'I don't know if I do it right.' By several accounts she did it simply, noisily and quite often, and talked about it in wonderful detail to husbands, lovers, doctors, drivers, snappers, snippers, masseurs, maids – who, in their turn, have generously passed it on. Marilyn said a lot. Maisie said nothing.

When it came to talking about sex Richard wasn't squeamish. He was happy to ramble on about Garrick and Kean, and Irving and Olivier, and the chaotic ups and downs of their lives between the sheets. He knew all the old stories, all the names, the mistresses, the bordellos, the law suits, the doses of the clap. Peg Woffington, David Garrick's Irish beauty, was a special favourite: 'in terms of allure, appetites and untimely death I'd say she was the Vivien Leigh of her day.'

Recollecting her several conversations with Richard on this score, Emma laughed her smoker's laugh, deep and dirty: 'I quickly learnt that one thing these great gods of the English theatre all seemed to have in common was an unhealthy obsession with the adequacy, or otherwise, of their equipment! You'll not be surprised to hear that I did not cross-examine Richard too closely on this delicate topic – though I do remember when he and Maisie were doing that terrible remake of the Errol Flynn *Robin Hood* – the one the public loved and I hated, *hated* – Richard was very taken with the fellow who'd worked on the original who came down to see them at Pinewood and revealed that Errol Flynn – *between takes* – would drop a pinch of cocaine on his penis as "an aphrodisiac and enhancer"!'

All Richard ever said to Emma about sex and Maisie was typically allusive: 'Since you ask . . . "It was roses, roses all the way."'

'Browning?'

'Yup.' He grinned. Emma knew he wouldn't say any more. She smiled at him indulgently. He widened his eyes and with an imaginary cane did his spinning-it-over-the-shoulder-and-catching-it routine. 'Yup, that first summer we learnt to fly.'

He did too. Literally. He went to the little flying school near Solferino and learnt on a Fiat R2 reconnaissance biplane. Perhaps it was part of his homage to Olivier. In New York, in the summer of 1940, the summer of the marriage to Vivien and the ill-fated *Romeo and Juliet*, Olivier took flying lessons in a superannuated sea plane, using the Hudson River as a landing strip – but then there had been a war on and Olivier had had ambitions to join the Fleet Air Arm. Richard had ambitions to make a movie of the life of Antoine de Saint-Exupéry. As Adam said to Maisie at the time, 'At least, that's his excuse.'

Long years later, Richard used a line from Saint-Exupéry to explain, to justify, the one ambiguous aspect of his behaviour towards Maisie. He claimed a fairy-tale marriage, a perfect match, a union like no other, yet he acknowledged that while he believed she told him everything – kept no secrets, spoke no lies – he was not always so open, so candid with her. 'I was true in all that I told her of myself, but of what I saw of the world and some of its darker corners I suppose you could say I told her the truth but not always the whole truth. It wasn't a matter of deception for deception's sake. It was more from a sense of duty, a sense of obligation. As the Little Prince says, "You become responsible, for ever, for that you have tamed. You are responsible for your rose."'

On the day the transcript of the coroner's report on the death of Maisie's mother reached Richard, Maisie neither knew he had been expecting it nor was aware that it had arrived. 'Still looking forward to what the mailman might bring is the acid test of whether or not you still want to be alive,' was a favourite Theodore Faber axiom, but the morning post had never meant much to Maisie. As a child at Dabney House she never saw it: Miss Cooper always got there first. (On Maisie's birthday there were cards, but they didn't come tumbling pell-mell through the letter box: she found them neatly arranged by her place at the breakfast table.) As a young married woman in Verona, she gave no thought to how the post arrived. Richard or Adam simply appeared holding a bundle of mail and if there was something for her –

an English magazine, a postcard from Odile – they handed it over. The tide of workaday correspondence – the flotsam and jetsam of domestic and professional life, bills, circulars, contracts – never reached her. The two men dealt with everything. That suited her fine. Even the messages in bottles – the unsolicited invitations, the unexpected offers of employment – were handled by them. Paperwork didn't interest her. When they asked her to read something, she glanced at it. When they asked her to sign something, she did.

Richard took the coroner's report into the bathroom, and leaning against the closed bathroom door, scanned it quickly, then read it carefully, just the once, and placed it in his jacket pocket, and returned to the kitchen where Maisie, in a white linen pinafore dress – but, apparently, nothing else – (this is Richard's account), was enjoying failing to come to terms with the electronic orange juice squeezer, declaiming above the din – with what Richard-the-voice-coach would have applauded as 'perfectly pitched plosives' – 'Is there no pity sitting in the clouds That sees into the bottom of my grief?'

'Good news,' bellowed Richard.

The grinding stopped. Maisie looked towards him, happy. 'Olivier will pre-record the Prologue?' Maisie knew her man.

'No.' Richard shook his head, suddenly embarrassed. 'I'm stupid. It's not that kind of news. It's just confirmation really of what we always knew.'

She looked perplexed. He went over to her and took both her hands. They were sticky from the oranges and (much later) he said the moment was one of the three or four times when he was overwhelmed by an immediate – shocking and shaming – awareness of the fact that Maisie was still a child. Quickly he said: 'Your mother did not take her own life. It was an accident. As we knew. A tragic accident. Nothing more.'

Maisie was baffled. Why this? Why now? Richard struggled on. 'When I was in London I went to get a copy of the death certificate. I should have mentioned it, but anyway . . . Now I've seen the coroner's report and it simply confirms it. Accidental death.'

She pulled her hands away and went to the tap to rinse them. 'Thank you. You are a very thoughtful husband and I love you.' As she dried her hands on a tea towel of the Leaning Tower of Pisa she moved back towards him: '"Come, gentle night. Come, loving, black-browed night. Give me my Romeo. And when I shall die, Take him and cut him out in little stars, And he will make the face of heaven so fine That all the world will be in love with night And pay no worship to the garish sun."' She said it all, all six lines, in one effortless breath with an upward inflection at the finish. She smiled and kissed him on the mouth and pressed her tongue against his.

She didn't ask to see the report. She had always known the truth: her mother, late at night and in the dark, had fallen down the stairs and, quite simply, broken her neck. The fall killed her.

Richard chose not to tell her that the coroner's report indicated a considerable quantity of lithium carbonate in her mother's system. What was the point? The verdict wouldn't change. Nor did he tell her that his own view was that Jack Rivers had probably pumped her full of drugs and then pushed her down the stairs himself. Where was the evidence? Richard told her what he told her to calm the demons, to allay her fears, to keep her safe. He was responsible for his rose, would protect and shelter it, always, whatever the price.

They had not spoken of Jack's letter since the day Maisie had received it. Now that Richard had brought this confirmation of what they had always known, they need not speak of it again.

Of Jack himself they spoke hardly at all. They read about him in the papers now and then – buying something, selling something, breaking something up – and, early in 1981, when he was invited by Margaret Thatcher to head up 'a task force to drive through the revolution of privatisation' there was a modest flurry of profiles, one or two of which made it beyond the business pages. Adam was impressed – 'Here comes the knighthood!' – but Richard said nothing because he wasn't sure what to say and Maisie looked at Adam to warn him off, to ensure that he had nothing more to say.

That same month, February 1981, Richard went to California to make a movie – just a TV movie, but according to Adam, 'a great script, a great part and a great deal of dosh'. *Charlie and the Kid* – eventually screened, after many rows, as *The Kid and Charlie* – told the story of young Charles Chaplin in the teens of the century, taking the hero from late adolescence as a barber's shop lather boy in London through his journey to America with Fred Karno and his early triumphs in Hollywood with Mack Sennett and the Keystone Film Company, but concentrating not so much on the one-reelers and Chaplin the silent clown as on his private life, Chaplin the noisome lover, husband and father. At the heart of the picture was his relationship with Mildred Harris, the simple-minded young girl he first bedded in 1916, married in 1918 and divorced in 1920. Maisie did not know that the part had been offered to her; nor did she know, because she didn't see the script and Richard didn't tell her, that, in 1919, Mildred Harris gave birth to Chaplin's child, a baby boy, grotesquely deformed, who died when he was three days old.

When Adam brought the news that the deal was done (it was the morning before the day that ended in the night that Richard and Adam secretly acknowledged the tiny crack, the beginning of the end) Richard said, 'Great', without sounding too convinced, and Maisie cried, sweetly, with conviction, 'Hollywood, here I come!' The men's averted gazes told their story. 'I can come, can't I?'

'No, Maisie . . .' Richard was screwing up his face and trying a bit of rather ropey aw-shucks-I'm-sorry-honey acting.

'Why not?'

'You know why not – the baby.'

'Piff-paff!' (This was an expression she'd got from Odile and had taken to using so much she even irritated herself by the frequency with which she uttered it.) 'Pregnant women are flying all the time.'

'Dr Spock doesn't recommend it.'

'Piff-paff! Who's he?'

'And it isn't only the baby, it's ...' Richard was floundering.

'The boredom,' said Adam, riding to the rescue. 'When you make your first movie you'll find the tedium of it is incredible. They get you up before dawn and then leave you sitting around all day with nothing to do. But at least you're making a movie. If you're the husband or the wife you're just an appendage – a hanger-on, a nobody, a nothing. It's hell. I know. I've been his manager for years – but at least a manager has a role, a purpose. A wife is nothing. And a pregnant wife is worse than nothing. She's a fucking liability.'

Maisie crumpled and burst into tears.

'Sorry.'

'Christ, sorry.'

They both said it at once and together they rushed towards her and put their arms around her, embraced her and each other, and stood as one, hugging, swaying, just as they had done on the night Adam had arrived.

Richard whispered into her hair, 'We won't let this happen again. Promise. We'll work together always. From now on. Always. We'll be together, every day, every night. Always.' She looked up at him and smiled. Her lips were swollen. Richard despised himself for thinking at that moment that the blotchiness of the tears was the only thing that ever robbed her face of its beauty. He closed his eyes and said, 'I'll just do this – and then it's done. It's only five weeks.'

'And I shall look after you,' said Adam, kissing her on the forehead, kissing her better.

'Yes,' said Richard and they broke the embrace and stood in a circle, like children playing ring-o'-roses, holding hands, 'Adam will look after you.'

'If I let you go,' Maisie said, looking at Richard, 'when you get back, can we go to Venice?'

'Yes,' said Richard, relieved. The storm was over.

They went to Venice, just Richard and Maisie, at the end of March, about a month before Sarah was born.

They stayed at the Accademia, not the famous gallery but a pretty seventeenth-century villa on a side-canal nearby, a tucked-away *pensione* on the Dorsoduro, much favoured by the English of a certain type and first 'discovered' by Theodore Faber in the 1950s. It only offered bed and breakfast, it only ran to a dozen or so rooms, but it possessed a charming little garden and the Henry James feel Richard had decided he was after. Maisie, naturally, had expected the Cipriani or the Gritti Palace – she was sixteen and she liked a grand hotel – but Richard, having had five weeks of Chaplin and Beverly Hills, chose to introduce his young wife to the delights of *La Serenissima* not as an international movie actor (that would come later) but more in the guise of a shy, charming, diffident, disarming, slightly donnish young man from a good Sussex family, a few years out of Cambridge, now climbing the ladder with Sotheby's. If you were casting it today it would have a touch of Hugh Grant meets *The Antiques Roadshow*. Whatever part her husband chose to play, so long as they were together Maisie was easy. And happy.

They did everything – or as much as you can do in the world's most extraordinary city when you have just seven days and six nights and one of you is expecting to give birth at any minute. Richard didn't talk about Hollywood and the movies. He talked about *commedia dell' arte* and the Bellinis. And Titian and Tintoretto and Veronese – and Byron and Browning and Max Beerbohm 'who, when he came to Florian's, always sat at that table – yes, Maisie, that table there. Don't ask me how my father knew, he couldn't see it anyway, but he swore it was so and I believe him.'

'I believe him too, Richard.'

When they'd done the obvious – the Doge's Palace and Harry's Bar and Santa Maria della Salute – they did the unexpected – the Bovolo Staircase, the dinosaurs at the natural history museum, Othello's house in the Campo dei Carmini – and wherever they went Richard talked and laughed and told tall tales of Venice's heroic past, and loved her more every minute, and Maisie listened and smiled and loved him too. 'She lov'd me for the dangers I had pass'd, And I lov'd her that she did pity them. This only is the witchcraft I have us'd.'

They were in the little theatre museum in Goldoni's House and Richard was about to embark on edited highlights from the eccentric life and times of the great playwright when suddenly she said, 'This is where we're going to live.'

'We can't live here, Maisie. It's too dark.'

'Don't be stupid, husband. Venice is where we're going to live. On the Grand Canal.' She could picture it all. 'We are the fabulous Fabers. Remember?'

'Yes, but, Maisie . . .'

'Where did Browning live? Where we went this morning.'

'Ca' Rezzonico?'

'Exactly.'

'It's a palace!'

'Exactly.'

'Maisie, my sweet . . .'

'Where's your ambition?'

'The Ca' Rezzonico is one of the world's great museums. It's not for sale.'

'But something will be. And I shall find it.'

And the next day, their last full day, she set off in search of Palazzo Faber. 'You're right,' she admitted to Richard over breakfast in the garden of the hotel. 'The Ca' Rezzonico's too big and baroque – I like that word, "baroque" – but there'll be something for us here. I know.'

While Maisie, amazing Maisie, sixteen-going-on-thirty, went house-hunting on the Grand Canal, Richard, thirty-going-on-God-knows-what, took his notebook and his camera and went meandering north towards the Ghetto. Why should Shylock be more than thirty-eight or thirty-nine? Jessica is just a child. He lost his way twice and a clock was already striking eleven as he crossed the iron bridge from the Fondamenta degli Ormesini and made his way to the little museum of Jewish history in the corner of the Campo del Ghetto Nuovo. He tried the door. It was closed, locked. He found the bell and, after a minute, a stout middle-aged woman with hennaed hair and a kindly face (easy casting) came to let him in. She mumbled pleasantly as she padded ahead of him, leading the way through the darkened exhibition rooms to the stairwell at the back. She smiled and nodded and left him to climb the stairs to the synagogue alone. The tall oak doors were half open. The sun was streaming in from a high window, turning the shafts of dust to gold, and, for a moment, blinding him, so that at first he didn't see the old man.

'I am here,' he said, and Richard looked up and recognised at once the ramrod back and Roman profile of the old professor from the university at Padua. 'Thank you for coming,' he said, putting out a hand of welcome. 'It is good that we meet again.'

They sat side by side in the panelled gallery and the professor, looking straight ahead, said, 'Do you know about the Venetian tradition of "denunciations"?' His English was impeccable. 'In the days of the Republic our citizens were encouraged to "tell" on one another. Have you noticed around the city, set into walls, on pediments, stone lions' mouths, like letter boxes? They are called *bocche di leone*, and there, at midnight, when all Venice sleeps, you post your accusation. I am grateful to you for coming to hear mine.' When he had finished his story they went out into the square and shared a coffee, and, before they parted, Richard took a photograph of the old man and the old man took Richard by the arm and led him back across the square to show him the brave, pathetic plaque that discreetly records the death of two hundred Venetian Jews among the six million slaughtered in the Holocaust.

When Richard and Maisie met up at the end of the day he kissed her and said at once, 'Guess who I met this morning?'

'Guess who *I* met?' she said. 'A wizened little man, like a monkey. Incredibly old, but so sweet. He wants me to play Gigi. He says he wrote it.'

'Colette wrote it.' Richard was amused. And relieved. The moment for telling his story seemed to have passed.

'No, I'm sure he said he wrote it. Anyway, he was at school with you and he's giving us dinner.'

They dined with Alan Jay Lerner at the Antico Martini, on the terrace overlooking the Fenice theatre, and took the great man's advice and had the duck with black truffles (followed by the iced mousse with raspberry sauce), warmed to his wisecracks, shared his passion for Saint-Exupéry, drank his wine (a strong, dry Recioto Amarone – 'I think you'll be amused by its after-effects'), discovered he had been at Bedales exactly thirty years before Richard, and courteously but firmly declined his invitation to play Gaston and Gigi in a revival of his masterpiece destined for the West End, the West Coast, and, 'hey why not?', Broadway. Over the third bottle Richard explained, a little pompously, that they were 'trying to resist revisiting too many things'.

'Haven't you just told me you're planning to do *The Merchant*?'

'Yes, but we're not doing *Return to Oz*.'

'What's that supposed to mean?'

'And we can't go to Broadway,' Maisie explained with pride, 'because when the baby's born we're going to live in Venice.'

'Great.' Lerner raised a dark enquiring eyebrow high above the rim of his glasses. 'I'm impressed. Where?'

'It isn't fixed yet, but on the Grand Canal. Of course.'

'*Bien sur*.' He laughed. 'And I suppose you will have your own gondola.'

'Yes,' said Maisie firmly. 'The fabulous Fabers will have everything.'

The lyricist leant over to Richard and put a nut-brown hand over his and squeezed it. 'Take my advice, young man, don't go for everything. Stick to one wife.'

'I'll drink to that,' said Richard, raising his glass.

'And I shall stick to one child,' said Maisie, 'and I shan't drink to that because my self-indulgent old husband says as a good mother-to-be I mustn't.'

When Sarah was born, three weeks later, Maisie was determined to be both a good mother and a good daughter. The day she got back from the hospital, with Sarah asleep on her stomach, she sat up in bed and wrote her father a long, loving, rambling letter in her funny arachnoid hand, and asked him to forgive her and not to forget her, and to bless her and her child and her husband, and sent it to him with lots of hugs and kisses and a rather old-fashioned photograph (taken by Adam) of mother and baby doing well.

She waited for a reply, but the weeks passed and none came. 'Piff-paff, I suppose I just have to accept that Daddy and I have said goodbye,' she said.

Richard said nothing. He did not tell her that her father had responded by sending an emissary to meet him. Jack Rivers had a series of creatures like Robert Annette: youngish lawyers, accountants, MBAs, potential high-fliers inexplicably ready to ground their souls, sacrifice their intelligence and promise, running errands for the great man. Money corrupts. Annette was naturally better suited to this servile role than most: he was a Canadian, precious about his nationality, jealous of his title – printed on his card: 'Mr Rivers' *chef de cabinet*' – and a person who needed to be taken seriously. This Richard couldn't do, partly because of the poor man's appearance (he had a washed-out albino look, thin lips and piggy eyes, the sickly mien of the committed health-food enthusiast), partly because Richard saw in him at once Caliban's desire to be bombastic whenever he got the chance knowing he'd crumble into a fawning wretch the moment he heard his master's voice or footfall on the stair, but mainly, of course, because Annette was Rivers' man. Their meeting – at Verona airport, at Annette's insistence, he was on his way from Rome to London – was brief, soulless and futile. Annette delivered his preamble as though he'd scripted it on the plane and, word for word, committed it to memory.

'Mr Rivers does not accept you as his daughter's husband, does not acknowledge you as the father of his granddaughter, and, as you know, has well-founded reasons for believing that you are neither suitable as a companion for Maisie nor appropriate as a guardian for Sarah.'

Richard was suddenly frantic with anger. Why was he there? Why had he allowed himself to meet this man? Why was he listening to this? 'No, I don't know,' he said. Why did he stay? 'What are these good reasons?'

'You abducted a child.'

'For God's sake—'

'You cannot be trusted with children.'

He closed his eyes. 'I laugh that I may not weep. This is absurd.' He looked at Annette. 'You are absurd.'

The *chef de cabinet* glanced at his watch and proceeded imperturbably to set out his proposal. It was a variation on the old one: in return for millions, Maisie and her child must be allowed home and Richard must give up his claims to each and both of them. Or face the consequences.

'Is that a threat?'

'"It's a promise" I think is the answer Mr Rivers would give you.'

Richard wondered later why he had not struck the man, smashed his face. He should have done. Adam was wrong. He didn't like danger. He was a coward. 'If you've said what you've come to say, go, get out. I don't know why I agreed to see you.'

Annette checked his watch again. 'Do you have anything you wish me to say to Mr Rivers on your behalf?'

'Yes. Tell him I know the truth about him.'

'Meaning?'

151

'And tell him he might as well accept the truth about me. I love my wife and she loves me and we will be together to the grave. We cannot be bought, we cannot be threatened. Do you hear me? I love my wife. I love my daughter.'

'Mr Faber, Mr Rivers loves his daughter too. That's the point.'

NINE

During the first dozen years of Sarah's life, the years that took Maisie from her teens through her twenties and Richard from the age of thirty to his early forties, the fabulous Fabers were at the height of their powers. Their success was astonishing, the range and quality of their work acknowledged even by the grudging and the envious. They became world famous. 'Richer than Croesus,' said Adam, 'more celebrated than Paris and Helen of Troy.' Year after year, for more than a decade, it seemed they could do no wrong.

They didn't, in fact, buy a house in Venice that first year. Maisie found one – on the Grand Canal, by the Accademia Bridge, a splendid palazzo, baroque with literary connections (Henry James had described it as the house rented by Milly Theale in *The Wings of a Dove*) – but it was too expensive for them at that stage and, according to Emma, 'Richard decided he had reservations about Henry James – and Milly Theale.' Anyway, after Sarah was born (a seemingly effortless production, in which Maisie took little active interest, apart from demanding an epidural, hiring a motherly Italian nurse, and equipping Richard and Adam each with his own copy of Penelope Leach's *Baby and Child Care*) and in the after-glow of the triumph of their *Merchant of Venice* in the Roman amphitheatre (an altogether more challenging production, and another sell-out; Richard as Shylock, Emma as Portia, Maisie as Jessica), in October 1981, they moved back to London and bought a big house in Little Venice. They called it 'La Fenice'.

'And what do we do with Adam?' asked Maisie.

'He can stay at St Pancras,' said Richard.

'Yes, but shouldn't he come with us? We love him, don't we?'

Adam came with them to Blomfield Road and lived in the coach house.

'I shall be like Michael Redgrave's boyfriend,' he said, 'with my own little hut at the end of the garden.'

It was far from being a little hut. It was a converted Regency coach house of some style. Downstairs was the company office, bright white and kitted out with high tech as modern as tomorrow, upstairs (and reached by a graceful wrought-iron spiral stairway) a spacious studio apartment with a lot of time for yesterday, light, airy, elegant – lots of Farrow & Ball off-white with splashes of saffron, polished floorboards with Indian rugs, huge vases anticipating great harvests of lilies – a flat for a man designed by a woman and one where Adam could bring his women with confidence. And did.

There were as many of them as ever, probably more. As the years rolled by, Adam's easy appetite for sex turned to a pressing hunger, and eventually to an obsessive gluttony, urgent and insatiable. However much he had, he was greedy for more. When Richard said lightly, 'There's a clinic in LA for people like you, why don't you give it a go?' Adam laughed for a moment and then whispered to his friend, in deadly earnest, 'Why don't you fuck off?'

Adam still had Emma whenever he wanted. As time passed, she rather surprised herself by not turning into the sad person she had expected. Her career was good and kept getting better. She got her kicks out of champagne and marijuana and as much work as she wanted and uncomplicated evenings at The Ivy and Groucho's with gay friends who made her laugh. She reconciled herself to settling at a size sixteen because she rather liked the coarse things Adam said about her figure and she accepted that her lot – now and always – was to be half in love with an unsatisfactory man who couldn't/wouldn't love and was only reliable in his unreliability. She decided to have no complaints. It was like having a life-long affair with a profoundly married man, no longer listening out for the three words he'll never say, no longer expecting him to leave his wife and children because you know he never will. 'It was pathetic, but it had its moments.'

*   *   *

At home or at work, there was nothing pathetic about the fabulous Fabers. After their first movie together – *Pride and Prejudice* – made in the UK with American money – Richard as Olivier, Maisie as Greer Garson – Hollywood beckoned. These were the years of *Chariots of Fire* and *Gandhi* and Dudley Moore and John Gielgud in *Arthur* and Richard and Maisie as the doomed lovers in *The Lost Mountain*. The English were coming and Faber and Rivers were leading the pack. The offers came thick and fast – and fantastic: one day *Lolita, Dallas The Movie* and *After the Fall* all arrived by the same post! – and Richard and Adam, in uneasy alliance, continued to be the ones making the decisions. Sometimes they got it wrong (they said no to *The French Lieutenant's Woman*, they said yes to *Princess Sisi*), mostly they got it right. They treated Maisie rather like a contract player from the bad old days when you belonged to a studio and you played as cast and, when you'd done, you said, 'Thank you, Mr Warner, "Juliet" was fun. What next? "Mrs Lindbergh"? Oh well, if you insist. And then a *mermaid* – you said a *mermaid*? That I like, that's good.'

She went along with anything – so long as Richard came too. 'We must be together always, all the time. I don't mind what parts I play, I really don't. You decide. So long as we're together I'm happy.'

'And are you happy – still?'

'Happier than ever. Since you ask. I love you more than ever. Since you want to know.' She put her hands up to his face and held him so he couldn't look away.

'In fact, there's only one thing we need out here that we haven't got.'

It wasn't Sarah. He knew that. When the Fabers came to Hollywood it was only ever for a matter of weeks, one movie at a time. Sarah stayed in London. Sarah didn't need to be unsettled. Sarah had nanny, who was lovely (Maria, 'Santa Maria'), and her routine, which was important, and, very soon, the very best Montessori nursery school, Mrs Tiggywinkle's, just around the corner in Maida Vale.

'What's that we haven't got?' Richard loved Maisie completely. He would grant her anything in his power.

'An apartment on Venice Beach. Near the pier. What do you say? I'm tired of hotels. We need somewhere just for us, our secret place.'

She slipped her hands around his neck and closed her eyes and they kissed exactly as screen lovers are supposed to do.

As the eighties progressed and the pace of their stellar ascent accelerated, the professional balance between them altered. In the theatre Richard always had top billing and remained the main attraction. It was his arena, his space, space he shared with Maisie, but shared on his terms. Essentially he was a stage actor of genius who became a film actor because of his talent and a film star because of his wife. The camera respected Richard Faber, but Maisie Rivers it simply adored. She was a true film star. On screen she was irresistible. Whatever 'it' is, she had. In terms of technique it's not easy to explain what she did – apart from look stunning and hit her mark – simply because she didn't seem to do that much. She hardly moved, she never blinked, she rarely seemed to speak above a whisper, but she made you feel strange things were going on in her head all the time. When she came into shot you looked at her and no one else, you couldn't help it, and, as often as not (especially when the music was right) your spine tingled, it really did. In close-up she could make her mournful eyes smile, all on their own, just for you. It was a look worth a million dollars, and it generated several.

The audiences – the money – the fame – they grew like mighty beanstalks and, in the glory years, our fairy-tale hero and heroine handled the voracious ogre of the press like sweet-talking giant-killers. They didn't hide or run away. They smiled back, they wooed, they welcomed. They were content to be photographed, almost anywhere, almost anytime, and if you wanted an effortless interview, engaging, gossipy, irreverent, apparently indiscreet, Richard Faber was your man. He played it (consciously, of course) as though he were a young David Niven, debonair devil-may-care, full of classy self-deprecation and good stories, and when he met the old David Niven, shortly before his death, frail and shaky but still with so much damn charm, Niven twinkled at him and said, 'I know what you're up to, you old bugger – and I'm deeply flattered.'

Richard talked, Maisie didn't. That was their rule and, generally, it was accepted and understood. After Maisie won her Oscar (for *Our Summer Sunday*, Truffaut's last film, Maisie's favourite), against her and Richard's better judgement (but because Adam was determined that she should) she gave her famous interview to Oprah Winfrey – who asked about Richard – who asked about Sarah – who asked about her father – and who, over thirty minutes, time after time, was given the same six-word reply: 'I am *not* talking about that.' The more often she repeated it, the more she giggled as she repeated it, the more she leant back and laughed and ran her hands through her mass of corn-gold hair and shut her eyes tight and shook her head as she said it, the more the studio audience whooped and cheered. 'I am *not* talking about that.' It was the last interview she gave.

According to Richard, their life together was a conspiracy: 'It was us against the world. When we were on parade, on the set, on the road, in rehearsals, at parties – Maisie loved parties, she was good at parties – we were happy and busy and it was fun, it was good, fun for us, good for business, but we were playing a part – all the time – and we both knew it. I suppose I saw myself, played myself, as a kind of leading man from the 1930s, black and white but bags of style, Gershwin music, a life choreographed by Busby Berkeley. Rumour had it that Maisie was into cocaine. Not so. Yes, Maisie got high, the adrenaline flowed, she could dance the night away – I think the Marilyn comparison pleased her, she played up to it, and as she got older she grew bolder, she *was* sexy and outrageous and flirtatious – but it was a game. We played a game with the world – and the world seemed to like it. We came on as a pair of glamorous shooting stars – carefree, incredible – and we performed our parts, let's face it . . . to perfection. You can't portray a character unless in some way you love the character you're portraying – it's quite impossible – and there's no doubt in many ways we loved the roles we'd designed for ourselves. But we knew what we were doing in public was play-acting. We knew it wasn't real. Our real life was our secret, ours alone. What we did in the dark, in our heads, only we knew.'

In April 1987, for their seventh wedding anniversary, Maisie bought Richard his own aeroplane, 'just a little one for my Little Prince, a toy for my boy', a two-seater Cessna Aerobat – 'combines the economy and versatility of the standard Model 152 with aerobatic capability'. On the envelope containing the log book she had written in block capitals: 'THE FABULOUS FABERS. *AND* THEY CAN FLY!'

Together they flew everywhere and anywhere the plane could reach. Richard said, 'We flew to fly – to ride the clouds, to touch the sun – actually we never flew that high: Maisie got nose bleeds around 6,000 feet – and we flew to places, of course, to get from A to B. I loved that plane.' The places were always *his* places, destinations he chose for his own reasons – looking for locations, revisiting old haunts, chasing up the past. London to Bristol was a regular run. Bristol he loved because of the old aerodrome's association with the earliest days of powered flight (he had a photograph of Saint-Exupéry in a Bristol Boxkite) and because, together, he and Maisie, at the height of their fame, could wander the streets, unnoticed, hand in hand, cocooned, retracing the long walks he used to take with Emma in their student days, around the docks, by the cathedral and the Old Council House, up through the villas and complacent mansions of Clifton (past the old flat) to Brunel's amazing suspension bridge with that incredible view of Nightingale Valley and the hanging Leigh Woods beyond.

Because the woods were strange and beautiful, to please Richard, Maisie took to calling them the Vivien Leigh Woods. She knew her man. Born in 1949, he belonged, in fact, to the Richard Gere/Sylvester Stallone generation, yet all his points of reference came from another era. When he worked with Al Pacino and Meryl Streep on Scorsese's *Trio* he loved them because, 'bless them', they shared his passion for Olivier, for the Barrymores, for Sarah Bernhardt. (The Faber apartment in Venice, on the gentle curve of Santa Monica Bay, was on the site of the old pier theatre which Bernhardt had inaugurated in 1904. That's why they were there.) Richard was a romantic locked in the past. And Maisie was quite content to join him there. Alone she would dance to Tina and Ike Turner; with Richard she danced to Cole Porter and Irving Berlin.

According to Richard, 'There was a timeless quality to Maisie. As an actress she could play any period, from Ancient Greece to space age, and you felt she was exactly right for that period. Where she was was where she belonged. While I know some people think there's something dated and stagey about me – perhaps they're right – Maisie was always contemporary.'

According to Adam, Maisie was 'of her time, apparently comfortable in her time, but she didn't epitomise it'. Faber and Rivers were the great stars of the eighties but in no sense did they define their age in the way, say, Marilyn and James Dean and the young Brando defined the fifties or the Beatles and Twiggy and Antonioni's *Blow Up* 'were' the sixties. The fabulous Fabers caught the public imagination because they looked so good, because they *were* so good at what they did, and because of their extraordinary love affair – handsome actor falls for beautiful girl, leading man elopes with child star, thirty-year-old marries teenage bride – *and it lasts!* As the publicist said, 'With Rivers and Faber, dreams come true.'

In 1988 Richard flew regularly between London and Bristol because he was using the Bristol Theatre Royal as the backstage location for *Touched with Fire*, his award-winning series of four television films on the lives of Garrick, Kean, Macready and Irving, in which he played each of his heroes in turn – and provided the voice of Robert Browning as the unseen narrator. John Mortimer and Frank Hauser wrote the scripts, but the approach, the structure, the research were all Richard's.

In pursuit of a first-hand recollection of Henry Irving, one Sunday in February Richard and Maisie accepted an invitation to visit Lady Brunner, Irving's granddaughter, at Greys Court just outside Henley-on-Thames. Their hostess was all that Richard had hoped for – bright, beady, birdlike, old, yet full of charming memories and the right kind of well-observed anecdote – but the occasion itself was alarming. Instead of the cosy *tête-à-tête* Richard had envisaged, it was a full-scale set-piece polished-sideboard log-fire English country Sunday lunch party: sherry, gin, soup, a roast, apple and black-berry pie, proper English cheeses, fine wines, weak coffee, the best crystal, the family silver, the nicely balanced cast – younger actor, older actor, senior politician, grandee from the National Trust, Assistant Chief Constable (plus wives) and, rounding up the dozen, and dominating the room, so at home he might have been the host, a world-class financier and, apparently, old friend of the family, Jack Rivers.

As they came into the room and saw him by the fireplace, holding forth, holding court, Maisie thought she would faint. 'We can't stay.' It was eight years since she had seen him. He looked just the same.

'We can't go.' Richard put his hand on her elbow.

'Please don't do anything, don't make a scene.'

'It's okay, Maisie. It's okay.'

'Yes. I know.' She took a deep breath. 'Piff-paff.' She pulled herself together. She was an actor too. Her father was looking at her, smooth, benign, knowing, *pater familias, homme du monde.* She smiled across the room, crinkled her nose and gave a little wave. Richard thought of his own father: '*La cortesia, mio piccolo, sempre la cortesia.*'

At lunch Maisie was seated at one end of the table,

next to Jack, and Richard at the other, next to Lady Brunner. Richard thought, 'We play this as Somerset Maugham or J.B. Priestley, don't we?' He did his stuff. Lady Brunner did hers. At their end of the table they talked at length of Irving, his genius, his method, his manner, his oddly shambling gait, jerky and eccentric, his curious voice, his stammer – the greatest actor of his age had a speech impediment! 'I can't use it in the film – they'll think I made it up' – his obsessions, his rivals, his knighthood, his drinking, his first great triumph – that never-to-be-forgotten first night of *The Bells.*

'My father used to say that night's victory delivered the English theatre into his hands.'

That was the self-same night when, travelling home together after the performance, Mrs Irving turned to her husband in the carriage and asked, 'Are you going to go on making a fool of yourself like this all your life?' They were crossing Hyde Park Corner. 'My grandfather told the driver of the brougham to stop. Without a word he got out and left his wife to continue the journey alone. He never returned to his home and he never spoke to her again.'

The politician's wife, chic and regal, was on Richard's right and on automatic pilot (why she was in the constituency on a Sunday and not at home in Northampton she wasn't quite sure): 'What is your favourite role, Mr Faber?'

'Is it too predictable to say Hamlet?'

'Of the twenty-seven I've seen,' said the older actor, who'd seen 'em all, known 'em all, and had a couple of good stories for each of 'em, 'yours, Robert Eddison's and John Gielgud's are the only three that *completely* worked.'

'Thank you,' murmured Richard, suddenly embarrassed, conscious that the table had fallen silent, that they'd reached the point in the meal when the half-dozen individual, disparate, overlapping duologues would cease and one grand group conversation would ensue. He had been watching Maisie and her father at the far end of the table. They had seemed to be chatting quite normally. Now Jack filled the silence, looked across the table and said to the politician, 'Did you ever go in for theatricals, Michael? I see you as a distinguished Claudius.'

'At least you had the good manners not to say Brutus, Jack.'

Another silence fell. Who goes next? Have we reached the dangerous corner? No, it's okay. The older actor (a definitive Polonius) rides to the rescue. 'There's a lovely story – true story – of the earnest young actor – deeply serious – intent on understanding the whole psychology of the part – who asked a much older actor if he thought that Hamlet had actually been to bed with Ophelia . . . "I don't know about the West End, laddie, but we always did on tour."'

The laughter subsided. 'I loved you in *Murderer*,' said the Assistant Chief Constable's wife (more Mike Leigh improvisation than J.B. Priestley).

'Thank you,' said Richard.

'This is a perfect house for a murder, isn't it?' she burbled on.

'Yes,' agreed the grandee from the National Trust who seemed to think the house was his. 'And wouldn't the Ice House be just right for the discreet disposal of the body?'

'Not as good as the Maharajah's Well. Do you know it? It's just down the road, the local curiosity. It was a gift from the Maharajah of Benares. It's about four hundred feet deep.'

'Taller than St Paul's.'

'Don't you mean "deeper"?'

'You know what I mean.'

The splendid old actor's splendid wife had heard enough from the Assistant Chief Constable's lady. She put down her glass with a bit of a clatter and surveyed the table with a wicked gimlet eye. 'Who would each of us like to murder?'

'And why?'

'And how?'

'Nice game.'

'Do you think so?'

'Who'd like coffee?' asked Lady Brunner, getting to her feet. She was a perfect hostess. The company adjourned. Coffee was taken, standing, in the schoolroom, so that the guests could study the portraits of Lady Brunner's parents, H.B. Irving and Dorothea Baird.

'She created the part of Trilby, you know,' said the older actor, with a satisfied smack of the lips. 'Rather fancied meself as a possible Svengali once. You and Miss Rivers should have a crack at it, Richard. It's heady stuff. Did you see John Barrymore in the film? Powerful. They did it again with Donald Wolfit. Mmmm. Rather less convincing.' He drained his coffee, shook his mane and went off in search of a cigarette.

For a moment Richard stood alone looking up at the picture of the actress and thinking about Trilby and Svengali. Maisie touched his arm. She had brought her father over. 'Here we are,' she said. 'I'm going to find the loo – and then, Richard, I think we ought to be on our way.'

'Well . . .' said Jack, watching her go. 'What now?'

'Are we to be friends?'

'I don't think so. Nothing has changed.'

'Hasn't it?'

'Not for me.'

Rivers was even smaller than Richard had remembered him. And, surprisingly, he seemed a little drunk. Richard looked at him, at his shiny, passionless face, at his smug, slightly watery eyes, and said, quite casually, 'You know, I met up with an old acquaintance of yours. In Italy.'

'Really?'

'Really. It was a while ago, but he had an interesting story to tell.'

Jack shrugged his shoulders.

'Giovanni Navi. That's his name. He asked to be remembered to you.' Richard took out his wallet and produced the photograph of the old professor that he had taken in the Campo del Ghetto Nuovo. 'I've been carrying this around for years, in case we ever met again. Don't worry.' He said it gently. 'Your secret is safe with me . . .'

Jack Rivers looked up at him, suddenly sober, white-faced, terrified.

'On one condition,' said Richard, smiling.

Richard told Maisie nothing of this, then or later. As they drove away from Greys Court – the last to come, the first to leave – he asked, 'What did you and your father talk about?'

'You, mostly.'

'I find that hard to believe.'

'It was easier than talking about me. And I didn't want to talk about him. All these years I haven't seen him, I haven't missed him. Not at all. I suppose I understand him better now. And I know why you don't like him.'

Richard began to protest.

'Sshh. There's no need to pretend. You despise him—'

'I—'

'You despise him and he hates you. He loathes you. My dad is Jack Rivers. What he wants, he gets. And what he gets, he keeps. That's the way he's made. He always wins. He has to. Except with you. He loses me – to you. And that he won't forgive, can't forgive. And that's why I don't want to see him ever again.'

'Maisie . . .' He put his hand out to her.

'He's my father, so I have to love him, technically, but I don't have to *like* him, do I? I wish him no harm, we will do him no harm, but I don't like him, we don't like him. He's not very likeable.'

'Maise . . .'

'It's true. I used to be frightened of him, but I'm not any more. He can't touch me now. I've got you. I'm safe.' She lifted his hand to her face and rubbed his knuckles against her cheek. 'Who needs the wrong father when they've got the right husband? Eh?'

The next day Maisie had a wonderful surprise. Just before lunch a large removals van arrived in Blomfield Road and Sir John Lavery's painting of 'The Beautiful Lady' was delivered to La Fenice with a handwritten note from Jack: 'Maisie, This is for you. God bless. Dad.' He never communicated with her again.

The pattern of Richard's and Maisie's year was now well set. A movie in the spring, another in the fall. They picked. They chose. They appeared together or not at all. August and September were kept clear – always – for their 'Shakespeare in English in Verona'. Most years, they also managed a production in the West End or on Broadway. (With *The Clandestine Marriage* they each won a Tony in '88.) And, on top of it all, when it suited, they did a little radio (poetry readings, *boulevard* plays from the thirties and forties, fading pieces Richard liked but accepted were uncommercial), and Richard, now and then, did a bit of TV. (Adam, still driving the business, was adamant: 'Maisie does not do television. Maisie Rivers is a film star. She has never, will never, appear on the small screen. It's different for Richard. He started on the box. If the right telly project comes along and we want him to do it, that's fine. Telly's fine for actors. For movie stars it's the beginning of the end. Did you see Burton and Sophia Loren on TV in the remake of *Brief Encounter*? Death.')

The lifestyle was well established too – private planes, chauffeur-driven limousines, the doorbell always ringing to mark the arrival of overflowing baskets of fresh fruit and vast bouquets of exotic flowers. Excitement, glamour, fame, fortune. They had all this. And Venice too.

In 1989 they made just one movie (*Vanity Fair*) and with the proceeds of that picture alone bought their house on the Grand Canal. The recession that beleaguered the Western world passed them by. The fifteenth-century Palazzo Contarini-Fasan, the little palace at the mouth of the canal, immediately facing Santa Maria della Salute, where Ruskin stayed and Turner sketched and Browning wrote, and from one of whose exquisite Gothic balconies Byron's mistress threw herself in despair, the house that local legend had long designated as the '*casa* Desdemona' – this was their house now. The fabulous Fabers had their own palazzo. They had their own gondola. They had their own gondolier. They had everything.

It was ridiculous, of course, quite over the top, more like a movie than a life, but for Maisie and for Richard it worked. And when Sarah was home from boarding school (from the age of eight she was packed off to Bedales) it seemed to work well enough for her too.

Sarah called her mother 'Maisie' and worshipped her as a child might idolise a film star. She called her father 'Daddy' and loved him with all her heart. 'Daddy always had time for me, always.' Venice was fun, but she liked the holidays at La Fenice best. Adam Waterson was ever-present, of course, and, by day, the house was full of servants, but none of them lived in, not one. 'When evening came, it was just the three of us. Daddy, Maisie and me. That was Daddy's rule: "When night falls, it's just us. Our secret place. Nobody knows what happens here."'

TEN

Over a dozen years the Fabers made seventeen movies: some good, some less good, some acclaimed, some panned – but even the dud ones made money for somebody.

Throughout their film careers they appeared together – except once. In 1997 Richard was invited to produce a season of classics of his choice to reopen the Saville Theatre in London's Shaftesbury Avenue and, coincidentally, Maisie was offered a picture on her own that sort of took her fancy.

Maisie was regularly offered pictures on her own – and Adam, equally regularly, urged her to take them. He sorted the deals and if you wanted Maisie Rivers to carry your movie the price now was $15 million – still less than Leonardo DiCaprio, Tom Cruise, Harrison Ford, John Travolta ($20 million), even Eddie Murphy

($16 million), but more than Demi Moore ($14 million), Julia Roberts, Sigourney Weaver ($13 million), a whole lot more than dear Meryl Streep ($8 million) or poor Goldie Hawn ($5 million), and – for Adam, this was the point – more than any other British artiste, of either sex, *ever*. And when you did a deal for Maisie Rivers these days Adam also insisted you budget that extra $250,000 for the 'comfort costs': the masseur, the trainer, the personal assistant, the make-up artist, the hair stylist, the assistant director designated to stand by the director, relaying by walkie-talkie to the star in her trailer the state of play on the floor. For some years Adam Waterson had featured on the credits of movies starring the Fabers. He was called Associate Producer. There wasn't any role that went with this title. It was just a bit of billing on which Adam insisted as part of the package.

The last solo offer Maisie had declined was the story of Grace Kelly. The producers didn't want Richard as Prince Rainier ('Who do they want? Danny de Vito?' 'John Travolta.' 'Oh, God, it might just work . . .') so, though the script was good and the money was fine, Maisie said no. Maisie still said, 'I appear only with Richard Faber.' Adam said Maisie was insane and later felt more than vindicated because, had Maisie done the film, it would have opened within weeks of the death of Princess Diana and, as he put it (he had caught the Hollywood *patois*), 'it would have been fucking colossal'.

Richard wanted to do the Saville season. Adam wasn't interested in theatre. Richard wasn't interested in Adam.

They were bound together by commerce and by a common past: they still maintained a civil veneer, a hollow framework of friendship, but the gulf between them was now a mile wide and evident even to outsiders. The only interest they truly shared was in Maisie.

Adam was obsessed with his self-styled role as Maisie's manager, mentor, Svengali. He openly acknowledged that he wanted her to be the most successful film actress of all time – his creation, not Richard's. And while Richard wanted everything good for Maisie he wanted too to get back on to a solid stage to tell a complete story in one night to an audience of real people. He was weary of flying around the world in abject luxury, sitting about in five-star trailers, hour after hour, waiting to distil his essence in a vacuum. He said, 'Shakespeare knew the movies, Shakespeare knew everything. He called it "an expense of spirit in a waste of shame". These last ten years I've measured out my life in two-minute takes and now I want to strut and fret again for six whole months in the same place at the same time, night after night, and twice on Saturdays, and, if they like what I do, hear 'em roar!'

So, without Richard but with his blessing, for $15 million, plus 'comforts', plus Adam, Maisie went to Hollywood to make *Real Mad Tango*.

'You're flying solo,' said Richard. 'Good luck.'

'Piff-paff. It's a mistake. I know it's a mistake.' She said it the moment she had signed. 'I shouldn't be doing this. We shouldn't be apart. This is madness. I don't want this. Please.'

'It's only a couple of months. We'll manage.'

'Will we?' He heard the panic in her voice, he saw the fear in her eyes, but he let her go. What else could he do? She had signed and the Fabers were professionals. If they promised, they delivered. And they couldn't go on expecting to appear in every movie together, could they? She was a film actress. She needed to do this. He was a stage actor. He needed to get back on the boards.

She called from the apartment on Venice Beach. 'Oh Christ, Richard, it's such a mistake.'

'Is Adam with you?'

'Yes, that's something. But they've started all that stuff in the press again.'

'Forget it.'

'Yes.'

'Are you managing?'

'Yes, but it isn't working.'

The movie itself was fine, it wasn't great, it was okay, but, from the start, Maisie's performance was all adrift. From week one, day one almost, it was clear something was wrong, something was missing. Perhaps it was Richard. Perhaps together they really were greater than the sum of their parts. Perhaps it was the fact that she was now thirty-three, but still playing twenty-six. Perhaps it was the acceptance on the set – and the nudges and winks in the American press, day after day – that her rumoured dalliance with Adam Waterson was now a full-blown affair. Who knows?

In London Richard launched his three-play season at the Saville with a revival of *Cyrano de Bergerac*, translated, quite beautifully, by Anthony Burgess, and directed, with overflowing buckets of swash, buckle and Gallic sentiment by Gerard Depardieu, Richard's old friend and exact contemporary. Richard, of course, was a natural for Cyrano and the piece opened to acclaim and played to capacity. The best of the notices contained useful words like 'dazzling', 'peerless', 'sheer genius', the worst acknowledged that 'Nobody gives us romantic middle-brow hokum with as much bravura style and proper *panache* as Richard Faber. Even in the nineties (or perhaps specially in the nineties?) it seems there's still a market for the old-fashioned English star.'

For the role of Roxanne, Richard and his director picked Kate Bingley, the new kid on the block, nineteen going on twenty-eight, with knock-out looks ('*C'est celle la, mon brave!*') and a potential talent to match ('*Ça va!*'). She didn't look like Maisie, she was darker, smaller, but she had a quality Richard remembered from Maisie when they first met: a sense that she knew completely who she was and that she was different, quite different, from anybody and everybody else. Depardieu saw it as a kind of knowing insolence that he found wonderfully attractive. Richard sensed, when she held him in her arms in the final scene, the moment before Cyrano dies, when at last she realises that he was the one who wrote the letters, whose voice she'd heard, the one she'd always loved without knowing it, Richard sensed then that he was a little bit in love with her himself. It was self-indulgent, but rather comforting.

After the performance on the second night, as soon

as she'd changed, she came to his dressing room. She knocked.

'Come.'

He was alone, seated at his dressing table, scrubbed and brushed and neatly attired in a charcoal grey pin-striped business suit. Now that off-stage he sometimes wore glasses, he thought that increasingly he was coming to look like Uncle Franco from the bank in Turin. That rather pleased him. Emma said he looked like a middle-aged Clark Kent, which pleased him less. His dresser – a novelty, a lady dresser, Maria, 'Santa Maria', Sarah's old nanny – had poured him his first glass of champagne, hung up his costume, taken his shirts off to wardrobe and gone home to Maida Vale.

'This is my reward.' He smiled at his visitor in the mirror, then catching his own ambiguity, laughed and quickly raised his glass. 'Come in, have some.'

'Where's everybody?' She stood at the door, peeping round it, glossy head to one side, bright eyes sparkling.

'You'll find the star's dressing room is often the quietest. No one dares knock.'

'I almost didn't.'

'Kate, you will dare everything. Have a drink.'

She came into the room and carefully closed the door behind her. She turned back to him and, as he found another glass and began to pour out her champagne, she put her hands behind her back and tilted her head again and said, rather formally, as though she'd committed the statement to memory, 'I just wanted to say thank you. It's amazing for me, being in the show. I'm awe-struck that it's happened. And that I'm here with you, face to face, now, it's quite wonderful. Dream-come-true time.'

Richard passed her her glass and smiled. He was used to this. Because he was so famous no one, certainly no one who had not known him and known him well since before he became famous, behaved entirely naturally with him. Every encounter was slightly awkward and unreal. He was aware that people who met him for the first time never forgot the moment. It was difficult to be normal with Richard Faber. He pocketed his spectacles and tipped his glass of champagne towards hers.

'You're pretty good too. Cheers! Welcome to the galaxy.'

She held the glass under her nose so she could feel the bubbles bursting. She took a sip, and then another, and then put her glass down on the dressing table, right next to his, so that the glasses were touching. 'Can I say something?'

'Yes,' he said. 'Yes. Anything.'

'You are the best actor in the world . . . and working with you is the best thing that has ever, could ever, happen to me. I love it. It's wonderful. But I'm frightened . . . I—'

He shook his head. 'Don't say it, Kate.'

'I'm falling in love with you, aren't I?'

He came and, with such tenderness, held her face in his hands. He gazed down at her and moved towards her so that his nose was almost touching hers.

'Do you want to kiss me?' she asked.

178

'No,' he said. 'I was just looking into your eyes, looking for something . . .'

'Anything in particular?'

'Yes,' he said, quite slowly. 'Maisie. Maisie Rivers. I'm looking for Maisie Rivers in your beautiful eyes.'

'Do you miss her?'

'Dammit, Kate, I do. I can't live without her.' He kissed the girl's forehead and backed away. 'But in three weeks, four days and ten and a quarter hours she is back. Back home. Back where she belongs.' He drained his glass and banged it down and said, 'Meanwhile, sweet Kate, bonny Kate, the prettiest Kate in Christendom, Kate of my consolation, a table for two awaits us, and the night is young, and a middle-aged actor-manager-johnnie is going to entertain you to an evening of stagey reminiscence and a repertoire of impressions of the great actors of yesteryear – and doubtless you will not have heard of a single one!'

Maisie flew into London on Wednesday 1 October, the most brilliant sun-filled autumn day London had known for a generation. Richard came to Heathrow to meet her and, at the airport, they gave a brief press conference in which Maisie said how excited she was to be coming home and Richard said how delighted he was to announce that in the second production of his season at the Saville Theatre, Marlowe's *Doctor Faustus*, Maisie would be making a special surprise guest appearance in the role of Helen of Troy. (*Cyrano* was a sell-out; the advance for *Doctor Faustus* was nowhere near as healthy.

According to Richard, it was Maisie's idea to give the box office a useful fillip by taking on the non-speaking role of Helen of Troy – exactly as Elizabeth Taylor had done when Richard Burton played Faustus at Oxford back in the sixties.)

On Thursday morning virtually all the papers ran the pictures of Richard and Maisie – looking good. Emma said, 'They *were* looking good, looking happy, really happy, and we all thought: "Great, that's what Richard needs." I didn't call her that day, but I called the next – and that was the first time I realised something must be wrong. She wouldn't take my call. I left a message, but she didn't call back. I went round to the house. Richard wasn't there, he was at the theatre, but the maid said Maisie was resting and couldn't be disturbed. It was about ten days before *Faustus* was due to open. It was odd, completely out of character. Maisie was back in town, but no one saw her. Friends called, but she didn't call back. She was expected at rehearsals, but she sent excuses. As ever, she was invited here, there, everywhere – but she didn't show.'

Adam had stayed on in LA for a further seventy-two hours and returned to London on the Sunday morning. He took a cab from the airport to Blomfield Road, dumped his bags in the coach house and walked through the garden to the main residence. From the rear La Fenice looked a little like an ocean-going liner from a bygone age. It was a fine, wide, low-built, late-Victorian villa, the stucco recently repainted bright white, and in the sharp mid-morning light it gleamed, prosperous, secure, utterly at ease with itself. Adam stopped to sniff a late-flowering rose, paused to pick a fig (yes, fresh figs in Little Venice in golden October sunshine – this was the life they led!) and climbed the wrought-iron steps and crossed the narrow verandah to the pretty little conservatory that must have been added in the 1930s. It was a room Richard particularly liked and used as a study – half house, half garden, he claimed it had a sort of mysterious A. A. Milne-J. M. Barrie feel. Adam put his key in the lock, turned it and found it didn't fit. He could see Richard inside, coming towards him. Richard unbolted the door and pulled it open.

'I've changed the locks,' he said. 'All of them.'

'Oh,' said Adam, lightly, stepping inside. They didn't shake hands. They never did. They were old friends. 'Why?'

'I'm changing lots of things. I'm going to ask you to move, to leave the coach house. No rush, but . . . you understand.'

'Do I?'

'Yes.' Richard had a jug full of Bloody Mary. He poured Adam a glass. 'How's Hollywood? How was the movie?'

'Hollywood's fine. The movie isn't good.' Adam took a sip of the drink and collapsed on to the wickerwork sofa on which, years before (he suddenly remembered this and wanted to smile), he had successfully seduced Maria, yup 'Santa Maria', and had realised at the amazing moment of penetration that no earthly conquest was beyond him. 'Darling Maisie was tired,' he said. 'Not at her best.'

Richard stood looking down at him. 'Don't talk to me about "darling Maisie".' He was white with anger. 'How dare you?' he hissed.

'Come on, Richard. Maisie and I—'

'Maisie and you – how dare you!' He was roaring now, instantly, startlingly ferocious. In a blinding fury he threw himself on to Adam, pounced, flung himself at him. The glass tumbled and smashed on to the tile floor and Adam, awash with Bloody Mary, lay sprawled against the cushions, ridiculous, as Richard, fists clenched, pounded at his head with all his might. Adam struggled, frantic, now screaming, shrieking, wriggling as his assailant grabbed hold of his hair and, locked together, the two childhood friends rolled off the sofa on to the floor. Over shards and splinters of glass they rolled, over and over, until they crashed into a heavy painted oak coffee table that brought them to a halt. Richard was on top, still gripping Adam by the hair as Adam yelped and scratched and scrabbled to push him away. Taking all his weight on his arms Richard pulled himself up and jabbed his knee sharply into Adam's stomach. He took his head – 'his ugly head' – and beat it rhythmically against the floor. One, two, three. *Les trois coups.* Suddenly he stopped, not (he said later) because he was appalled by what he had done, but because he was suddenly disgusted with himself for bothering with Adam at all.

'Get out!' he yelled. 'Get out now!'

When the first night of *Doctor Faustus* arrived, Maisie's

name was out front, in lights, and in the programme, with photographs, and when the memorable moment came for what Marlowe describes as 'the spirit taking the form of Helen of Troy' to appear in Faustus's study ('Was this the face that launched a thousand ships, And burnt the topless towers of Ilium?'), there she was, matchless, amazing, breath-taking, still the world's most beautiful woman: Maisie Rivers. 'Sweet Helen, make me immortal with a kiss . . . Come, Helen, come, give me my soul again.'

As spine-tingling theatre the moment worked wonderfully well, but it was immediately evident that Maisie wasn't actually there. It was a sensational illusion, a most impressive special effect: brilliant lighting, dry ice and her image, Maisie Rivers as Helen of Troy, filmed among the clouds and back-projected on to a giant screen.

Maisie's non-appearance stole the notices. The broadsheets had fun speculating if this was a taste of things to come. ('Some years ago we were offered a hologram of Sir Laurence Olivier in a musical with Cliff Richard. Can we now expect a succession of Hollywood stars to take to the boards without having to go through the tedious business of coming to the theatre? Why struggle through the West End traffic at rush-hour when you can stay by the pool, pre-record your performance and have it sent over by satellite? At last we'll be able to see Sean Connery's Macbeth. "Beam me up, Scottie!"') The tabloids had fun simply speculating. Where was Maisie? Why had she gone to ground? Was she having a breakdown? Or a face-lift? Was she having an affair?

Old pictures began to surface of Maisie with Adam – 'her manager and close friend'.

Richard carried on regardless. He went about his business as if nothing was out of the ordinary. He began work on the third and final production in the Saville season, *Waiting for Godot*. And, without reference to Adam, he signed up for another movie: *Catch a Falling Star*. Rivers and Faber together again, the bankable duo back in harness, a remake of a cops and robbers caper set on the French Riviera, a throwback to the fifties, yes, but possibly just right for the dying days of the sentimental nineties. Maisie herself declined to comment, refused to surface, failed to show, so the rumour-mongering went on, the fuse of speculation continued to burn. With the staff at La Fenice, with colleagues at the theatre, Richard affected not to be noticing what the papers were saying and managed to do so almost convincingly because people knew that nowadays he didn't read the papers, hadn't done for about a year.

When Jack Rivers telephoned, Richard was perfectly civil. Jack asked to see him, pressed him, said he knew Richard would understand. Jack would come over to La Fenice. Right away. No, said Richard, he did understand, but Jack need not come to him, he would call on Jack later that day, on his way in to the theatre.

'Will you bring Maisie?'

'No.'

'Why not?'

'I will tell you when I see you.'

When he arrived at Dabney House, Richard found

Miss Cooper still in attendance and everything much as he remembered it from all those years ago. On the landing at the top of the main staircase, in place of 'The Beautiful Lady', was a large Edwardian water-colour, a sentimental picture of a young girl in a long white nightdress, holding a night-light, climbing the stairs to bed.

Miss Cooper avoided Richard's eye and led him, in silence, to her master's study. Jack too didn't appear to have changed. ('What a funny little man you are.') He had been staring out of his window, down into the garden, towards the ilex tree. As Richard arrived, and Miss Cooper retreated obsequiously, pulling the door to behind her, he turned and said at once, briskly, as though concluding a business discussion, 'Whatever you think of me—'

'You know what I think of you,' said Richard. He didn't come into the room. He stood by the door, the door handle within reach behind him. 'As you know, I know the truth.'

'And Maisie?'

Richard smiled. 'Maisie knows nothing. I have told her nothing. I shall keep my word. She knows nothing of what I know of you, but she knows herself. And she knows she does not want to see you again. It's as simple as that.'

'It is not as simple as that. I am her father.'

'Oh, yes, you are her father.'

'Where is she?'

'Where she wants to be.'

'Where is she? What have you done with her? Why is

there all this – all this *shit* in the press? What's happening, Faber? For Christ's sake, what's going on?'

'I am not accountable for the press. Thank God.' He thought of saying so much more, of trying to explain, but instead he turned to go.

Jack moved away from the window and walked towards the fireplace. He kept his back to Richard and looked at him in the mirror. 'Let me tell you who I am.'

Richard put his hand on the door. 'Do you know who you are?'

Jack turned and looked steadily at his son-in-law. 'I know who I am and I know who I have become. I am one of the richest and most successful people of our time. There are quite a few of us, of course. You're one too, I accept that. In a different way. So you'll know how it's done, this getting to the top, this getting what you want. Not by magic, but by graft. Not by chance, but by single-minded pursuit. Not by luck, but by judgement. It's all about energy, isn't it? Harnessing energy, your own – and other people's. It's about energy, determination, ruthlessness if you like. Knowing what you want – and getting it. You stole my daughter. You turned her against me. I shall not forgive you – ever. You know that. But what you need to know also is that I shall pursue you until I get at the truth, the whole truth and nothing but the truth – so help me God.'

Richard gave a little sigh and opened the door. 'Mr Rivers, you're clearly not averse to clichés, but frankly I don't think you are very comfortable with the truth. Goodbye.'

That same night, Emma came to find Richard in his dressing room after the show. Kate Bingley (as far as Emma was concerned, controversial casting for Marlowe's 'Good Angel') made her excuses and left. Richard handed Emma a glass of champagne. She lit her cigarette. 'How long have we known each other, Richard? A long time, isn't it? We are old, old friends. We are comfortable together, aren't we? Tell me . . . tell me the truth. Where's Maisie?'

He paused, refilled his glass, waited for 'Santa Maria' to collect the shirts and go. Eventually, he said, 'She's at home, where she wants to be.'

'Is she okay?'

'She's fine. She's happy. She's good.'

'Only Adam says—'

'Fuck what Adam says.'

'He says he loves her.'

'But *she* doesn't love *him*.'

'Are you sure?'

'Emma, Emma, don't you know anything? Maisie is mine, all mine. Now and for ever. "I love her with the breath, smiles, tears of all my life. And if God choose, I shall but love her better after death." Remember?'

Emma looked up at him and thought, however ridiculous it was, she still loved him too.

'Remember?'

'Mrs Browning?' she said.

'Good girl.' He poured more champagne into her glass. 'We are as one, don't you see? Adam is nothing. Let me tell you: I know my wife, and I love her to *distraction*!'

Emma drank as heavily as Richard. She drained her glass and said softly, 'Then let me tell of one that loved not wisely but too well.'

Richard was opening a second bottle. 'I can never do Othello, you know. I saw Olivier. Of course, you know I saw Olivier, I've banged on often enough about it down the years. But it's not because of him. I just don't think a white actor can do it any more. Pity. Maisie would be a perfect Desdemona. You could give us your Emilia and – indeed – Adam *would* be interesting as Iago.'

He replenished the glasses. 'Let us get drunk together. Old friend.'

He kissed her on the forehead. 'Agreed.' She laughed and lit another cigarette. 'How's Sarah?'

'Sarah's fine. And beautiful.'

Sarah *was* fine. And beautiful, like her mother. She was now sixteen, at Bedales, and she too, of course, had read the papers, heard the rumours, caught the gossip. She called home. Her mother couldn't be disturbed, her father was at the theatre. She decided, almost for the first time in her life, to write to Maisie. 'I never normally wrote to her, and she never wrote to me. Maisie didn't write letters. Daddy taped a letter to me every week when I was at school. Without fail. Wherever he was, London, Venice, LA, he always recorded a letter for me – usually in the car, he kept a little Dictaphone in the car, always, "just for my letters to you" – and they were long, funny, newsy letters, letters full of love and gossip and jokes and plans, letters full of encouragement and kindness, and what he called "unsound advice". I think Daddy found it easier to talk to me on the tape. When you were with him he was always performing really. I think he was natural only when he was with Maisie – or when he was drunk. Maisie didn't answer my letter. I didn't expect her to. Daddy did. Daddy told me to ignore the press. He said Maisie sent all her love. She was fine – and more beautiful than ever. That's what he always said.'

When Sarah got home for the holidays, on 22 December, La Fenice was all dressed up for Christmas. There were fairy lights in the windows, a huge wreath on the door, holly, ivy and mistletoe everywhere. There was magic in the air – the old Faber and Rivers magic.

'Daddy said, "I've sent all the staff packing for Christmas, got rid of the lot – even Santa Maria. They've all gone. It's just us, for a whole week."'

Maisie stayed in her room. Richard made all her meals (she was eating almost nothing) and took them up to her on a tray. Sarah could hear them talking, laughing, playing, working on their lines.

'I stood outside the door, listening to them, and felt so guilty. Once or twice I thought I heard crying, but I wasn't sure. I said to Daddy, "Won't Maisie come down – at least for Christmas?" "Of course, she will," he said, "for Christmas – and for you. I promise."'

Richard and Sarah prepared Christmas dinner together. 'This is an easy one for father and daughter to do – smoked salmon and caviar, followed by roast Tom turkey with all the trimmings. Conventional, but cosy.' At one o'clock he opened a bottle of Maisie's favourite champagne and set out three glasses – 'not our customary champagne flutes, fine as they are, but on this special day, our champagne saucers. According to my father, Max Beerbohm and Aubrey Beardsley *and* Oscar Wilde have all drunk from these!' He filled the glasses to the brim. 'Are you ready?'

'I said, "Yes, Dad, I'm ready."'

'Good,' he said. 'I'll go and fetch her. You wait here.'

A moment later Sarah heard him calling from the landing. 'Sarah. Sarah. Come and see your mother. She looks lovelier than ever – my matchless Christmas rose.'

Sarah went out into the hall and looked up and saw her father standing at the top of the stairs, on the landing by the painting of 'The Beautiful Lady'.

'Isn't she perfect?' he said with his sweetest smile.

Of course, there was no one there.

PART TWO

'There, that is our secret: go to sleep! You will wake, and remember, and understand.'

Robert Browning

ELEVEN

What I have told you so far is what I have pieced together from reading the cuttings and from conversations, over several months, with Richard and Sarah, with Adam Waterson, Emma Irving, Jane Stanhope, Ursula Cooper and others. I believe it to be accurate, but I was not there. For all that follows I can vouch personally: I was involved; I saw most of it happen; and, at the end, I was there. I did not witness the actual arrest, but Sarah described it to me.

At exactly twelve noon on Friday 2 January 1998, three police cars swept into Blomfield Road, sirens silent, blue lights flashing, and seven police officers called at La Fenice, searched the house, removed books, boxes, files, recording equipment, clothes, and arrested Richard Faber in his study.

His protests were more bewildered than outraged, more in sorrow and amazement than in anger. 'This is absurd. Is this some sort of game – apprehending the actor in the conservatory? Why not the doctor in the dining room? Or the butler in the pantry? This isn't happening.'

But it was. They took him to Maida Vale police station where he was cautioned and charged with the murder of Maisie Rivers.

Sarah stood in the drizzle at the top of the steps, clinging to Maria, 'Santa Maria', as her father was bundled into one of the police cars and driven away. On the far side of the road, the canal side, Jack Rivers and Adam Waterson sat in the back of Jack's Bentley surveying the scene.

As the police had bustled him through the hall, Richard had smiled and said to Sarah, 'Don't worry, baby. It's fine – there's nothing to worry about. Maisie's fine. We love you. It'll be all right. I promise. Look after Maria.' As the car door opened he turned back and blew her a kiss.

When cautioned and charged, Richard had said, 'This wasn't meant to happen,' and nothing more.

He knew the form, of course. In *Murderer* he had played this scene – this exact scene, on location in authentic interview rooms in real-life police stations – a dozen times, at least. But now it was real, it didn't feel real at all, more like a rehearsal than a performance. Where was the camera? Where were the lights? What about the script?

He was trying to cast the officer in charge. The look was easy – youngish Peter Lorre or Herbert Lom: moon-faced, baggy-eyed, thin-lipped, balding – but the manner was disconcerting, unexpected: modern, courteous, businesslike. This wasn't Morse or Dalgliesh or Columbo, or any of his other favourites: this was crisply effective middle-management with an MBA in murder studies. No easy eccentricity to latch on to, no lurking angst, no hinterland, just: 'There's a job to be done, let's do it.'

'It's funny,' said Richard, polishing his glasses, volunteering small-talk, 'I've played a number of murderers, but not many detectives. I've done Sherlock Holmes, of course, and I've just been offered the new Inspector Clouseau. I think my friend Monsieur Depardieu turned it down. I suspect I'm going to turn it down too. Did you like the Peter Sellers' films?'

Superintendent Higgins smiled politely. 'This is a very serious charge, Mr Faber. Do you have a solicitor?'

'Thank you. I've already been through that with your people upstairs. Allen and Overy look after my business affairs – but I don't want them. I really don't. Thank you. Mustn't mix business with pleasure.'

'Pleasure?'

'Well, this is a game, isn't it? A charade. I can't treat it any other way. This can't be real. I haven't murdered my wife. That is absurd.'

'Shall we get you a solicitor?'

Richard shrugged.

They sent for the duty solicitor and my husband, Tom Dalton, was on call, so Tom turned up.

It's difficult for me to describe Tom. We had been married for thirteen years and when you live with someone you can lose sight of them. At university Tom was every mother's dream – fair, friendly, Christian, kind. He wasn't so much handsome as wholesome. He was sandy-haired and sunny, sweet and so *so* steady, Mr Moderation-in-all-things. A pint and a half, that's my lot, just one lump, lift-the-seat, join the TA, double-lock, cross at the lights, neither a borrower nor a lender be. Deliver your daughter to Tom Dalton and you were delivering her into a safe pair of hands. I have just been reading a book about romantic love – I'm afraid that's what a midlife crisis does for you – it was a book Richard recommended, he had come across it when he directed that first *Romeo and Juliet* in Verona, he said it fascinated and infuriated him by turns – and its central message is that being in love is fine – and fun – and thrilling – and important as a gateway – but it doesn't last. Can't last, won't last, mustn't last. It's immature. Loving is what lasts. If you expect, always, to be in love, life is going to let you down. Romeo and Juliet are in love. It's a tragedy and ends in tears. 'Being in love is a sensation, not a way of life,' said the book. 'Oh, but being in love is *the most sensational* way of life!' protested Richard. Richard, of course, was in love with Maisie, from start to finish. 'That's the point,' he used to say. I don't know that Tom and I were ever 'in love', even on our wedding day. We were loving, yes; he was so affectionate, decent, doting – Labrador as lover – soft and snuffly – nice 'n' normal – dull as ditchwater – irritating as hell. It's so unfair, I know.

Tom arrived home about quarter to eight that night, late by his standards. I was upstairs, in the bath. I heard his feet on the stairs and, as usual, despised myself for letting my heart sink a little. There was a key but I hadn't locked the door because somehow I felt to lock the bathroom door against your husband betokened the beginning of the end. In he came, knocking first, cheery, fresh-faced, freckled, keen.

'You look good.'

'Thanks.'

'You look fantastic.'

'Thanks.' I didn't want to be looked at at all. He clicked his fingers, both hands at once. That meant he was happy. You could read Tom like a book. I closed my eyes. I knew what was coming next.

He peeled off his clothes – at once, without a word – and climbed into the bath. The water was tepid. There wasn't room. I was ready to get out. He sat facing me, beaming, his back to the taps, his ridiculous red knees bumping mine. 'This is nice,' he said, and widened his eyes. 'You'll never believe who I met today?'

'Richard Faber,' I said, spoiling his surprise.

'How do you know?' He didn't mind. He never minded. At least, he never let it show.

'I saw you on the news. In the background. They didn't say it was you, but it was.'

'Yes, it was.' He reached for the soap. 'It's been an amazing day.'

That night Richard sat alone in his police cell, while, outside, the world went mad. It had certainly been an amazing day. The coverage was massive and quite extraordinary. The death of Maisie Rivers, '*Murderer*' on murder charge, it was the lead story across the globe.

Tom had wrapped me in a bath towel and was rubbing me dry. He was careful, gentle, you couldn't fault him. 'This is going to be the murder trial of the century. Move over Louise Woodward, eat your heart out OJ. Play your cards right, Jo-bug, and you could be defending him.'

'What on earth do you mean?' I twisted my head round to look at my kindly, fresh-faced, means-so-well-but-never-gets-it-*quite*-right husband of thirteen years.

'He doesn't want to be defended. He's insane. A complete screwball.' Tom patted me on the bottom. 'But he'll take you.'

'He's a film star, Tom. He's one of the most famous people on the planet. He must be worth millions. He's not going to want me.'

'Oh yes he is.'

Tom was not in the least ambitious for himself. He had a settled belief in recognising one's potential and accepting one's limitations. When we were both twenty-one he said, 'I am what I am, middle-class and middle of the road. I've got red hair and I like golf and rugby and you. I'm going to get a 2.1 if I'm lucky and you, Jo Benson, you're going to get a First. You're the high flyer. I know that. You can't have two high flyers in one family. You're going all the way, Jo-bug, and I'm going to be with you all the way. If it's okay with you, you can count on me.' I could count on Tom, always. In many ways, my husband was what every working woman wants and needs: a traditional wife, devoted, supportive, compliant, loyal. Within five years of him qualifying as a solicitor and my arriving at the bar, my income was twice his. Within twelve years, it was four times or more. I had a number of friends in comparable situations. They told me that, however much their husbands denied it, the imbalance in professional income created domestic tension. Truly, it wasn't like that with Tom. 'Your success makes me glow with pride,' he said, and seemed to mean it, so of course I couldn't lock the bathroom door.

Tom also told the truth. I had had ten good years at the criminal bar and my proper share of murders, but Richard Faber was a star and deserved the star treatment. Carman, Robertson, Mansfield, any one of the firmament could have been at his disposal, but he had said to Tom, 'You're here and I'm grateful, but I don't need to be defended. I don't want to be defended. There's nothing to defend. To begin with, if there's been a murder, where's the body?'

They didn't have a body. 'We don't need a body,' said Superintendent Higgins who had both ambition and expertise. 'It's a mistake murderers make. I'm sure Mr Faber must have played John "Acid Bath" Haigh in that famous series of his. That's where Haigh went wrong. Thought he was safe because he'd disposed of the body in a bath of sulphuric acid. Boasted about it. "Mrs Durand-Deacon no longer exists! She has disappeared completely and no trace of her can ever be found again!" Great mistake. You don't need a body to secure a conviction.'

But it helps. They would have liked a body. For weeks they searched for the body of Maisie Rivers – in London, in Venice, in LA. They virtually dismantled La Fenice; they dredged the canals of Little Venice; they pulled up floorboards at the Saville Theatre and the St Pancras Hotel. At the suggestion of Jack Rivers – who funded a worldwide advertising campaign appealing for any information as to the whereabouts of his daughter and, under the auspices of the police, made two heart-rending television appearances pleading for anyone who knew anything to come forward and help – they searched the Ice House at Greys Court and, at Henley-on-Thames, lowered a diver four hundred feet to the bottom of the Maharajah's Well. Scores of men spent hundreds of hours and many thousands of pounds and dollars and lire, but they didn't find a body.

They didn't need a body, but they did need evidence of murder. And, in time, that they found, in the cockpit of Richard's aeroplane.

'You'll be wanting a brief,' said Tom, 'and I have one for you. She's the best.'

'Oh,' said Richard, 'a lady. I like that.'

Richard told me later that he had decided to play all this as Cary Grant. 'This is what actors do, you know. Hide behind masks. It helps you through the nightmare, being someone else. You don't need to look like them or sound like them. It isn't meant to be an impression. It's just an idea, a ready-wrapped persona you can lock into your head. Gives you a route map, points of reference, a means of escape. My mother, bless her, had two favourite movie stars, Marcello Mastroianni and Cary Grant, and for my sins, in my time, in my head, I've tried to slip into both. Mastroianni she knew quite well, she'd worked with him in the late forties, in *Angelica* and something else – they were the same sort of age. He came to stay in Verona once and my mother got so cross because he and my father got wildly drunk and he told my father he only had three phrases in English: "How are you?", "I love you" and "Where is your hotel?" It was one of my father's favourite stories. Mastroianni was a beautiful actor and I think now – O, hindsight, hindsight! – if I'd played it as Mastroianni at the start it might have been better, more credible – that touch of melancholy, the uncertainty, the diffidence, that would have made more sense to Higgins and his kind. But somehow I got it into my head as I was being driven from La Fenice to the police station that Cary Grant was who I needed. "How old Cary Grant? Old Cary Grant fine – how you?" Cary Grant would see me through. Over the years I'd talked to people who knew him and they all said the same: off-screen he was charming, debonair, sophisticated, serene, but utterly private – there was no way in. And, of course, on screen, the joke line was that the only real drama in a Cary Grant film was seeing whether the star could be made to lose his wry, elegant, habitual aplomb! You couldn't crack Cary

Grant. You couldn't resist him either. At least, that was the idea.'

By the time I had my first case conference with Richard Faber, he had been questioned for many hours but had said next-to-nothing. With the police he was unfailingly courteous and comprehensively uncooperative. The detectives working on the case were initially fascinated by him but gradually repelled. They failed to be charmed by the Cary Grant carapace. They came to see Richard as bloodless, calculating, unreal.

'What have I got to say, Mr Higgins, except I'm innocent?'

'What can I say, Mr Faber, except this isn't a game.'

'We seem to be on a different wavelength.'

'Different planet.'

His chosen manner was more effective with the prison officers than the police. Richard decided he didn't want to apply for bail. 'I'm fine here. If I'm out there it'll just be a media circus. Maisie's fine. She's safe. And there's no one else I want to see. Sarah's back at school now. She'll be safe there. They had Oscar Wilde's children at Bedales, remember. They're used to this sort of thing.'

In prison the officers and the inmates were excited by Richard's celebrity: it is exciting to have a star in your midst, there's electricity in the air. It's how royalty used to cure the scrofula. A little touch of Harry in the night. The officers found Richard easy to handle: he was no trouble. His fellow remand prisoners found him easy to talk to. He was ready to tell stories, drop names, sign autographs, do tricks. They spent hours watching old movies on television and, when it came to the stars, it seemed the fabulous Fabers had known them all.

The first time I met Richard Faber, face to face, I was immediately overwhelmed. Inevitably. You were. You couldn't help it. He was *world* famous. He was *wonderful* to look at. And when he took off his glasses and looked you in the eye and carefully deployed old Theodore Faber's three rules of charm – be courteous, be carefree and concentrate – he was *irresistible.*

That's how he'd made his fortune, after all. It was hardly surprising that the magic should work on me. Except, of course, that he was charged with murder. It was all wrong, I saw that; unprofessional, self-indulgent; I knew I should resist him, but the moment I set eyes on him I knew at once I wasn't even going to try. It was like arriving at a party with the best intentions and then deciding, suddenly, there and then, 'I'm going to get drunk tonight; it doesn't matter; nothing matters; I'm not driving; I can sleep on the floor.'

We met over many weeks and for hours on end we prepared his case and I suppose I felt a little drunk throughout. I was certainly intoxicated with something. I kept thinking how odd – and wonderful – it was that this was happening and how ridiculous – but right – I was to be allowing myself, to be letting myself fall in love – gently, sweetly, madly, lightly – with this strange, impossible, impenetrable man. It was all unspoken, all unsaid, in my head – and safe, like loving your teacher or your priest. Or Cary Grant. I fooled myself it was innocent too. After all, my husband was in the room most of the time.

'Jo – may I call you Jo? – Jo, I don't want to be defended because there's nothing to defend – but since you tell me this trial is going to go ahead come what may, and you and Tom seem keen to take on the venture, why not? The three of us against the world.'

'Richard, you can have the finest legal minds that money can buy—'

'I hope that's what I'm getting.'

'Thank you. What I mean is that I'm just a junior, you should have—'

'I want you, that's all I want.'

'Okay. I'm not sure the world will understand.'

'Bugger the world.'

He had told the police nothing. At our second meeting he said to me, 'I'll tell you anything you want to know. If I can.'

'Tell me about Maisie.'

'You know about Maisie. You've read the papers.'

'No, tell me about you and Maisie.'

He told me their story – much as I have tried to tell it to you here.

'Where is she now?'

'Where she wants to be.'

'Where's that?'

'Where she's safe.'

'Why won't you tell me more, Richard?'

'Because it's our secret. That's the point.'

Where was Maisie? Was she alive and in hiding? And if so, where? And why? And if she wasn't alive, how had she died? In an accident? Or had someone killed her?

Had Richard murdered her? Or had she killed herself? I asked him, 'Do you think she might have taken her own life?'

He laughed. 'Look, she's alive. She's fine.'

'If she's alive, if she's fine, as you say, why won't she get in touch?'

'Because . . .'

'Yes?'

'Because – because she's going to do it her way now, our way. She doesn't belong to the world. She doesn't have to do anything she doesn't want to do. She's free.'

'Do you know where Maisie is now?'

'Yes.'

'Where is she, Richard?'

'To tell you would be to betray her. Don't you see? She wants to be alone. It's not that difficult to understand, is it? Almost since the day we met, certainly since the day we got married, she's been public property – owned by the world, picked over by the press. Mostly they've been on her side. She hasn't complained, she doesn't complain, but if she doesn't want it any more, that's for her to decide, isn't it? No one else. No one.'

'Can I ask you something?'

'Yes?'

'Maisie's mother?'

'Yes?'

'Did she commit suicide?'

'No.'

'I know the verdict was accidental death, but what do you think? Suicide can run in families.'

'I know. I've never played one – unless you count Hamlet – but I've known several suicides. Maisie befriended Margaux Hemingway you know. We met her in LA. She was drunk, but still rather beautiful. I think she said that her grandfather, great-grandfather, great-uncle and great-aunt had all killed themselves – and her brother had tried. Must have been some sort of record. But I don't believe Maisie's mother killed herself. I think she was murdered.' He paused. He was, of course, an actor of the old school. He held his pauses. He smiled and looked straight at me, 'I think Maisie's mother was murdered by Maisie's father.'

'That's quite an allegation,' I said.

'It's not one I'm making public. I'm just telling you, as my *confidante*. I've got no proof. It's just a hunch, an idea. A wild surmise. She was on lithium, for manic-depression, and had been for several years. It kept her stabilised, it got her through. Taking it, day in, day out, would have been part of her routine, the dosage didn't vary. But the autopsy showed three times the amount in her system there should have been – not enough to kill her, hardly enough to look suspicious, but more than enough to blur her vision, make her drowsy, weaken her muscles, make her giddy. She wouldn't have taken an overdose by mistake. I believe Jack Rivers did it somehow – slipped her triple the dose, then waited, then pushed her down the stairs.'

'But why? Why should he want to do that?'

'Because somehow she had learnt his secret.'

'What secret?'

He hesitated. 'What I tell you goes no further?'

'Not without your authority.'

'I believe Maisie's mother discovered that her husband, Maisie's father, was not the person who he claimed to be. And that discovery cost her her life.'

'What do you mean – he's some sort of schizophrenic?'

'Far from it. I mean Jack Rivers is not Jack Rivers.'

'Who is he then?'

'His proper name is Arnold Gadd.' I looked incredulous. Richard smiled. 'I agree. An unfortunate name, but his own. Arnold Edward Gadd.'

'Do you have proof of this?'

'Oh yes. This I know. And Maisie's father knows I know. This I've researched quite carefully. Over many years. This I've got right. For a time I even thought it might make a movie, but there isn't really a part in it for Maisie. It's a war story. Before my time, of course. Before your time too. Long, long ago – July 1943: the Allied invasion of Sicily. An amazing operation, four hundred and seventy-eight thousand troops, British and American, safely landed on one small island in just three days. The resistance from the Italians was fairly pitiful – their heart wasn't in it any longer; the Germans were hopelessly outnumbered – there were sixty thousand of them, no more. It took just a month to take the island, more or less. And the price? British casualties: 7,939 wounded, 4,904 missing or dead – not bad, apparently, as these things go. The point of the story is that the casualties included two young soldiers, corporals, one handsome, one less so, one brave, one less so, one that lives, one that doesn't. They are, as you'll have guessed, Jack Rivers and Arnold Gadd, the pride of the Eighth Army, the young heroes of the assault on the bridge at Catania.

'On the night of twelfth July, barely forty-eight hours after they have landed just south of Syracuse, these two young men are sent on a mission behind enemy lines. It's a reconnoitre critical to the attempt to capture the all-important bridge the following day. It's a hazardous mission, through uncharted terrain, conducted in the dead of night, a thousand miles from home. At just after one in the morning, within a stone's throw of the bridge itself, as they scramble through the undergrowth on the edge of the river Simento, a siren sounds and a search-light begins to sweep along the river-bank. Jack Rivers, the real Jack Rivers, lies utterly still, unseen, unheard, while Arnold Gadd, poor pathetic lad, suddenly gripped with terror, loses his nerve, loses his head and starts to run – to run away. He runs, he turns, he trips, he stumbles, he rolls, he falls head-first towards the water. He's caught, trapped. His legs are imprisoned in a tangle of roots at the river's edge. He is lying face downward. He is going to drown. His comrade sees him, and, as the citation would have it, with total disregard to his own safety and in the face of enemy fire, goes to rescue him – and, yes, is immediately caught in a furious barrage of gunfire from the unit guarding the bridge. The gunfire ceases, the arc lamps go out, silence falls, and by the light of the silvery moon we can discern that Rivers has rescued

Gadd, but, poor bastard, has been fatally wounded in the attempt.

'Gadd is soaked and breathless and terrified, his ankles are badly twisted, but apart from that he is uninjured. To his credit, he doesn't abandon his comrade-in-arms – at least not yet. Slowly, painfully, he drags him up the bank, over the top and towards a small stone shepherd's hut beyond the hill. It's no more than a thousand metres away, but it takes an hour to reach. That's where Jack Rivers actually died – in that shepherd's hillside hut – and that's where Arnold Gadd took – removed – stole – his friend's identity papers. Perhaps it's wrong to say he stole them. Maybe he took them then just for safe-keeping. That I don't know. Anyway, it was as he was searching his colleague's clothes in this shepherd's hut that Gadd was suddenly surprised by a young boy – no more than ten or eleven. It's the boy's father who told me the story. Gadd held a gun to this child's head and demanded sustenance and shelter. It was mid-July. It was four in the morning. Day was breaking. As the pair of them crept from the hut, a mortar descended – instantly destroying the hut, severely wounding Gadd, devastating his face with burns, but hardly touching the boy at all. God is merciful, as my witness says. The boy struggled with the wounded soldier, got him home, to a secure farmhouse at the edge of the wood, and there Gadd stayed, in agony but at least in safety, for several days.

'By fourteenth July the Allies had captured the bridge – a parachute brigade delivered the goods – and, as the boldest and the best of the Eighth Army broke through into the Plain of Catania, and Alexander applauded and Montgomery purred, Arnold Gadd came stumbling down the hillside claiming to be Jack Rivers and was shipped home, a hero, a brave soldier cruelly disfigured in the fight for freedom, a selfless friend who risked his life to save a comrade from drowning.

'When I first heard the story I couldn't understand why he had done it. Why steal Rivers' identity? Why not simply claim the credit for the heroics himself? Then I did some homework on Arnold Gadd – discreetly, enquiries here and there, Maisie never knew – and gradually it began to make sense. It turned out there wasn't that much to discover. Arnold Gadd was really a nobody from nowhere, a lad from Lincoln, whose father was a bookmaker who drank a little, whose mother was a drudge. He had a much younger sister, but not much else. Certainly he had no prospects – a poor school record and a brief history of trouble with the police. By letting "Arnold Gadd" die he gave his poor parents a son they could be proud of – and he gave himself a chance. The real Jack Rivers was an only child with no parents. Arnold knew that. Jack's family were respectable, but nothing special. His father had been a solicitor in Accrington: he died of cancer when Jack was about eighteen. His mother was killed in an accident, a motorbike in the blackout. The point was that Jack had a modest trust fund and prospects and ambition. He had told Arnold all about them. He had shown Arnold what life might be like. Jack was handsome, Jack had potential, Jack was a hero. By becoming Jack, Arnold could leave his drab past behind and build himself a brighter future. He could realise Jack's potential. Jack had sacrificed his life to save him: the least he could do was live that life and live it to the full. When he published Jack's war diaries as his own he told himself he was doing it as a kind of secret tribute to the man whose identity he felt he had not so much stolen as inherited. Oh, I can see how he rationalised it all to himself – Jack was dead, what harm could it do to him? And all his achievements since the war, they're real enough – he's made those billions from next to nothing, he's done it – it's remarkable, admirable in its own way. But at the same time, our Jack Rivers, the Jack Rivers the world now knows, has built his life upon a lie. The first lie is the one that counts.

'I met the man who knew the secret quite by chance. He's a professor now. Distinguished, delightful, a nice part to play – Gielgud twenty years ago. He had no idea what became of the young English soldier he and his family had sheltered during the fateful summer of '43 until years later, when he was in England, around the time of the Coronation, early fifties, and he chanced to see a photograph of "Jack Rivers" in the paper with a long article detailing his heroic exploits during the famous raid on the bridge at Catania. The professor knew that the English corporal he had sheltered was called Arnold Gadd. He knew Jack Rivers was the soldier who had died. He was intrigued to find that Gadd now claimed to be Rivers, but he did nothing about it, told no one. Why should he? It was none of his business really. Over the years, whenever he came across a reference to "Rivers" and his astonishing wealth and ever-growing international empire, my friend, the professor, Giovanni Navi, would read the story and smile. He didn't think about it much, but then, one day, sitting in a café in Padua, he happened to see me and Maisie together – it was soon after we were married – and he introduced himself, said he couldn't resist it. Because he had met my mother a few times – even claimed to be a little in love with her – he had followed all the hooha in the press about our running away together – the tale of the outraged father and the fly-by-night young lovers – and he had decided he was on our side.'

'Did – does – Maisie know all this?'

'No, Maisie doesn't know.'

'Are you sure?'

'Yes, of that I am certain.'

'If you believe Maisie's father may have killed Maisie's mother because she had discovered this life-lie of his, because he feared exposure, couldn't he have killed Maisie for the same reason?'

'Husbands kill wives. Fathers don't kill daughters.'

'Did you kill Maisie?'

'No. No. Never.'

'Do you think someone else could have murdered her? Adam Waterson?'

'Adam is irrelevant.'

'Are you sure?'

'Jo, listen to me. Maisie is alive.'

'If you didn't murder her, Richard, where is she?'

'I cannot tell you where she is, but I do tell you I did not murder her.'

'If you did not murder her, it would be wrong if you were to be convicted and imprisoned?'

'Yes. Of course. But you can't be convicted for a crime that hasn't taken place.'

He laughed. He made me laugh. He had told this extraordinary story, he was faced with a charge of murder and yet he sat facing me with a look on his gorgeous face of studied charm bordering on insolence. 'You're insane. Do you know that?' I wanted to kiss him. I wanted to kiss my client. I wanted him to kiss me. These are not thoughts that the Bar Council encourages. Was I out of my mind too? 'We could say you're insane. We should say that. You are insane.'

He shook his head and ran his fingers through his hair. 'But I'm not.'

'That's what you say. A jury might think differently.'

'I'm not insane, Jo – not in the least. Well, I suppose, slightly. Actors are all a little mad. Good ones. Besides the jury will know me, won't they? They'll be fans. Surely? They'll know I'm not mad. When they hear what I have to say they'll see that I'm sane, totally sane.'

'They won't hear what you have to say. They won't hear you speak. You won't say a word. We're not putting you in the witness box.'

'Oh, no, no, no, my beautiful brief. You've got it all wrong. Tell her, Tom. If I stay silent, that's an admission of guilt. I am pleading not guilty. I am not guilty. I did not do it. I have nothing to hide. I have nothing to fear.'

'This isn't a play, Richard.'

'Isn't it? No, not yet. But it will be a movie, a wonderful movie. And if Maisie doesn't fancy the part, you can do it yourself. You're very good, Jo. Very good indeed.'

TWELVE

What's in a name? Nothing and everything, of course. It is illogical and entirely sentimental, but for me, all my life, the name Richard has possessed a certain magic. If you are called Richard, come what may, to me you're special and I'm on your side. Yes, I know, it's absurd, quite unjustifiable, foolish even, certainly not what's expected of a thirty-five-year-old barrister-at-law, quite as naïve as reading your horoscope each morning in the *Daily Mail*, (I do that too, furtively but without fail, and when the newspaper's prediction matches my mood I think, 'Mm, yes, there are more things in heaven and earth than are dreamt of in your philosophy', and when it's a mile off – which it isn't often – I shrug and mutter to myself, 'The stars incline, they do not foretell', and hope for something more encouraging in the *Evening*

Standard). My father was called Richard, as were both my grandfathers, and all three of them were lawyers. Had I been born a boy I would have been a Richard too. As a child Richard the Lionheart was my special hero and in my early teens I took up the cause of King Richard III, a great man misunderstood by history, travestied by Shakespeare. I joined the Richard III Society and wrote to its patron, the present Richard, Duke of Gloucester, and was thrilled, aged fourteen, to receive from Kensington Palace – on thick, creamy paper, gloriously embossed – a wonderful, long, courteous, scholarly reply. My father had a special friend, Richard Du Cann (they were in the same chambers), and on my eighteenth birthday Richard D C gave me a small book he had written called *The Art of the Advocate*. I loved it for its subtle wisdom and for the tales it told of the forensic heroes of yesteryear. In a way it was the book that changed my life because, under its influence, I abandoned my settled plan to train as a solicitor and decided to follow in the family tradition and read for the Bar after all. It was this Richard too who first told me of another Richard, the legendary Sir Richard Muir, leading Treasury Counsel at the Old Bailey at the end of the nineteenth century, of whom it was said that the lucidity of his argument and the clarity with which he stated the facts in his opening remarks invariably wove a net so tightly round the prisoner in the dock that he could never afterwards escape from it.

I don't think Richard Muir QC, who appeared for the Crown in *R* v *Faber*, was in fact related to his namesake, but he shared something of his reputation and managed to combine this awesome perspicuity with a deceptively mild manner (not unlike my father's) that came over as an odd mixture of diffidence, deference, self-deprecation and rather fruity old-world charm. Colleagues were not fooled, but juries were entranced. His particular trick was to bend over backwards to see the other side's point of view. To any impartial observer Richard Muir seemed to be the personification of clear thinking, fair play and sweet reason, with just a touch of dottiness inherited from a bygone age.

At three minutes before eleven on Tuesday 15 September 1998, in Court Number One at the Old Bailey, Mr Justice King-Lovell presiding, Richard Muir rose to his feet and with a courteous nod to the bench and a welcoming smile to the jury, in his easy, measured way, began: 'I appear for the prosecution; my learned friend, Mrs Dalton, for the defendant.' He glanced around the courtroom, packed but utterly still. He seemed momentarily puzzled. He turned back to the jury and shook his head. 'This is an extraordinary day. In thirty and more years at the criminal bar I don't believe I have known anything like it. The streets outside are thronged with people, the massed ranks of the world's media have descended on the Old Bailey, hundreds of them, reporters, photographers, journalists, a whole caravanserai of camera crews, radio cars, outside broadcast units, surrounding the building, stretching down the road to Ludgate Hill, almost as far as the eye can see. Extraordinary scenes. And why? Because of the extraordinary interest in this case – an extraordinary interest arising from the fact that central to the case are two extraordinary people. The victim, Maisie Rivers – you can picture her, can't you? We all can – extraordinary in her beauty, her brilliance, her style. I heard someone say on television the other day – you may have heard it too – "We have lost an angel." We have lost an angel. Maisie Rivers. And the accused? Richard Faber, the man in the dock, an actor of extraordinary ability, with an international reputation originally built on his television series *Murderer*. The angel and the murderer. You can see the headlines, can't you? Well, ladies and gentlemen of the jury, that's not how I see it at all and I don't believe it is how you should see it either. This is a trial involving film stars, but it is not being played out on the silver screen. Miss Rivers and Mr Faber may have worked in a glamorous trade, but there is nothing glamorous about this case. There may be extraordinary scenes taking place outside, but here in this court I submit that the case you are to hear is, in truth, quite ordinary. When it comes to murder, tragically, there is nothing more commonplace than the man who murders his partner, the husband who kills his wife. This case is not a drama about film stars; it is an all-too-common tale of a jealous husband driven to murder a much younger wife whose affections have turned elsewhere.

'It is my purpose and duty to explain to you, as clearly and as concisely as I can, why the Crown believes that on the first of October last Richard Faber did wilfully, knowingly, and with premeditation, murder his wife,

Maisie Rivers, disposing of her body that same night off the Bristol coast in the Irish Sea. We will tell you why it happened. And how. And when. And where. And at every stage it will be my purpose and duty to produce evidence to substantiate every claim I make – and your role and duty to weigh that evidence with all due care.

'Why? Why did Richard Faber murder Maisie Rivers? Were they not famously in love? Once upon a time, possibly, but just as this case isn't a melodrama for the big screen, nor is the story of the Fabers' marriage a fairy tale in which the prince meets his princess and they live happily ever after. Real life isn't like that. We might wish that it were, but it isn't. Sadly, all too often, love does not last the test of time. Miss Rivers was a girl of fifteen when she met Mr Faber. He was already thirty, a man of the world, an established star of stage and screen, and he swept her off her feet. Perhaps it was too good to last? He was twice her age, after all. Who knows? What is certain – and I want only to deal with what is certain – what is certain is that nearly twenty years later, whatever the public veneer, the marriage had turned sour. That is the bitter truth. And you will want evidence of it – not newspaper tittle-tattle, not Hollywood gossip, but evidence that you can weigh, assess, evaluate. I will produce in evidence a letter from Maisie Rivers in which she describes the condition of her marriage, the state of her true feelings about her husband and her fears for her own safety. You will hear evidence from Mr Adam Waterson, Miss Rivers' lover and companion in the months and weeks leading to her death. He will tell you of their relationship, of how Miss Rivers feared for her life, of the fight that took place between Mr Waterson and the accused – a violent struggle clearly overheard by members of staff at the home of the Fabers in Little Venice, members of staff who will be in court to testify. In the privacy of his home Richard Faber was a violent man and, realising that his wife no longer loved him, knowing that she had taken a lover, driven by jealousy, spurred by wounded pride, he determined, callously, cruelly, to end her life.

'He did so on Wednesday first October 1997. That morning Miss Rivers flew in to London airport on a British Airways flight from Los Angeles. Mr Faber was waiting at Heathrow to meet her. Together, in a VIP lounge set aside for the purpose, they took part in a pre-arranged photo-call and press conference. At its conclusion Mr Faber and Miss Rivers, who had only hand baggage with her, left the airport alone. As you will hear, this surprised the VIP handling staff at Heathrow who were accustomed to looking after the Fabers and could not recall either of them coming to the airport previously without, at least, a chauffeur or personal assistant of some kind in attendance. Mr Faber and Miss Rivers then collected Mr Faber's distinctive blue Mercedes from the car park at Terminal Four and together they drove not, as expected to their home in Little Venice, but around the M25 and then on to the M1 to Luton Airport, north of London, where Mr Faber was then keeping his Cessna Model 152 Aerobat two-seater monoplane. At one twenty-two that afternoon, according to air traffic control, the Cessna was cleared for take-off and set out along the agreed route for the short flight to Bristol. Witnesses who saw the Fabers arrive at Bristol airport that afternoon will testify that the couple appeared both relaxed and happy – but, of course, when it comes to actors, appearances can be deceptive. That is, after all, their stock-in-trade and, in public, at least, the Fabers always maintained that their marriage was a perfect one.

'There were several sightings of the couple that after-noon – in the centre of Bristol, near the Theatre Royal, down by the docks, up Whiteladies Road near the BBC. The last time they were seen together for certain was by a witness who observed them crossing the Clifton Suspension Bridge, apparently going towards the Leigh Woods beyond. That was the last time Maisie Rivers was ever seen. At some time between this final sighting at around six o'clock and the early hours of Thursday morning, Richard Faber murdered his wife. He killed her with a single shot from a Welrod pistol, a weapon dating back to the Second World War, a simple blowback automatic pistol with one special feature: a wonderfully efficient silencer built on to the barrel. The gun, the murder weapon, which is almost entirely silent in operation, will be produced in evidence. It bears the fingerprints of the accused. At around one am, this time without clearance from air traffic control, Mr Faber flew his Cessna out across the Bristol Channel and disposed of his wife's body by tipping it into the Irish Sea. Traces of blood matching that of Miss Rivers have been found on the aeroplane and witnesses will testify that Mr Faber was alone when he landed the Cessna back at Luton in the early hours of Thursday morning.

'I have no doubt you will find that the defence makes much of the fact that the body of Maisie Rivers has not been recovered. We do not need to produce the body of the victim to establish the guilt of the accused. Since most crimes are committed in secrecy, it is inevitable that, in many a criminal trial, direct proof of guilt is lacking and much of the evidence is indirect or circumstantial. Ultimately, in the absence of evidence directly proving the facts in issue, the accused may be convicted solely on circumstantial evidence. That is what the law allows. In a case of murder, there may be a conviction notwithstanding that the body is never found, provided there is sufficient circumstantial evidence to convince the jury that the facts cannot be accounted for on any rational hypothesis other than murder.

'Members of the jury, in the coming days you will hear evidence both direct and circumstantial and it will be for you to assess the strength of that evidence, for you to decide whether the case the prosecution makes is well founded or not. We do believe that the facts cannot be accounted for on any rational hypothesis other than murder, but, when you have heard all the evidence, if there is any real doubt in your minds, the accused is not merely entitled to the benefit of that doubt – he is entitled to acquittal. The Crown has to prove to your satisfaction that the accused is guilty. The onus is on us. If you are reasonably convinced, taking the evidence as a whole, that Richard Faber has murdered his wife for the reasons and in the manner I have described, then according to your oaths and your duty to society, you will find him guilty. If, on the other hand, you have doubts, real doubts, justice requires that you acquit the accused of the terrible charge laid against him. I began by describing this senseless domestic tragedy as an ordinary murder, and so it is. But weighing the evidence that is set before you is no ordinary responsibility and I know you will undertake it with the closest attention and the most extraordinary care.'

The jury – eight women, four men, one Asian, one Afro-Caribbean, a range of ages but overall older rather than younger, we were content with the mix – looked suitably attentive, careful and impressed. Richard Muir had done his stuff. He had buttered them up, and laid his ground, anticipating our defence, acknowledging the circumstantial nature of much of the evidence, sowing seeds of doubt about the trustworthiness of actors, 'appearances can be deceptive – that is their stock-in-trade', making a meal of it yet managing to present it as a run-of-the-mill murder at the same time, an awesome responsibility but really an open-and-shut case. It was all much cleverer than it looked. And it wasn't easy to answer.

Richard sat impassively in the dock. We had decided that the bank manager from Turin was the look to go for. There was much of the prosecution's case we couldn't and wouldn't dispute. We accepted that Richard and Maisie had flown to Bristol and that Richard had returned to London alone. We accepted that Maisie had not been seen in public since. We did not dispute that the traces of blood found in the cockpit of the Cessna were Maisie's. Our explanation was that she had had a severe nose-bleed during the flight.

Taken at face value both Maisie's letter and Adam's evidence-in-chief were highly damaging. The letter was addressed to Adam, typed on the old electric typewriter Richard kept in his study at the apartment on Venice Beach, and signed by Maisie. We didn't dispute the authenticity of the signature or the fact that Maisie occasionally used this machine to type letters and notes to friends. It was the content of the letter that was the problem. It sounded the way the jury might think Maisie might sound.

> Adam dearest,
>
> You know I love you. I think I always have. I used to love R, of course I did. I loved him desperately once. But he's changed, hasn't he? You know that. He was always completely wrapped up in himself and his acting, but now there isn't room for anything else – for anyone else. He's jealous of you and he's obsessed with me. If ever he found out about us I don't know what he might do. You will look after me, won't you? If anything happens to me, you will kiss me better, won't you? I'm frightened.

There was a full page of it, several hundred words,

closely typed, declaring love for Adam, suggesting that Richard had threatened her before and stating, in terms, that she now feared for her life. In giving his evidence Adam elaborated on all this, allowing himself a little too much relish in his descriptions of the apparently passionate affair.

In my cross-examination I wanted to lead the jury to wonder why on earth Maisie Rivers – still regarded by many, by millions, as the most beautiful woman in the world – should want to have an affair with Adam Waterson. If she was looking for an extra-marital dalliance, she could have had the pick of the planet. George Clooney was her co-star in the movie. Why sleep with Adam Waterson, a man no younger than her husband, certainly no more handsome or more gifted, and a man with an unenviable reputation as a serial womaniser? I wanted the jury to question the very existence of the affair.

'Did other people in Hollywood know about your relationship with Miss Rivers?'

'Yes. There were stories in the press.'

'Do you believe everything you read in the newspapers, Mr Waterson?'

'Of course not.'

'How did these stories get into the press?'

'I don't know.'

'Have you any idea?'

'Not really.'

'Did you tell anyone about the affair?'

'Yes, possibly.'

'"Yes, certainly", don't you mean? If you were having an affair with Maisie Rivers you might be rather proud of the fact. Any man might be.'

'I did not talk about it widely.'

'Did Miss Rivers talk about it?'

'I don't know.'

'To the best of your knowledge, is there anyone to whom Miss Rivers confided that she was having a relationship with you?'

'We were seen kissing in the elevator.'

'Please answer the question, Mr Waterson. Did Maisie Rivers confide to anyone that she was having an affair with you?'

'I don't know.'

'I think if she had done you might have produced such a person to give evidence, don't you?'

'Maisie was in love with me. She told me so. I don't know if she told others. You've seen her letter.'

'Ah yes, the letter – written on the Fabers' typewriter, on Miss Rivers' own notepaper and personally signed by her. When did you receive the letter?'

'I found it waiting for me in her apartment when I got back from taking her to the airport for her return flight to London.'

'She didn't mail it to you? You found it?'

'Yes.'

'There are fingerprints on the letter. Did you know that?'

'I hadn't thought about it. I suppose there would be.'

'Can you imagine whose fingerprints they might be?'

226

'Mine?'

'Yes, your fingerprints are all over it.'

'I read the letter many times. It was precious to me.'

'And who else's fingerprints are on the letter?'

'Maisie's?'

'No, Mr Waterson. There are no other fingerprints on the letter. None at all. Don't you find that odd?'

'I don't know.'

'And Miss Rivers' signature – isn't there something odd about that as well?'

'I don't think so. It is her handwriting.'

'Oh yes. It is certainly her handwriting, that is not in dispute, but take a look at it – members of the jury, you will find copies of the letter in folder A at divider three. What is unusual about it?'

'Nothing.'

'Come now, Mr Waterson. What does the signature say? What are the words she has written?'

'Maisie Rivers.'

'Yes, Maisie Rivers. That is certainly her name, but do you customarily write a letter to your lover and sign your name in full?'

'I don't know.'

'I put it to you, Mr Waterson, that you never had an affair with Maisie Rivers, that your relationship with her was solely professional and that anything more intimate than an affectionate actress's comradely kiss in an elevator was a figment of your fevered imagination.'

'No. No.'

'I suggest to you that Miss Rivers regularly signed

professional correspondence at your request and that this letter was a letter you had written for your own warped reasons and presented to her secreted amongst a variety of others. I suggest that you turned over the pages and invited her to sign her name in the usual way. She never wrote this letter. She never read this letter. She never even touched this letter. You were holding the papers. She was holding the pen. It is her signature, but it is not her letter. I am right am I not, Mr Waterson?'

'No, you are wrong.'

'Thank you. No more questions.'

Richard Muir may have anticipated my line of attack. In re-examining Adam Waterson he immediately asked: 'Had Miss Rivers ever written to you before?'

'No.'

'This letter was deliberately left somewhere where you could not fail to find it?'

'Yes.'

'It is almost like a confession, is it not?'

'I suppose so.'

'It's a declaration of love, but more than that. There is something formal about it, isn't there – like a will or a last testament? As far as we know, it was the last letter she wrote.'

'Yes.'

'In the case of a confession or a declaration or a last will and testament, if you were signing them you would sign them with your full signature, would you not?'

'Yes.'

*   *   *

Maisie's father was to prove a tougher nut to crack. He was due to give his evidence on the fourth day of the trial, the Friday morning, and on Thursday night I said to Richard, 'It's going okay. Don't worry.' He didn't look in the least worried: tired, neutral, not completely engaged, but I couldn't see fear in his eyes, or anxiety.

'Don't you worry,' he said gently, with a little smile. He ran his fingers over my clenched knuckles. 'You're doing well. Thank you.'

Tom shifted his chair so that it scraped loudly against the stone floor of the interview room. Tom's clerk leant forward and refilled our paper cups with water. I pulled my hand away and said, 'The jury won't have liked Adam, they won't trust him, but the father of the alleged victim – that's different. If we can, we should undermine his credibility at the outset.'

'Agreed,' said Tom.

'Meaning?' asked Richard.

'Muir's first question to his witness will be: "You are Jack Rivers?" and if the answer he gives is "Yes", according to your account, he's perjuring himself.'

Richard spread his arms wide and tilted back on his chair. 'No, no, Jo, we can't do that.'

'If we can expose him, we should. It will change everything.'

He sat forward again and looked straight into my eyes. 'We can't do it.'

'Why not?'

'Maisie doesn't know the truth about her father. She mustn't know.'

'Richard, Maisie isn't here.'

'She is.' He said it with a quiet emphasis that brooked no debate. His tone was always rational. He appeared so even-tempered, gently amused, naturally in control. He seemed so sane.

'Do you mean she's in this room here with us now?' Tom asked the question.

'No!' Richard shook his head and gave Tom a sharp look of mock-scorn that hissed what-kind-of-fruitcake-do-you-take-me-for? 'No! But I promised her I would never say anything to damage her father, and I won't.'

'But he will damage you.'

'No matter.' He looked around at us and with his forefingers softly drummed the table. 'Sorry. Sorry. I promised Maisie. What's more, in a way, we did a deal. He bought my silence. With a picture. Maisie's favourite picture.'

When Jack Rivers took the witness stand he was impressive. He was old now, in his mid-seventies, but when the judge invited him to give his evidence seated he said he was grateful but preferred to stand, and he addressed all his replies directly to the jury in a manner that came across as dignified, human yet quietly commanding. You could see he had presence; you could believe he had been a war hero; you knew that he loved his daughter. As Richard conceded later, 'Not a trace of Charlie Drake: this was Alec Guinness at his finest.' He spoke clearly and simply and, shrewdly, he took care not to overstate his case.

'Do you like Richard Faber?'

'No, but I respect his talent as an actor.'

'Did you regard him as a suitable son-in-law?'

'No, but only because my daughter was fifteen when they met and he was a man twice her age. He took her from me and he kept her from me.'

'Following her marriage to the accused, how frequently did you see your daughter?'

'I saw her rarely. I wrote to her, but she did not reply. I believe he prevented it.'

'What do you think was the state of the marriage at the time of your daughter's disappearance?'

'It was bad. She was unhappy. And fearful.'

'Why do you say that? Because of what Mr Waterson told you?'

'Yes, that – and a father's instinct.'

We could not understand why Jack and Adam were conspiring together. Was it merely a mutual loathing for Richard? Or did they share some darker secret? The gun, of course, the alleged murder weapon, was the pistol Jack had dropped in the church in Verona. Ballistic evidence established that a shot from the gun had been fired recently, but we needed the jury to accept that the fingerprints on the gun, indisputably Richard's fingerprints, were nearly twenty years old. Richard forbade me to question Jack's identity, but, reluctantly, he conceded that we had no choice but to cross-examine him about the gun.

'Do you own a gun, Mr Rivers?'

'No.'

'A pistol, a rifle, a firearm of any kind?'

'No.'

'Have you ever owned a gun?'

'No.'

'Are you sure?'

'Yes, of course. I have no interest in guns.'

'But you have handled a gun?'

'In the war, yes. But that was a long time ago.'

'And since then?'

'No.'

'Think carefully before you reply.'

'I really know nothing about guns, nothing at all.'

'The gun that the Crown alleges is the murder weapon, the one Mr Waterson found in his office in the coach house at La Fenice and handed in to the police – Exhibit Two. Have you seen it before?'

'No, never.'

'It dates from the Second World War – in which you played an active and distinguished part.'

'Yes, thank you, but it's not a gun I would have used.'

'Why not?'

'I was never a member of Special Operations and the Welrod was developed for them.'

'I thought you said you knew nothing about guns, Mr Rivers. You seem surprisingly well informed about this one.'

It was something, but not much. At the end of the

232

day, it was Jack's word against ours. Who would the jury believe?

'I think they'll believe me,' said Richard.

It was Friday night. The first week was over and, I felt, had gone reasonably well. 'We don't need you to give evidence,' I said. 'We really don't. The onus is on them. Yes, they can show that Maisie has disappeared, vanished without trace. Yes, they can prove that you were the last person seen with her. They have a gun, they have some blood, but can they establish, beyond reasonable doubt, that you, and only you, could have killed Maisie? I doubt it. Put you up as a witness and what do we gain?'

'They'll see me for what I am.'

'Richard, once we make you and what you are central to our defence, everything about you, your character, your past, *everything* can be brought into question. They can attack us from all sides. And they will. It's a risk you don't need to take. Why do it?'

'I want to tell them the truth about Maisie.'

THIRTEEN

Jo Dalton: You are Richard Faber?

Richard Faber: Yes.

JD: You live at La Fenice, Blomfield Road, London W2?

RF: Yes.

JD: In April 1980 you married Miss Maisie Rivers, the daughter of Mr Jack Rivers of South Kensington, London SW7?

RF: Yes.

JD: When did you first meet Miss Rivers?

RF: On 30 October 1979. She came to audition for me.

It was an open audition, at the London Palladium. She just turned up.

JD: You have a precise recollection of the date—

RF: It was my thirtieth birthday. But I would hardly forget the date. It changed my life. Meeting Maisie changed my life. It may sound improbable, or absurdly romantic, but the moment I saw her I was enraptured. It was love at first sight.

JD: Maisie Rivers was how old at the time?

RF: Fifteen. But I was not conscious of her age. There was nothing childish or childlike about her.

JD: But she was obviously young.

RF: I suppose so.

JD: And soon after meeting her you took her off to Italy?

RF: Some months later we went to Verona together, yes. We were married there.

JD: Without her father's consent?

RF: I am afraid so. I don't believe he would have given his consent.

JD: Do you understand how a father, a single parent in this case, a widower, might resent a man twice the age of his only child taking that child to a foreign country and marrying her without his blessing?

RF: Yes, I do understand that resentment. And I believe it explains his appearance in court and the evidence he has given.

JD: You believe Mr Rivers has harboured a grudge against you?

RF: Yes. Understandably so. I do not complain about that.

JD: Is there something that you do complain about?

RF: The allegation that I used the Welrod pistol to kill his daughter, to murder my wife. It's a vile allegation, obscene, unfounded. The gun belongs to Mr Rivers, not to me.

JD: You are not suggesting that Mr Rivers killed his own daughter, are you?

RF: No, of course not. No one has killed Maisie Rivers.

JD: If no one has killed Maisie Rivers, Mr Faber, where is she? Why is she not here in court to help you clear your name?

RF: My wife is where she chooses to be. She chooses not to be here. Her fame has made her a public figure, but she is not public property. She can come and go as she pleases.

JD: Mr Faber, you will have heard one of the prosecution witnesses testify that he saw you and your wife together at around six o'clock on the evening of Wednesday 1

October last. He says you were crossing the Clifton Suspension Bridge in Bristol. Do you accept that is where you were on that date at around that time?

RF: Yes.

JD: Your wife has apparently not been seen since. Do you accept that?

RF: She has been seen by me.

JD: When you crossed the bridge that evening where did you go?

RF: For a walk in the woods.

JD: A walk in the woods? At six o'clock in the evening at the beginning of October? It was getting rather dark for a walk in the woods, wasn't it?

RF: It had been a beautiful day and we know the Leigh Woods well. We had a lot to talk about. My wife had been away for several weeks in the United States. It was the longest period we had ever been apart.

JD: What did you talk about?

RF: What we talked about is none of your business.

JD: Mr Faber, I am trying to be helpful. You are being tried on a very serious charge – none more serious—

RF: I apologise. I don't mean to be difficult. It's just that our lives belong to us – not to you, not to the court, not to the world. Our work belongs to the world.

When we put ourselves on show and ask you to pay money to come to see us, of course, you can come and you can judge us. And you can say what you like. But when we leave the stage, when we walk out of the spotlight, our lives become our own again. They must. What we talk about when we are alone together is nobody's business but ours. Where my wife is now is nobody's business but hers. Suddenly, as rare things will, she vanished. *Voilà*. That does not mean that I have murdered her.

JD: Mr Faber, how would you describe your marriage?

RF: How do you mean?

JD: Was it, is it, a good marriage, a happy marriage?

RF: My wife is an angel – she is perfection.

JD: But I take it your marriage has had its up and downs like any other marriage?

RF: I do not know about any other marriage. I don't think it is possible to understand anybody else's marriage. It's not always possible to understand one's own.

JD: How did your relationship develop over the years? Did it grow stronger, weaker?

RF: Stronger, much stronger, and deeper.

JD: Can you say why?

RF: Because we have grown to love one another more and more – and, perhaps too, because we have come to love the world at large rather less. It's strange being famous. No one is quite normal when they are with you – no one at all. It's strange too leading a fairy-tale life. No one wants to believe it's possible, but it is. Despite Mr Muir's cynicism, it is quite possible to fall in love at first sight, to sustain that love, even to live happily ever after. Please believe me.

Richard Muir QC: Mr Faber, you are an actor, a very distinguished actor, internationally recognised for your work on television and in the cinema, but I'd venture to suggest most widely acclaimed for your award-winning work in the theatre. Am I right? Would you describe yourself first and foremost as a stage actor?

RF: Yes, I would.

RM: The theatre is your first love?

RF: Yes.

RM: Would it be fair to say that you live for your work? That you find it wholly engrossing, all-absorbing, that in many ways you are quite obsessive about it?

RF: I don't know about 'obsessive', but certainly I have a passion for my work, yes.

RM: Can you tell the court something about your approach to it?

RF: How do you mean?

RM: About your technique as an actor. When you appear

in a play where do you start? From the outside in or the inside out? Is motivation important? When you arrive on stage, are you conscious of where you are coming from, where you are going to?

RF: Usually I am coming from the Number One dressing room and I am going to the Ivy.

RM: That's very droll. Very droll. I must say, Mr Faber, you are mighty cool under fire. Mighty cool. It makes me wonder, are you in fact acting now?

RF: I don't know what you mean.

RM: I mean that you are an actor and could therefore be acting here and now in a way that might not be possible for others. What do you say?

RF: I don't know. I suppose if I'm candid—

RM: We would be grateful. You are on oath.

RF: What I mean is that to the extent that this is an unnatural situation and, in a way, being on the witness stand is being on show, comparable to appearing on stage, then, yes, I am performing – but I am also telling the truth. Good acting is about telling the truth.

RM: And about making the lines your character speaks ring true?

RF: Yes.

RM: When you met Maisie Rivers you were auditioning her for what part?

RF: Alice.

RM: As in *Alice in Wonderland*?

RF: Yes.

RM: This was your own adaptation in which Maisie Rivers appeared both as Alice in the story and as Alice Liddell, the girl for whom Lewis Carroll created the story?

RF: Correct.

RM: And you played both Lewis Carroll and the Mad Hatter?

RF: Yes.

RM: You are, of course, aware of Lewis Carroll's particular fondness for young girls.

RF: It was not a feature of the play.

RM: Oh? I have a copy of the script here – I think it is called the 'prompt copy' in theatrical jargon. According to this, you have your part, Lewis Carroll, say right at the beginning of the piece, 'I am not omniverous. I am fond of children, except boys. Boys are not an attractive race of beings to me.'

RF: Those were Lewis Carroll's own words. He preferred young girls to young boys, but his interest in girls was entirely innocent.

RM: Yet he took photographs of them naked, did he not?

RF: With their parents' permission.

RM: But not altogether with their approval. Didn't he abruptly stop taking such photographs?

RF: I don't see the relevance of this. It did not feature in my play.

RM: You had Lewis Carroll photographing a partially clothed girl in the prelude to the play, didn't you?

RF: It was an innocuous tableau. It was lovely. The girl wasn't Alice. It was Ellen Terry. The actress Ellen Terry. She and Lewis Carroll were friends. Theirs was an extraordinary friendship. They were remarkable people.

RM: No doubt. And when Lewis Carroll was thirty I think Ellen Terry was fourteen – about the same age difference as that between yourself and Maisie Rivers at the time you met.

RF: Not that I see the relevance of any of this, but Lewis Carroll's interest in girls was entirely innocent.

RM: That is your view. Others felt differently. Including, of course, the parents of Alice Liddell. They stopped her seeing him, didn't they? Maisie Rivers was fifteen when you met her. Did you see her naked at that age?

RF: Why do you ask?

RM: Did you?

RF: Yes.

RM: You have also played Mark Twain, have you not?

RF: Yes, on stage and in a radio play. Was he interested in young girls?

RM: Yes. You did not know? The radio play in which you appeared was called *Angel Fish*.

RF: I cannot recall.

RM: Let me refresh your memory. Mark Twain had a circle of young female friends, aged between thirteen and sixteen. He called them his 'Angel Fish' and gave each one an angel-fish pin. When one of his Angel Fish abandoned Twain's little club, preferring the company of a young man more her own age, Twain became obsessionally jealous.

RF: Before you mention it, Mr Muir, I have also played the part of John Barrymore . . .

RM: In a one-man show of your own devising.

RF: And devised by me because he was a fascinating character to play – a weird and wonderful self-destructive actor with a rare talent – not because he had an affair with Mary Astor when she was sixteen.

RM: I think some of his conquests were considerably younger.

RF: Possibly. There may well be actors who take an unhealthy interest in young women. I am not one of them.

RM: But Maisie Rivers was only fifteen—

RF: I can play a child molester without being one, I can play a murderer without being one—

RM: And you can play an innocent victim and not be one! You are a consummate actor, Mr Faber, we have established that. Is it correct that you were offered the part of Humbert Humbert in the recent film version of Vladimir Nabokov's controversial novel *Lolita*? In the event the part was played by your friend and contemporary from the Bristol Old Vic Theatre School, Jeremy Irons?

RF: Yes.

RM: You were advised against taking the part?

Judge: Mr Muir, I think you have been pursuing this line rather a while now. I am not entirely sure where it is leading.

RM: My lord, I am seeking to establish a possible motive for the murder of Maisie Rivers. If a man has a particular interest in, obsession with, young girls and finds that his child bride turns from a nymphette into a woman and then turns away from him altogether, what might his reaction be? I have nearly concluded.

Judge: Very well.

RM: Mr Faber, would you take a look at the document that is item twenty-three in the list of evidence. The jury will find it at divider sixteen in folder A. Do you have it, Mr Faber?

RF: Yes.

RM: Do you recognise the handwriting?

RF: I think so.

RM: It is yours, is it not? And your fingerprints are on the original of the letter.

RF: If you say so.

RM: Please read to the court what it says.

RF: 'The most beautiful form of human life is the very young girl just starting to bloom.'

RM: 'The most beautiful form of human life is the very young girl just starting to bloom.' Are those your sentiments?

RF: No.

RM: But they are in your handwriting?

RF: Adam Waterson provided you with this, didn't he?

RM: Please answer the question, Mr Faber. The handwriting is yours?

RF: Yes, certainly. But the words are Charlie Chaplin's! And I wrote them when appearing in a television film about Chaplin's early love life. Certainly Chaplin had an unhealthy interest in pubescent girls, but I cannot believe that Adam Waterson has—

RM: We will come to Mr Waterson in due course. Let us stick with this for the time being if you don't mind. You accept that you fell in love with Maisie Rivers when she was just fifteen and you were twice her age? You accept that you have been offered and have taken, or have sought and secured, a number of parts playing older men with an interest in very young women? Your own daughter is now sixteen, I believe. What would you think of a man twice her age who wanted to sleep with your young daughter?

Judge: Mr Muir—

RF: I am quite happy to answer. If my daughter met and fell in love with a man and loved him truly and he loved her – as I love my wife and she loves me – age is completely irrelevant. How old was Juliet, for God's sake?

RM: The same sort of age as Romeo, I seem to recall.

Judge: Mr Muir, I think we need to move on now.

RM: Of course, my lord. I don't wish to weary the court by going through Mr Faber's career role by role, but I do believe the parts he has played are of significance because Mr Faber acknowledges that in many respects his life and his work are inextricable. Mr Faber, have you ever been asked to play the Prince of Wales?

RF: The present Prince of Wales?

RM: Yes.

RF: I hope you are not going to suggest he has an unhealthy interest in younger women.

RM: Again, amusing. One would almost think you were playing to the gallery – except that you are here charged with murder. You turned down the part of the Prince of Wales?

RF: Yes. It was meretricious.

RM: This was to be a Hollywood film about the death of Diana, Princess of Wales?

RF: Yes.

RM: What was the essence of the plot – in a nutshell?

RF: That Diana had not died in the car crash in Paris, that somehow the accident had been contrived to enable her to be spirited away to find peace and tranquillity, and freedom.

RM: Where is your wife at the moment, Mr Faber?

RF: Where she chooses to be.

RM: And has she found peace and tranquillity, and freedom?

RF: I hope so. For her sake, I am glad that she isn't here.

RM: No, she isn't here. She's vanished, disappeared.

RF: She's disappeared from your gaze, Mr Muir. She prefers to be alone.

RM: Like Greta Garbo?

RF: If you like, like Greta Garbo.

RM: But Miss Garbo was sighted now and again, wasn't she?

RF: Very much against her will.

RM: When did you first meet Adam Waterson?

RF: At school.

RM: And you were friends?

RF: Close friends, best friends.

RM: And later you became partners?

RF: Yes.

RM: And has the partnership been a success?

RF: Commercially, yes.

RM: In other ways?

RF: Less so recently.

RM: Meaning?

RF: As Maisie and I have become more successful, better known, more famous, Adam's attitude has seemed to change. I think he became more and more envious of me – and he became obsessed with Maisie. He had to 'have' every woman he wanted. And he wanted Maisie.

RM: And did he have her?

RF: No, of course not. No way.

RM: Are you sure? You had a fight with Mr Waterson,

didn't you? You came to blows. With your best friend. Wasn't it because you were jealous?

RF: No, it was because I was angry.

RM: Angry with Mr Waterson because he was having an affair with your wife?

RF: Angry because he was presuming to suggest he was having an affair with my wife. My wife has only had one affair.

RM: Oh?

RF: With me! With me, Mr Muir, only with me! Adam became a kind of stalker in our midst. His so-called affair with Maisie was a sad fantasy – pathetic, unrealisable. The whole world would want to have an affair with Maisie Rivers – but what would Maisie want of the world? Adam had nothing to offer Maisie. Maisie and I and Adam, we were once close, so close, but as friends, nothing more. I do assure you. We two stood there with never a third.

RM: 'We two stood there with never a third.' Isn't that a line of Robert Browning's? You quoted Browning earlier in your evidence, didn't you? 'Suddenly, as rare things will, she vanished.'

RF: Yes.

RM: You are a great admirer of Browning's, I know.

RF: He was a genius.

RM: You have played him?

RF: The story of Robert and Elizabeth Browning is the most touching true love story I know. And Browning was a fascinating man. A giant. Prolific, profound, passionate. I have first editions of virtually all his works. I collect Browning memorabilia. I have a small Browning museum at my home in Venice. As you say, Mr Muir, I admire him greatly, I have written about him, and, yes, I have played him – more than once. But he had no interest in young girls.

RM: He was interested in murder though, wasn't he?

RF: How do you mean?

RM: You have described *The Ring and the Book* as his greatest achievement. What is it about?

RF: It's an epic poem, running to twenty thousand lines or more.

RM: And its theme?

RF: It's an account of the trial of an Italian count, Guido Franceschini, who is charged with the murder of his wife.

RM: You have played a number of murderers in your time.

RF: I don't deny it – but I don't see the relevance.

RM: In your television series *Murderer* who was the very first true-life murderer you portrayed?

RF: I portrayed so many.

RM: Think carefully. The first? Could it have been Donald Hume?

RF: Yes. I believe it was.

RM: So, you remember playing Donald Hume who, of course, shot his victim, dismembered his victim—

RF: I would never dismember my wife. Why are you saying this?

RM: And then threw the remains of his victim out of an Auster sports plane. Did you not shoot your wife on the night of first October last and then dispose of her body by throwing it out of an aeroplane, your own aeroplane?

RF: No. No. Why should I?

RM: Because she was no longer a nymphette, no longer your beautiful ideal, because she was no longer your unique possession, because she was now the lover of your oldest friend. And because you could no longer possess her as once you had—

RF: No, no.

RM: You of all people, Mr Faber, will recall Chesterton's line that when Elizabeth Browning died Robert 'closed a door in himself, and none ever saw Browning upon earth again, but only a splendid surface'. That's what you're showing us here, Mr Faber, aren't you – a splendid surface, an actor's mask, hiding from us – and, heaven knows, from yourself as well perhaps – the terrible truth that in cold blood you killed the fickle woman who was your wife because she was no longer the entrancing child who had been your bride?

RF: No, no. You are quite wrong.

RM: I think we'll let the jury be the judge of that.

FOURTEEN

The trial had lasted nine days and could have ended neatly on a Friday afternoon – enabling the lawyers to get away to the country and the Sunday papers to have a field day – but for Mr Justice King-Lovell's elaborate yet necessary rehearsal of the niceties of *R* v *Onufrejczyk* ('The fact of death is provable by circumstantial evidence, notwithstanding that neither the body nor any trace of the body has been found, but the circumstantial evidence must be so cogent and compelling as to convince you that on no rational hypothesis other than murder can the facts be accounted for') and the jury's consequent inability to come to a quick conclusion. The judge, a man more fastidious than his rambling-rose eyebrows would suggest, wanted a unanimous verdict and felt one could be reached, so gave the jury the weekend for further reflection.

I was not sure what outcome to expect. Saturday and Sunday, alone with Tom, were awkward days.

'What do you think?'

'I don't know.'

We had exhausted ourselves on the case and hadn't anything left to say. We had talked it out over so many months – it had sustained us – and now it was almost over, I was confronted, suddenly, with the realisation that the very moment it was we would simply be faced with each other again and nothing to sustain us, only an uneasy emptiness. Tom had recognised my infatuation with Richard, took it on board, kept his distance, let it happen. Tom's view of life's dark clouds was simple: give them time and they pass by, always have, always will. He said nothing, but I could hear him thinking, 'Don't worry, Jo-bug, it'll blow over.' At night I would lie in bed rigid with anger – enraged with myself for allowing myself to be overwhelmed with a sentimental obsession ('Richard is thrilling; Tom is dull'), furious with Tom for his benign, understanding acceptance of what was happening.

On Sunday night, on my own, I went over to La Fenice to see Sarah. During the course of the case we had become good friends. She was, in fact, seventeen now and lovely – lovely to look at (she was her mother's daughter), lovely to be with: easy, open, unselfconscious yet amazingly self-assured. She could cope. She *was* coping. Brilliantly. Reading about Maisie, knowing Richard, it sometimes seemed that Sarah was the true grown-up in the Faber household. While they were strange, she was normal; while they were dangerous, she was safe. Her world-famous mother had disappeared, her beloved father was charged with murder, her home was besieged by media from the four corners of the earth, and there she was, standing in the kitchen with her gentle look-alike boyfriend, Ben, giving pasta and Rioja and comfort and encouragement to those who, nominally, were there to give comfort and encouragement to her.

She hugged me. 'It's going to be all right.'

'I hope so.'

'I know so.'

Sarah wouldn't come to court on Monday. 'It'll be a circus. I'm going to stay here, get the house ready. Dad's coming home. I know he is.'

I didn't say, 'And what about Maisie?' but I thought it – I thought it all the time – and Sarah knew what I was thinking and said, 'I don't know about Maisie. Don't ask me. I've blanked it out. If Dad says it's okay, it's okay, but that bit, I don't understand.'

At eleven forty-seven on Monday morning Richard Faber stepped into the dock at the Old Bailey for the last time. He sloughed off bank manager from Turin, removed his spectacles, lifted his shoulders and stood, defiant, expectant, heroic, as a narrow shaft of brilliant sunshine came through the clerestory window to provide him with his spotlight at the moment of triumph. The verdict was unanimous: 'Not Guilty'. In the pandemonium that followed Richard stayed quite still. The press were scrambling for the exits. In the public gallery there was a confusion of anger and applause.

Through the hubbub the judge murmured his thanks to the jury and rattled us through the rest of the ritual. In a matter of moments, it was all over.

'Well done, Joanna.' Richard Muir put an avuncular hand on my shoulder. 'Putting him in the box worked. It shouldn't have done, but it did. Donald Hume got off too, you know. Jury couldn't agree. In due course, he confessed, spilt the beans to the *Sunday Pictorial* for a few pieces of silver and fled the country. Changed his name to Brown and went to Switzerland – where he murdered somebody else. Ended up in the bin.'

It was bedlam too in the street outside the court. There were hundreds of them: photographers, camera crews, hacks, gawpers, fans, all jostling for their vantage point. For a naïve moment we thought we might have outwitted them: one of Tom's clerks had arranged for a taxi to come into the courtyard at the back of the building and pick us up behind closed doors. We clambered aboard – just the three of us, Richard, Tom, me – with Richard insisting on perching on the jump seat: 'You two have done all the work – thank you – thank you both' – but as the great black gate swung open the cab driver chose to turn not away from the maelstrom but towards it. The taxi was engulfed at once and, at walking pace, we nosed our way forward through the pressing mass of poking lenses and prying eyes. Suddenly, amid the forest of flash guns and jiggling grinning faces, we saw Jack Rivers and Adam Waterson, standing close together on the pavement, no more than a yard away, their whole bodies contorted with loathing. They were chanting, rhythmically, with

256

jabbing fingers: 'Murderer! Murderer!' Richard closed his eyes and turned away.

'Oh, how they hate me.'

I put out my hand and touched Richard's knee. Tom stared back at them. 'It's their obsession, it's eating into them.'

'But they believe it. They believe I murdered her.'

'They manufactured evidence.'

'But only to prove what they knew to be true, what they believed to be true. Using the gun, firing the shot, somehow the end could justify the means. They couldn't get me any other way.'

'They didn't get you.'

'No.' He smiled.

In Blomfield Road, the length of the street, the chaos was much the same. 'I'll keep the cab, I'll sort it out,' said Tom. 'You two go in. Okay? See you later, Jo-bug. Well done, Richard. It's over now.'

We stepped out of the taxi and Richard held my hand as we ran the gauntlet, through the gate, up the steps, notebooks waving, shutters clicking, voices shouting. 'How do you feel, Mr Faber?' 'What are your plans?' 'Can you tell us where your wife is?' Richard said nothing, but as we reached the top, he let go of me, turned and gave them one shot, one wave, one enigmatic smile. Then we were inside.

'Yeesss! That's it! Never again. Pull up the draw-bridge.' He looked at Sarah, suddenly wary. 'There's no one here, is there?'

'No one,' she said. 'Just us.'

'Thank you, dear girl. Thank you. Come here, come to Daddy.' As they stood together in the hallway, hugging, rocking, laughing, she laid her face against his chest and I watched him looking over her shoulder up the stairs to the landing, to the painting of 'The Beautiful Lady'.

Sarah broke away. 'There's champagne on ice, all set.'

'Wonderful!' cried Richard. 'My first for months and months. I hope you notice the slimmer line, the svelter look?' He took us each by the hand and led us into the drawing room. Sarah had laid out four glasses on the tray – Richard's favourite tray, the one he claimed had been a prop in the original Paris production of *Salome* by Oscar Wilde.

'Did you know that the shape of the champagne saucer is based on the breast of Madame de Pompadour? That's what my father used to maintain anyway. Then my father always added, "What we want to know is what inspired the shape of the champagne flute!" God, it's good to be home.'

He filled the four glasses and handed us ours. 'Here's to my beautiful daughter, here's to my brilliant brief.' He picked up the remaining glasses. 'And now, if you'll excuse me, ladies, I must go and tell my angel the news.'

We watched him go, and wondered.

Sarah, embarrassed, glanced at the tray and muttered, by way of justification, 'I thought Tom might have been coming.'

'No.' I should have said something more, but all I could manage was a graceless shrug.

'Does he know you are falling in love with Daddy?'

'Yes.'

'Doesn't he mind?'

'It's all a bit confusing. Why can't you love two people at once?'

Sarah, seventeen-year-old Sarah, looked at me and smiled. She did not sit in judgement. She was guileless and kind. I felt ridiculous. I was ridiculous. I could hear myself and I sounded so winsome, so coy, so *silly*. Infatuation is absurd. Love is blind and baffling and embarrassing and a poor respecter of age and station. For all I know Mr Justice King-Lovell had a crush on his neighbour's wife. And, once upon a time, didn't the Lord Chancellor himself run off with the Scottish Secretary's sweetheart? Whoever you are, falling in and out of love can make you seem and feel and be so foolish. I ought to know better: I was old enough to be Sarah's mother – indeed, had her father been sent to prison I had promised to keep a motherly eye on her, and Richard had asked Tom to set up a trust fund for her and help manage her finances, together we were to be *in loco parentis* – and yet here I was maundering on like a self-indulgent schoolgirl, Confused of King's Bench Walk. 'Sorry,' I said.

Sarah got up and refilled my glass. 'I'm the same,' she said. 'I don't know what to feel now about anything. We've been waiting for this for months and, suddenly, it's over. It's so odd. What happens next?'

Richard was standing in the doorway. 'We take a little holiday. We take a little break. We deserve it. You deserve it.' He came into the room. He looked so good, so easy.

'I hear you have a boyfriend, daughter. I understand he's called Ben and he's beautiful, gentle and wise. I have my spies.' He was near me now, so close. He put his hand on my shoulder. He beamed indulgently at Sarah. 'Bring him. Bring Ben. We shall introduce him to the delights of *La Serenissima*.' He looked down at me and stroked the back of my neck. 'You come too, Jo. If Tom can spare you. Please.'

Venice was golden. As always. Venice never fails. If you are unhappy in Venice you have brought your unhappiness with you. I thought I knew the city well – it was where I spent my gap year, it was where Tom and I went for our honeymoon, and for three anniversaries after that – but Richard knew it like a Venetian, loved it like Browning, spoke of it like Ruskin. We had ten days and for each one he planned a programme – one day Thomas Mann's Venice, Byron's the next, then Baron Corvo's, then Woody Allen's, turn-of-the-century Venice, Shakespeare's Venice, Death in Venice – 'today we go to San Michele to see the graves of Diaghilev, Stravinsky, Ezra Pound' – every excursion had a theme, every glorious building, every palazzo, every *calle*, came with an anecdote, a quotation, a trip down memory lane – and each evening over dinner (always somewhere different, sometimes grand, sometimes simple) the wine flowed and our inexhaustible guide set up the next day's delights. He talked all the time, he never stopped, he was Scheherezade, spinning ever-more-fantastic yarns to postpone the evil hour. We listened, we laughed, we loved him, and we played the game. We were his audience: he spoke the lines; we applauded. The trial we never mentioned. About the future we never asked.

On the eighth night of our holiday, by chance, I stumbled on the truth about Maisie. We had gone to bed early – Venice goes to bed early – and I sat alone at the window of my room at the top of the Faber palazzo, the *casa* Desdemona, gazing down at the Grand Canal and marvelling at its beauty and my own stupidity. I had drunk too much and my conscience wasn't clear. Sometimes God moves in a fairly obvious way: my head was thumping. Across the water the chimes of Santa Maria del Giglio struck twelve. I pulled on a dressing gown – it was one of Maisie's, flowing silk, snow-white, with a resplendent phoenix embroidered on the back – and went in search of an aspirin, Disprin, anything. The house was quite still. Like a furtive child, I crept down the stairs to the floor below. The main bathroom was immediately opposite Richard and Maisie's bedroom. The bathroom door was just ajar. I pushed it open. I flicked on the light. There was a small mirrored cupboard above the basin. I pulled it open and inspected the two narrow glass shelves neatly packed with assorted medicine bottles, pills, packets, potions. I picked one out at random. It was a bottle of tablets: Priadel, lithium carbonate. It was clearly marked. It was Maisie's.

Richard was at the door, wide awake, still dressed, still with a glass in his hand.

I stared at him in the mirror. 'This is Maisie's,' I said.

'No.' He was smiling. 'It's mine. An experiment.'

'This is Maisie's, Richard.' I turned to him. 'I see it all now. Why didn't you tell me, Richard? Manic depression. Like her mother. Why didn't I guess? She stopped taking the lithium, didn't she? And the depression returned. And then she took her own life. That's what happened.'

'No.'

'And you can't face it.'

'No.'

'Or won't face it.'

Richard breathed a tiny sigh, and laughed at me through it, not unkindly, almost sweetly. Slowly, patiently, he said, 'No, Jo. Maisie's not dead. How many times do I have to tell you? Maisie Rivers has never been more alive. I'll prove it to you, if I must. But not tonight. I'm tired now. I'm going to bed. You go too. Sleep tight.'

The next day was a Saturday, the last full day of our holiday. Richard had planned a special treat: the Faber launch would take us to the tiny island of Torcello, not to explore the faded glories of the Byzantine basilica (that was an optional extra) but to indulge us with a farewell lunch in the shaded garden of the legendary Locanda Cipriani. We were expected. The welcome was effusive. Richard matched it in manner and appearance. He played the international movie star: dark glasses, white linen suit, silk shirt, absurd broad-rimmed panama with, inscribed inside the hat in large letters: 'Like hell it's yours!'

'Not my joke,' he explained with a mock-bashful

shrug. 'Mooney Lynn's.' He raised an enquiring eyebrow at Sarah and Ben. 'And who was Mooney Lynn?'

'I know,' said a gravelly female voice from the bar. 'The man from Nashville who married Loretta Lynn when she was just thirteen and taught her all she ever knew.'

'Emma! Ye gods, this is glorious!' Richard swung round and there she was: Emma Irving – Glenn Close meets Mae West – perched on a bar stool, cigarette in one hand, her second Bellini in the other. 'This is wonderful. This is Emma, everybody! My oldest friend, my flat-mate. "The wheel is come full circle!" Sarah, you know. This is her friend, Ben Knight – a writer, not an actor so there's hope. And this is Joanna Dalton, my brilliant barrister – without whom . . .' We shook hands, we kissed, Richard put his arms around her. 'This is so good, Emma, so good. You're going to join us? You must.'

'I have a friend,' said Emma, in stage *sotto voce*. 'He's in the loo.'

'Who is it? Do I know him?'

'You know him, but don't worry.' She stretched out her hand and stroked his cheek. 'It isn't Adam. It's all over with Adam.'

It turned out to be another actor, Michael Gambon, and the six of us shared a table – and a feast – and what seemed like that season's entire harvest of Soave – and Sarah and Ben and I (outsiders, observers) sat wide-eyed, amused and grateful as the three middle-aged thesps made happy caricatures of themselves.

Funny voices, funny faces, funny stories, funny friends.

'"From quiet homes and first beginning, Out to the undiscovered ends, There's nothing worth the wear of winning, But laughter and the love of friends." Hilaire Belloc dined here. Probably at this very table. With Max. With my father.'

Emma, mouth full of risotto and Soave, winked at Ben and Sarah. 'The fabulous Fabers have known them all!'

Gambon – Richard called him 'The Great Gambon' – narrowed his rheumy eyes and distorted his vowels to mutter darkly, 'Woi've been reading rather tew much about the fabulous Foibers lately, 'aven't we?'

'We have! We have!' wailed Richard. 'Or rather, *you* have. I stopped looking at the papers a while ago. Even before the trial. When they started running all that garbage about Maisie and Adam Waterson – and there was nothing we could do, *nothing*. You can issue a denial, of course, but that just fuels it. You can give your own interview, but then you're playing their game. And they don't write about what you say, they write about what you don't say. They come to talk about your project – your play, your movie, your wretched part – and let you ramble on for an hour, plying them with coffee and charisma, and then off they go, all smiles, and write up what you muttered as an aside while showing them to the door and how carefully you pick your nose. God, they're shit. No more interviews. Ever.'

'I hate them,' Gambon said lugubriously, skewering an outsize chunk of squid.

'You don't do interviews,' said Emma. 'And no one wants to interview *me*, of course.'

'The less people know about you the better.'

'Thank you, sweetie.'

Gambon gave a wheezy laugh and wiped a fleck of olive oil from his beard. 'Darling, I didn't mean that personally. I mean *ideally* an actor should be a blank canvas. Otherwise you walk on as Mark Antony and the fellow in the front row whispers to his wife—' new funny voice – '"Ya know 'e collects toy trains – 'e's got 'undreds of 'em, 'undreds!" I don't do interviews because I can't be trusted. The devil gets inside me. I say what I shouldn't.'

Emma coaxed: 'Tell them the Wilde story.'

'Yes!' cried Richard. 'Cue the Wilde story!'

The Great Gambon played it straight to us. 'When I did Oscar Wilde on the telly – it was years ago – a lad from the *Birmingham Post* asked me if I found it difficult playing the part of a homosexual. "No, it comes to me quite easily," I said, "I used to be one." He said, "Oh, really?" And I said, "Yes, but I was forced to give it up." He wasn't looking at me, he was scribbling away with his pencil. Eventually he said, "May I ask why?" And I said, "Well, it made me eyes water."'

They roared. They cheered. They drank. They told their Olivier stories. Gambon had carried spears for Olivier in the inaugural season of the National at the Old Vic. Richard had carried Olivier's crown from the film of *Henry V* in the procession at the Memorial Service in Westminster Abbey. Emma had been kissed by Olivier – on the lips.

'You can't top that!' she smirked.

'When was this? You never told me.' Richard was always proprietorial about Olivier.

'A terrible movie. I was terrible. He was terrible.'

'Olivier was never terrible.'

'I tell you, Richard, he was terrible – awful – embarrassing. And he knew it!'

Richard was laughing. 'This is sacrilege!'

'What's the part he never played and should have done?'

'Good game! Prospero?'

'Captain Hook.'

'*You* should do Captain Hook,' said Gambon, poking a forkful of *anguille in umido* at Richard. 'You live in Never-land.'

'Did you see Dustin? In the film? Oh, dear . . .'

'*And* he cut off his right hand for the part!'

They roared. They cheered. They drank some more. I looked at Richard and wondered if, perhaps, with these people, he was himself. Was this for real? Was he happy now?

'Why are you two here, for God's sake?' he asked, all of a sudden. 'You've not told us.'

'You didn't ask,' said Emma.

'We're doing a movie,' said The Great Gambon with dignity.

'I don't know why they call it a movie. It's for the telly. It's a movie for the telly. Not terribly distinguished . . .'

'But big wodges of dollars.'

'Bravo!' Richard raised his glass.

'And you?'

Richard leant towards them. 'No more movies. Been there, done that.'

'Wow,' said Emma very softly.

'We were going to do some cops and robbers caper, but the trial killed that.' He put out his hands and squeezed theirs. 'Thank you for not mentioning the trial.' He loved these people, he trusted them. 'And I tell you, Maisie's had enough. No more movies for Maisie Rivers. She'll never again be seen on the silver screen. Leave 'em wanting more.'

'Quite right,' said Gambon, gently fingering the heavy bags under his eyes. 'She's going to be like Garbo or Marilyn or Bardot – caught for ever in her prime. Brilliant.'

'And wise,' reflected Emma, who seemed to be moving gently from the mellow to the maudlin. 'Once upon a time films were so special, secrets we shared in the dark. Now they're just car chases and clichés, all spectacle and special effects. Video fodder. There's no intimacy, no feeling, no point.'

Suddenly Ben, Sarah's gentle Ben, who'd said hardly a word so far, leant forward and, with a sweet earnestness, asked Richard: 'Who's the greatest director you've worked with?'

'Film director? I don't know. I don't understand films really. Maisie would go for Truffaut. No contest. We did two pictures with Monsieur Truffaut. He used to say–' Depardieu accent – '"I make films that I would have liked to have seen when I was young." Maisie was charmed by his philosophy. "The director should give the audience a promise of pleasure." That was his line. "The curve of life is not pleasure promising. It goes towards decadence, decrepitude, illness, oblivion." Maisie plans to defy the "curve of life". She's doing it her way – going for a happy ending.'

'So – what next? Your memoirs? We can take it you've been offered a fortune since – since – you know – all this . . .' Gambon waved his fork about.

'Yes, but no – no memoirs, no interviews, no movies. However – one more challenge.' He widened his eyes. 'This is a happy encounter because I can share with you my news.' He raised a glass with ceremony, as though about to propose a toast. 'Friends, family, you will be pleased to know that for my next role I plan to follow in the footsteps of The Great Gambon himself.'

'Oh God, not a singing detective!'

'No. No singing, no dancing – mountaineering. An assault on Everest.'

'Oh Lord.'

'I'm going to do *King Lear*. Produce it. Direct it. Play it.'

'Oh Christ.' The Great Gambon wheezed and spluttered. 'It's a bugger. For God's sake, Richard, don't.'

'I'm going to cast it to the hilt.'

Gambon closed his eyes. 'I will *not* play Gloucester. I am *not* available.'

'I suppose I'm too old for Goneril.' Emma puckered her lips and fluttered her eyelids.

'I don't know.' Richard was playful, smiling.

'And Cordelia? Kate Bingley?'

'Oh no,' Richard said firmly. 'No, no. Listen to this, Jo. Maisie Rivers is going to give us her Cordelia. Yes, I am probably a bit too young for Lear and she is arguably a smidgeon too old to play my daughter, but we are actors after all, so, dammit, we might just pull it off. And it'll cause a little fluttering in the dovecotes, don't you think?'

It caused more than a fluttering – there was a mighty beating of wings – and Richard certainly pulled it off. The production, back at the Saville, was a virtual sell-out the moment it was announced. Richard gave no interviews – Richard never spoke directly to the press again – but the proposed casting was advertised and, even without hype, the hoohaa was extraordinary.

What were we going to get? Maisie Rivers in person? As a hologram? On video? In rehearsals Sarah stood in for Maisie. Richard apologised, but Maisie wanted to work on her part at home. He hoped everyone would understand.

In the event, on the opening night, Maisie did not appear, but we heard her. Richard provided a tape with her reading the part of Cordelia. It was unmistakably her and she read it beautifully and, though you couldn't see her, the actors and the audience all looked to where she would have been and, oddly, incredibly, you did feel she was there.

The final scene, when Lear brings on his daughter's body, was almost unbearable. Richard cradled the empty air, cradled and caressed it.

'We two alone will sing like birds i' the cage:
When thou dost ask me blessing, I'll kneel down,
And ask of thee forgiveness.'

At the end of the evening, in the sudden darkness of the auditorium, there was a moment's pause while a thousand individuals dried their eyes and took deep breaths and then, as one, gave in, rose to their feet and roared. 'Those of us fortunate enough to find ourselves at the Saville Theatre last night – we few, we happy few – were privileged to witness the finest classical actor of his generation giving the finest performance of his career. After a year of trial and trauma, Richard Faber returned to the London stage with a performance about which there can be no controversy and only one verdict. This is the greatest *Lear* since Lear himself.'

In the dressing room we hugged the star, kissed him, squeezed him, slapped his back. It was bizarre. We seemed to be pretending this was a triumphant first night like any other. When the passing trade had been and cheered, blown their kisses, whooped and gone, there were half a dozen of us left: Sarah, Ben, Gambon, Emma and Maria, 'Santa Maria'. 'Champagne for the home team,' said the hero of the hour. We stood around him in a circle. He gazed at us with lion eyes. He played the old-fashioned star. 'All I want on stage is cues and elbow room. All I want now I have here.' We raised our plastic beakers and told him how magnificent he had been.

'Yes – yes – but Maisie – wasn't Maisie amazing?' he asked.

And we said, 'Yes, amazing.' What else could we say? The audience had joined in the conspiracy. It had worked.

The party broke up a little before twelve. We each went our separate ways. Sarah went off to Ben's place – she was living there now – and I returned towards Muswell Hill. I was going back to Tom, coming home. The madness had all but gone.

Richard drove home towards Little Venice alone and, as he was turning out of Oxford Street into Gloucester Place, he noticed the time and switched on the car radio to hear the midnight news. The remains of a woman's body had been found, washed ashore at Battery Point, near Bristol, where the mouth of the Avon meets the mouth of the Severn. Details of her identity were not expected before morning.

FIFTEEN

At the end of Gloucester Place, he turned left into
Marylebone Road and drove straight up on to the West
Way, towards the M4 to Bristol. As he drove he dictated
a letter, on his little Dictaphone, a letter to me and to
Sarah, to both of us. His voice was clear and certain,
full of strength and energy, and warmth. 'This is for
both of you, because I love you, because I want you
always to be friends. I'm going to say goodbye. I've
got to move on. It's okay. You'll manage. You will.
Nothing lasts. Remember *Brief Encounter*? If you've not
seen it, Sarah, see it. It's wonderful. Celia Johnson in
that quaint, clipped, period English voice: "Nothing
lasts, really. Neither happiness, nor despair. Not even
life lasts that long." My mother loved that film. And
I loved my mother. And she was killed. And I loved

272

my father. And he died. And Miss Stanhope loved him too, and, as a child, I loved her, but it didn't last. And I loved Adam, man and boy – and look what happened to him! Nothing lasts. That's life. I'm not going to think about Adam any more. And don't you either. Forget him. The business is half his. So be it. Let it go. You'll have more than enough. You'll have the houses, all those houses, Sarah, and the pictures. Adam doesn't matter. Jack Rivers doesn't matter. The tinpots and the tosspots – forget 'em!

'I hope you can hear me. It's started to rain. It's bucketing down. I must tell you what happened. I want you to know. That day, the first of October, when Maisie flew in from LA and I met her at Heathrow, after we'd done the press conference, as we got into the car, she said, "Let's not go home. Let's go to Bristol. Let's fly." So we went to Luton and we climbed aboard our little plane, our little two-seater, and we flew. "The fabulous Fabers. *And* they fly!" Piff-paff, nose-bleeds and all, Maisie loved to fly. And when we were there, up in the air, up in the clouds, up so high in the azure sky, she said, "Little Prince, this is where I want to stay. Don't laugh." I didn't laugh, I didn't cry. I listened to her, my girl, my Maisie, and I understood. She didn't want to grow old. "I don't have to. I'm different. *We're* different. Remember? We don't need the world, we have each other."

'We got to Bristol and, hand in hand, all day we walked the streets. We visited all the old haunts. We told each other all the old tales. And when night came we crossed the bridge and clambered down the bank to the woods.

"We're Hansel and Gretel," she said. We lay there in each other's arms and I looked into her eyes and I knew all I ever wanted, needed, lived for, was there. I had met a girl and she was the girl for me, my one and only. It happens. If it happens to you, don't let it go. "I love you," I whispered it to her, "I love you." "I love you," she whispered back, "I love you so much." "Thank you," I said, and I kissed her tears, her warm, salt tears. "Thank you for everything." "We're just beginning," she smiled. "You know the line—" "The best is yet to be—" "And we must believe that we have life not just here on this scrap of mud flying through space but for all eternity – for all eternity, you and I, me and you, my funny old-young man, my Richard, my old-fashioned star. I have learnt so much from you. And we're just beginning. I love you with the breath, smiles, tears of all my life, I love you to the breadth and depth and height my soul can reach! I love you, husband, now and for ever!"

'They got it all wrong at the trial. We left the woods and went back to the plane together. It must have been midnight when we took off. The sky was so clear. I flew back across the city. Maisie loved the twinkling lights, night-time in fairy-land. I flew back towards Clifton and then down, down, as low as I could go, over the bridge, right over it, along the estuary to the river mouth and then, as we reached the sea, she turned and looked at me with those amazing eyes and smiled and said, "Come when you're ready. There is no hurry. I'll be waiting, Little Prince."

'And with one hand she released her safety belt and

with the other she levered open the aircraft door and she was gone.

'Everyone suddenly burst out singing;
And I was filled with such delight
As prisoned birds must find in freedom
Winging wildly across the white
Orchard and dark green fields; on – on – and out of sight.

'She wasn't mad, that I know. Oh yes, she had some of the symptoms of manic depression – the highs anyway. I had them too: the mind that raced, the eye that gleamed, the spirit that soared – but if that's madness who wants sanity? Yes, she had highs – and she had lows – the lithium was hers, but she couldn't see the point of it. It made no difference. She did not suffer from the numbness, the nothingness of true depression. Her lows were rational: she felt trapped, locked in to the repetitiveness of the movie-making treadmill, caught in the glare of the public gaze, weary of the attentions of the world, but disconcerted when they waned. Mixed-up Maisie, not crazy Maisie. At times she loved our jet-set life, at times she hated it, at the end she'd had enough of it. That was all.

'She was not mad and I did not murder her. Of course, they'll say I did. They'll say this proves it. "This is remorse." Well, you can tell them what really happened. Up, up in the sky, so close to heaven, that October night. Maisie jumped – and I flew on, alone.

I flew without knowing where I was flying, I flew in a haze, a daze, a dream, and then, slowly, as the sun rose and the sky turned from charcoal to cobalt to the palest pink and blue, I flew back to reality, I flew back to earth, back to Luton – Luton, God save the mark! – and as I flew I thought of the Little Prince: "You become responsible for what you have tamed. You are responsible for your rose." I knew the world would get it wrong and I wanted to protect her, so I kept her secret. Olivier used to say, "What is acting but lying, and what is good acting but convincing lying?" I would live the lie. It was another part to play. The man with the invisible wife. It was like the best light comedy when you've got a really good house – rather fun at the time. Getting film of Maisie for *Faustus* was easy, and I knew Cordelia would work like a dream. It's all illusion anyway. We could have done more, we'd taped so many plays, ourselves, at home, as try-outs, for the hell of it. *Lear*, *Othello*, *Private Lives*. Maisie wasn't interested in acting, but she went along with it to please me. She pleased me so much. She never let me down. Not once.

'The Chippenham turn-off. We're nearly there. Nearly through. Jo, you know your learned friend Mr Muir was right – not about the murder, but about the door I had closed so that none would see me on earth again, "only a splendid surface". But the surface has cracked and I can't go on. I can't act this out any more. I've done with acting. I've done with lying. Sarah, can you hear me? This is your old dad speaking. Down the years I've loved doing these tapes for you. We've had some fun,

GYLES BRANDRETH

haven't we? I love you, my baby. Always will. And you'll love me, won't you? You'll miss me – I hope – but not for ever. It'll hurt for now, but not for always and not too much. You've got Ben, you've got tomorrow. You don't need me now – and I need Maisie. I need her so much. You see, we are one and we cannot be apart. I am going to find her again. She's waiting. There, that is our secret. Now you know.'

I was in my car coming up through Highgate when I heard the midnight news. I turned back towards Little Venice. When I reached Blomfield Road two police cars, blue lights flashing, were already outside La Fenice. I drove straight on. I drove towards Bristol too. I knew that was where he would be going. I drove hard and fast as the sky opened and the rain came tumbling down.

I reached the place a little before three and found his car parked carefully on the near side of the bridge. At once I saw his outline silhouetted against the sky. I ran towards him. And then I stopped. He was balanced on the rim of the parapet. He didn't see me. He didn't know I was there. I watched him as he threw his twirling cane high into the air, and caught it, and held it, and laughed, and stretched his arms out wide and then, quite suddenly, threw himself into the night air. He leapt off the Clifton Suspension Bridge like a dancer. What happened next you may choose not to believe, but I was there and it is true. As Richard Faber fell from the bridge I heard him shout, loud and clear, 'Now and for ever!' and I saw Maisie – amazing Maisie,

277

lovelier than ever – Maisie Rivers, The Beautiful Lady, rise up out of the water, floating, flying, laughing, crying. I saw her wings open and unfurl as she came towards him. I saw her fold him safely in her arms. I saw them kiss. The fabulous Fabers.

And they lived happily ever after.

Yeesss!

WHO IS NICK SAINT?
Gyles Brandreth

Apparently, Nick Saint is a charming 28-year-old teacher at a small private school in South Carolina. In reality, he doesn't know who he is or where he comes from. He has no papers, no passport, no past – only a recurring dream and an alarming obsession about who he was, or might be.

Who is Nick Saint?

That's what psychotherapist Kirsty Macdonald, who has come East in search of happiness and fallen in love with this secretive Adonis, needs to know. Is he simply the most perfect man who ever was? Is he Superman or Peter Pan – or a dangerous psychotic on the run? Whoever he is, together they set out for New York and Philadelphia on a quest to establish Nick's true identity.

'A first novel of style, wit and confidence . . . Not merely, like all the best after-dinner speakers, does he know how to spin a yarn; unlike most politicians, he has a touching access to the secrets of the human heart'

Anthony Holden, *The Times*

Warner Books now offers an exciting range of quality titles by both established and new authors. All of the books in this series are available from:

Little, Brown and Company (UK),
P.O. Box 11,
Falmouth,
Cornwall TR10 9EN.

Fax No: 01326 317444.
Telephone No: 01326 372400
E-mail: books@barni.avel.co.uk

Payments can be made as follows: cheque, postal order (payable to Little, Brown and Company) or by credit cards, Visa/Access. Do not send cash or currency. UK customers and B.F.P.O. please allow £1.00 for postage and packing for the first book, plus 50p for the second book, plus 30p for each additional book up to a maximum charge of £3.00 (7 books plus).

Overseas customers including Ireland, please allow £2.00 for the first book plus £1.00 for the second book, plus 50p for each additional book.

NAME (Block Letters) ....

....

ADDRESS ....

....

....

☐ I enclose my remittance for ....

☐ I wish to pay by Access/Visa Card

Number ☐☐☐☐☐☐☐☐☐☐☐☐☐☐☐☐☐☐

Card Expiry Date ☐☐☐☐